THE NETWORK

AN URBAN FANTASY TRILOGY WITH TWISTS
AND TURNS

E. G. BATEMAN

CORNERDOWN PUBLISHING

PROLOGUE

Previously, in *FADE*...

My awakening—my introduction to the world of trackers and faders—happened about a year and a half ago in the courtyard of a Glastonbury bookshop. But my experience was different to most. I was at the center of an electromagnetic pulse and energy wave which destroyed digital devices near me, toppled furniture and set off car and house alarms in the distance. I had gained the Sight *and* seen my first fader, Connor.

A day later, while I was spending time with my friend, Gill, my home exploded and my father was presumed dead. I was taken to the military academy where my dad had previously worked, and there I learned that I had the ability to be a tracker. What would I track? faders!

At the academy, I was taught that faders were monsters. They looked like humans, but could make themselves invisible. I was also told that faders were responsible for murdering my father, so I was happy to learn how to hunt them. Because my awakening had been unusual, and I could now affect electrical objects around me, the agency also wanted to investigate my potential abilities.

At the academy, I began to rebuild my life. I trained and made new friends: Marcus, Orla, Zoe and Nathan. I became particularly close to Marcus.

I learned that the fader who had killed my dad was still after me and, in an attempt to get to me, had murdered two of the other students at the academy, including Zoe's boyfriend and Marcus's best friend, Nathan. I was moved for my own safety to another academy in Colorado. My friends, Marcus, Orla and Zoe, came to Colorado with me. We made a new friend, Hannah, who became Zoe's girlfriend, and life carried on...

Until I learned that my dad hadn't died in the explosion at all; he had been saved by the fader, Connor. I also discovered the reason we had the special ability to see faders was because we *were* faders. The agency was giving us a drug which stopped us from developing fully, and had been doing this to trackers for at least seventy years. It's amazing what you can get away with when you control the narrative —the victor had well and truly rewritten history.

The agency scientists inserted a special inhibitor into my head which allowed them to study my abilities, but I wouldn't be able to access those abilities myself. However, we still managed to escape from the Base—Orla, Marcus, Zoe, Hannah and I—and I met another person I'd presumed dead: my grandmother, Vanessa. She had also been a tracker, but had been able to develop into a fader.

We were hiding in a safe house in Arizona when I found Zoe and Hannah seemingly dead with Connor crouching over them. Marcus, telling me he believed something was off about Connor, escaped with me into the Arizona night. That night, Marcus also told me that he had always known we were faders, but he didn't care. He was happy to hunt them down. He was addicted to a special kind of energy that faders produce, but he was so sensitive to it, he could sense it in trackers and regular humans too.

I also learned that it had been Marcus who had murdered his best friend Nathan and tried to drain the energy from Zoe and Hannah. In the dark, I escaped from Marcus, but broke my ankle in the process. Marcus found me, but so did Connor. To stop Marcus from killing Connor, I slashed at the back of my neck and removed the inhibitor. Using my ability I killed Marcus and saved Connor.

We spent a couple of weeks at a farm where my ankle was treated. Finally, we traveled on to a vineyard in a remote area of California. There were many faders hiding out there, and we were invited to join a resistance group called the Network. They were planning to fight back against the agency.

I was tired and in physical and emotional pain. But as I looked at the faders around me, men, women and children living in perpetual fear, I became angry...

1

We stood in a row, Orla, Zoe, Hannah and I, all facing the wall. Behind us, Dad and Jason sat at a long, ancient-looking wooden table, while Connor leaned against a bookcase in the corner of the room.

"So, this is it?" asked Zoe.

"Yes," said Dad.

We continued to stare at the wall.

"It's a map with lines drawn all over it," said Orla.

"Correct," said Dad.

"Okay, Dad, you've had your fun. Show us the Network," I said.

"You're looking at it. Look closer!"

"Do these lines represent secret tunnels?"

"No, they're not secret tunnels."

Dad wasn't giving much away. It was like he wanted me to get it without his help.

"But..."

"It doesn't matter how many times you ask, this is it," said Connor.

"It's a grand map," said Orla, nodding her head as though she understood it.

"It looks sort of familiar. I've seen a map like this somewhere before." I continued to look at it, squinting and turning my head this way and that.

"Here it comes," said Dad.

"Are they… are they ley lines?" I asked.

"There it is!" Connor grinned.

"I told you she'd get it."

"So, the Network is a network of ley lines," I said.

"You got it," said Connor.

"And not a network of heavily armed, technologically advanced cyborg faders?" asked Orla.

"Nope," said Jason.

"Not a network of secret underground lairs?" I asked.

"Sorry, Beautiful, but we're not Ninja Turtles."

I flicked an annoyed look at Connor. He kept calling me that.

I turned to my dad. "But, in Glastonbury, you said ley lines were nonsense. I thought you were going to thump that strange-smelling hippy who was 'Feeling the ley line energy, Man.' You called him a doped-up imbecile."

"I was wrong about the ley lines, but in my defense, he was a doped-up imbecile. The last time I saw him, he was standing in a water fountain, trying to flush himself into the Ministry of Magic."

I turned away from the map on the wall, dropped into a chair at the table and rested my head on my arms on its surface.

"We're all going to die, aren't we? My new granny is a crackpot, and we're going to die."

Dad rolled his eyes. "I need coffee," he said. Scratching his beard, he stood.

"Hey, do you want to fade over there?" asked Connor.

"I thought you'd never ask," said Dad, shaking himself out like he was about to exercise.

Connor put his hand on Dad's back, and the two of them disappeared.

"Oh my God, that's so funny," said Orla. "Your dad gets such a kick out of fading. That's the third time this morning Connor's faded him from one room to another."

"Yay! Comfort break," said Hannah, grabbing Zoe by the hand and walking quickly through the double doors out onto the deck.

Orla dropped into the stout wooden chair next to mine. "How are you?" she asked.

"Oh, I'm grand, so I am," I replied in a rubbish attempt at an Irish accent.

"That was a rubbish attempt at an Irish accent," she said.

I smiled.

"Let's have a wander-slash-hobble onto the deck. I can't look at that liney map anymore," said Orla.

I looked over to where Connor and Dad had faded, blinking in to see a yellow mist trailing off through the wall. I was relieved Connor had left the room. Ever since the night Marcus had died, he had been following me around, either trying to talk to me or just watching me. It was getting on my nerves.

We got up and went out. I glanced over at Zoe and Hannah, who were holding hands down at the corner of the deck, looking out at the rows of grape vines which seemed to stretch for miles. Orla looked at them too and tutted.

"What's wrong?" I asked.

"Zoe's emitting again," Orla said, shaking her head.

"I don't think it ever stops now," I said.

I blinked in and saw Zoe was lit up like a Christmas tree. I looked down at myself, but there was no yellow mist.

"Is it my imagination or has the radius of that yellow mist actually grown?" asked Orla.

"And it looks brighter than usual," I said.

My inhibitor had been switched on and off so many times by Doctor Philipson during his tests, it was odd that Zoe had started emitting within a few days of having had the capsule cut out of her. It made me realize I could have begun emitting at any time. They'd have killed me at the academy the second that happened. I shuddered.

I thought back to a couple of weeks before when Marcus had attacked Zoe and Hannah. He'd got as far as removing Zoe's capsule when he'd been disturbed by Connor. Otherwise, he'd have killed them—just as he had killed his best friend, Nate—to syphon their energy.

I touched the back of my neck where my injury was healing. I was lucky not to be horribly scarred. The memory came to me of hacking at myself with the edges of a broken mirror, gouging out my own inhibitor to free my ability and use it to end Marcus's life as he tried to murder Connor. Immediately, the thought of Marcus hanging from the roof of the cave invaded my mind. I reached out for a glib comment to push it away.

"Maybe we could put baubles on her," I said.

"I see it in your eyes, you know," Orla said. "Right before you make some silly joke."

"I guess there's no hiding it from you."

"There's no hiding it from anyone. We can all see you're hurting, but *you're* trying to hide from *it*. Also, the screamy nightmares are a bit of a giveaway, but well done for not exploding things anymore."

"Sorry. I asked if I could sleep in the basement, but Nanna said no."

"If she hears you calling her Nanna, she'll probably shoot you. And why would you want to sleep down in the gym? You'd be woken at some ungodly hour every morning by a bunch of grunting blokes."

A little girl came squealing around the corner of the building with an older girl of roughly twelve years. They were chasing a cat as it jumped at a small plastic ball.

"Those kids have stolen my cat," I said.

On hearing my voice, Felix stopped and looked up at me. A light breeze caused the ball to move again, it became the cat's primary goal once more, and the little girl resumed her squeals.

I sighed and looked back to Orla. "I miss him. I keep having dreams where he's lifting me up and kissing me, and I'm so happy. Is that weird?" I asked.

"Who, Felix?"

I looked at her with an eyebrow raised and shook my head.

"Marcus was your boyfriend, and you loved him. How can that be weird?" Orla asked.

I counted the points off on my fingers. "He was an unhinged killer. He killed Nate. He would have killed all of you, and eventually me, I suppose. Every memory of him I have is tainted. When he hugged me and I felt giddy, it was because he'd been syphoning my energy. I thought that was how love felt." I shuddered. "Do you remember, he said he wanted to be a physiotherapist like his dad? I see now he just wanted an excuse to syphon people."

"Don't torture yourself with these thoughts," said Orla. "Anyway, that's not the worst part. Your dad told me that Marcus's father was a bloody milkman."

My jaw dropped. "Aren't you angry? You and Zoe knew him for five years. He fooled you both."

"Well, I always thought he was a bit tactile. I guess that makes sense now. But I don't think that's really what's bothering you."

"Of course that bothers me. But you're right. I killed him, Orla. I mean, he'd have died in minutes anyway with his head stuck in that rock. But that didn't kill him. I did, and I can't stop thinking about it. So yes, I make jokes. I'm trying to keep out those thoughts."

I turned around, leaning my back on the rail. Orla did the same.

"How's that working for you?" she asked.

"Not so well." I barked a bitter laugh.

"The only way around it is through it."

"Oh God, you sound like Helen." I rolled my eyes, thinking of the counselor from Hilltop tracker Academy back in England.

"Maybe you could call her for a consult. What could possibly go wrong?"

"Five hundred agents turning up at the door?"

I turned at the sound of footsteps approaching us along the deck.

"We're heading back in," said Hannah.

"Oh yes. The liney map. I can't wait," said Orla as we followed.

It had helped to talk to Orla. I decided I'd try to focus more on our current problems during meetings and deal with the past another time.

We assembled before the map again.

"So, how do these things figure into this mystery plan?" I said, pointing at the lines.

Dad stood beside me and smiled, indicating he could see my head was back in the game.

"You know the story. There are ley lines around the world which are supposedly pathways of energy between ancient sacred sites. It's mostly pseudo-science and has never been proven. But it appears that when you get a fader near a ley line, it does have an effect."

"What kind of effect?" asked Zoe.

"For most faders, not very much. You know that feeling when the hairs on the back of your neck stand up?"

"Yes," said Zoe.

"I think so," I said, feeling my eyebrow rocket to my hairline.

"Well, apparently most faders feel that quite strongly near a ley line, and they tend to emit more than usual."

"Are we, by any chance, on top of a ley line right now?" asked Zoe.

"I'm afraid not, Zoe," said Dad. "That's all you."

Zoe slumped. She'd started looking tired lately.

"Okay, so how are these ley lines going to help us?" asked Hannah.

"Good question," I added. "I get that strange feeling whenever a fader or tracker is looking at me while they're blinked-in. I always have."

"Really? I used to wonder how you knew you were being watched," said Dad. "I just assumed you were unusually observant. Although you never seemed to observe when your bedroom needed tidying."

"Dad! Really?"

"Sorry Litt... Jenna."

I took two steps and hugged him. I couldn't be mad at him—I'd spent months thinking he was dead, and I would never take him for granted again. I kissed his cheek. Actually, I kissed just under his eye because I struggled to find some face that wasn't covered in his new scratchy beard. Then I stood next to him, and he turned his attention to Hannah.

"As you know, some faders have other abilities. Those are usually amplified on a ley line."

Vanessa, my grandmother, entered the room. "We've already tried it with Connor. His ability to fade other people increased so he didn't need to be touching them. They only needed to be standing near him. We know you have an ability, Jenna. We need to see how it is affected near the ley lines."

"So what's next?" I asked.

"For you? Healing. Then we're planning a field trip," said Dad.

"There's a ley line which crosses a hundred or so miles from here. We're going to pay it a visit when you've recovered," added Vanessa.

"Don't you want to get started straight away? I can get around on crutches if I need to."

"It's okay, we hope to use the time to resolve another issue. In the meantime, we need to work on making you all less recognizable."

The meeting broke up, and I went to rest my leg on the sofa.

"Hey," said Connor, walking in.

"Hey," I replied with my face intently in a book. I hoped he'd get the message and keep walking. He stood around for about a minute, then tried again.

"How's your ankle?"

He wasn't going to leave me alone. I dropped the book down with a sigh and faced him.

"Broken and painful."

"You don't spend enough time keeping it elevated. You need to rest more."

"Thanks for the diagnosis," I said, picking up my book again, trying to signal an end to the conversation.

"The first one's free," he said.

I was opening my mouth to make some snippy reply when I heard a scream. It was Orla. I flew off the sofa, as well as I could, and hobbled through the vast house. As I went, my mind flooded with memories: Orla's scream at the place in Arizona; Marcus pulling me away into the night. I shook the thoughts away.

Connor had instantly faded and raced ahead of me. By the time I arrived up on the next floor and down the east side of the house, he, and pretty much everyone else, was already there. A woman I'd seen around but didn't know was standing outside the bathroom with a pair of scissors in her hand.

"Come on, you're being silly," she called through the door in a Spanish accent.

"Keep that crazy slasher woman away from me," shouted Orla from inside the room.

The woman raised her arms in exasperation and turned away from the door. She looked at Hannah and pointed at her with the scissors.

"You, come with me, now," she said.

She marched off down the stairs, and Hannah looked at me, shrugged her shoulders and trudged after the woman.

I had no idea what was happening. I looked at Connor, who had been leaning against the wall when I arrived. He shook his head and wandered off.

I knocked on the door.

"Orla? She's gone. Can I come in?"

I heard the click of the lock and entered the bathroom. Orla leaned against the sink and folded her arms.

"What on earth is going on?" I asked.

"Look, I know all this is very 'life and death' and everything." I had to hide a smile. Orla had actually drawn air quotes around the words life and death. "But that woman is not touching my hair with those scissors."

"Oh! I see. Well, don't worry. She's got Hannah for now."

"She can dye it, and she can straighten it, if she must," Orla continued. "But if she tries to come near me with a pair of scissors again, I'll smash her face in."

"Okay. Point taken. What color do you fancy—blond?"

"No bleach. I'll go brown, but no other color."

After a few seconds, she put her head in her hands and sighed.

"I suppose I'd better go find Sofia and apologize to her."

"Sofia?"

"The woman with the scissors. I shouldn't have been so melodramatic, I suppose. I think I could love it here, you know? I miss my family like crazy, but I know as long as I don't try to contact them, they're safe."

We'd only been here a day, but having Jason back had altered Orla. She had an optimistic outlook that I envied.

I sat down on the side of the tub.

"I hate it," I said.

She looked at me with her mouth hanging open.

"Okay, I don't hate it. It's just... Have you seen the way some of these people look at us? They know we were with the agency and they hate us. Some of them have lost family because of us. I don't blame them. I hate myself for it."

"Well, yes. Things might be a little difficult for a while, but they'll get to know us, and they'll see we're not bad people. Vanessa was a tracker..."

"A hell of a long time ago. And since then, she's given them all this." I waved my arm out to indicate the house, the vineyard, the safety—everything.

"Jason was a tracker, and they like him. They seem to get on well with your dad. Give it time, and don't forget, we're going to help them, aren't we?"

"I want to, more than anything."

"We've been on the inside of the base. We've got information that can help them. We know the faces of Agents and trackers. That kind of thing must be of help."

I nodded, and we went to sacrifice ourselves to Sofia Scissor-Hands.

An hour later, I was sitting with my head in a plastic wrap. Sofia had calmed Orla enough that she was able to take a fraction of an inch off the ends of her hair. My hair loss was a little more dramatic: a good amount of it was on the floor. When Sofia had finished, gone was my long, fine dark-blond hair. Instead, I had a sharp, edgy graduated bob which grazed the back of my neck and came down into sharp points just past my jawline. Also, my hair was now black. I was confident that Dad was going to hit the roof.

I left Orla and Sofia arguing over colors and went to find my dad to horrify him with my hair. I found him on the deck with Vanessa. Dad looked up as I walked out and did a double-take.

"Well, that'll take some getting used to," he said. "Very pretty, though. You look like your mum." I tried to shake the feeling that I had somehow been cheated out of a girly scream of horror from Dad. "Take a seat, we were just talking about her."

Vanessa had begged Dad for every memory of Mum that he could think of.

"I'm sorry I can't show you any other pictures of her. Everything went up in the explosion. I've just got that one of her in my wallet."

"I took the pictures from your office, but I had to leave them in my room," I said. "It would have been noticed if I'd taken them with me on the night we escaped. Sorry."

"Would you mind waiting here a moment?" Vanessa asked, and walked into the house.

I sat next to Dad and hugged him. "You smell like the jumper," I said.

"The one from my office? Marcus said you kept it in a ziplock bag until the night you escaped."

I flinched at Marcus's name.

"Sorry, Little Duck," he said, kissing the top of my head. I could tell he wanted to talk about Marcus, but didn't know how to approach it. I was relieved.

Vanessa returned with a large black plastic box. Dad swept magazines from the table-top, and she placed the box down and took off the lid. Inside were thousands of pictures of Mum as a baby, a little girl, a teenager. There were wedding photographs of Mum and Dad, and more. Photos of our family, even pictures of my friends and me.

"Where did you get these?" I asked.

"A few of the baby photos were in my purse the day I met the faders," she said. "Later ones came from various criminal activities. Fading into the local pharmacy at night for photographs developed for her adoptive family, until she was taken to the UK. I had a local contact who would do the same at your local pharmacy before everything went digital. Later, hacking Jenna's social media accounts."

I looked at her in shock.

"What is it you kids say these days, dear? Sorry, not sorry."

I barked a laugh. Diving into the box of photos, I couldn't believe I had all these pictures of Mum, Dad, Gill and me, and other friends; I had accepted that I would never be able to access my social media accounts again. Dad was already lost in a wedding picture.

I looked up from the photos to see a girl standing at the balcony on the deck, looking out towards the vines. I hadn't heard her come up. She had straight white-blond hair all the way down to her waist. Most people here were strangers to me; it made me a little nervous.

I looked down to see she was wearing boots. She was wearing Orla's Ugg boots.

"Orla?" I said, shocked. She turned around with a massive smile across her face. "Holy smoke! I didn't recognize you."

"I know, right?" she squealed. "I couldn't believe the length when she straightened out the curls. It's ridiculous! What do you think, Mr. B?" She swished her hair about.

"Well, it was very nice before, but it's lovely. It does the job—you look like a different person."

"Do you think Jason will like it?" Orla asked me.

As though he'd been summoned up, Jason appeared around the corner of the deck, walking towards us.

"Have you seen...?" He glanced at Orla, and then looked back at her again. "Mother of..." he was silent for two seconds, then recovered "...dragons." He took two steps to her, lifted her up and kissed her. "My Khaleesi," he boomed.

Orla squealed again as he marched away with her in his arms.

"Oookay then," I said.

Dad and Vanessa returned to the photos.

"I'm going to get some water. Want anything?" I asked.

"No thank you, dear," said Vanessa, and Dad just shook his head while he gazed at the pictures.

In the kitchen, I found Zoe and Hannah. Zoe's hair hadn't been touched, but Hannah's hair was candy-floss pink.

"You look like Selena Gomez in her pink hair phase," I said.

"That's what I said," said Zoe.

"I didn't say that, because I'm too self-deprecating, but I thought it," said Hannah.

'Erm... what's going on with your makeover?"

Zoe shrugged. "She says I have to wait."

"Apparently, Sofia has other plans for Zoe," said Hannah.

"I don't mind waiting. I don't have the energy for it anyway. I'm going to lie down."

Zoe's eyes looked heavy. As she walked towards the sofa, Hannah and I exchanged looks of concern.

I hobbled my way up the staircase to our room, stopping to look at my new hairstyle in a mirror on the landing. Loving it, I smiled until I noticed the reflection of a man watching me from a doorway across the wide staircase. He sneered, stepped back into his bedroom and closed the door.

2

As the days went by, I spent more time in the bedroom than anywhere else. I felt like I was in everyone's way downstairs, and some of the women wouldn't even talk to me, so I was beginning to feel very uncomfortable around them.

A week after arriving, I was settled on my bed reading when I heard a light knock on the bedroom door.

"Yes?"

The door opened and a girl came in. I recognized her as the older girl who had been playing with Felix.

"Hi, I'm Ava-Jean, or just Ava, or Ava-Jean Reynolds if I'm in trouble."

"Hi, Ava, I'm Jennifer—Jenna. Was that your sister with you the other day?"

"Yes, her name's Milly. She's six."

Ava continued to hover by the door.

"You can come in."

"Why are you in here alone?" she asked.

"Because I broke my ankle, and apparently, it will heal faster if I keep it rested."

"What happens to faders who get caught?" she asked in a tiny, hesitant voice. "Do they get killed?"

I opened and closed my mouth a few times. This conversation had taken an unexpected turn.

"Come and sit down," I said. She sat on the edge of the bed. "What have you been told so far?"

"Nothing. I keep asking, but the grown-ups change the subject or give me chores to do."

"Okay. Well, I'll be honest with you. I don't know for sure what the agents do with the faders. I don't think they kill them, but I think they keep them asleep."

"Like Sleeping Beauty?"

"Maybe."

This was awkward. No one had told me what I could and couldn't say. Maybe someone here knew better than me what did happen. I didn't know if I was giving this girl false hopes.

"I will tell you this," I continued. "If I discover that I'm right, and the agents are keeping them asleep, I'm going to do everything I can to get them back, or I'll die trying."

She looked at me for some moments. "I think you're telling the truth."

"Damn straight I am," I said.

"Why did you used to work with them?"

"They lied to me—to all of us—and when we found out the truth, we left."

"That's good." She nodded like she had made up her mind about me. That was one down, the rest of the household to go. "Oh, Vanessa wants you downstairs," she said as she stood up. "Do you need help?"

"Thank you," I said. I didn't really need help, but it feels nice to help people. I wanted to give Ava that.

As we reached the bottom of the stairs, the man who'd

sneered at me days earlier came out from one of the rooms, looking angry.

"Ava," he shouted, "come away from there."

Ava looked at me. "She's in her office. Can you get there okay?"

"I'm fine. Thanks for your help," I said and watched Ava walk away with her head down. The man looked at me like I was dirt, then turned away.

I hobbled down the hall to Vanessa's office. The door was open. Vanessa was in an armchair and patted the chair next to her. She had placed a stool in front of it for my foot.

"Thanks," I said as I closed the door behind me.

"You don't need to hide up in that room all day," said Vanessa.

"It's easier for my leg."

"I'm sure it's easier for a lot of reasons." She looked at me, knowingly.

"How did you get on with the faders when you first met them? Didn't they hate you?"

"Some did. It took time."

"You said they captured you. What happened?"

"They only knew about me because of my husband, Tom. They weren't organized, they were terrified. One of the students survived, for a while at least, because Tom sacrificed himself."

"Survivors? I thought the only survivor was an agent who was saved by a student." I thought about what I'd just said. "I guess that wasn't true."

"No, it wasn't. Initially, there were two survivors, David and Kim. But we think they became separated in the woods, and Kim was probably killed shortly after the initial massacre. I met David the next year; he was with the group of faders who came looking for me."

"But he never met Tom?"

"No. David witnessed my husband's murder, but he never met him."

"I'm sorry," I said.

"David was profoundly damaged by the incident. He was a nervous wreck when I met him. It's possible he witnessed Kim die too. He didn't talk about it. The woods at the perimeter were littered with mines; she could have encountered one of them. David's fader friends rescued him. For months, he remained rolled into a ball, muttering, 'So much red' over and over. It took years for him to be able to function properly again. He couldn't cope with the guilt."

"The guilt?"

"David believed the massacre at the Washington State Academy was his fault. When he'd learned the truth—that he was actually a fader—he'd stopped taking the pills, and a few weeks later, started emitting. He told his friends, but the agency had the place bugged. So, a year later, when they found me, the faders took a different approach. They didn't want to wait for the pills to wear off; they injected me with a solution which I suspect was made up by some second-grade chemistry student. They thought it would work immediately. It didn't. In the end, I was missing for a week before I started emitting. By then, it was too late. I couldn't go back. It seemed safer for Tessa if I just stayed away..."

The door burst open. It was the horrible man who had sneered at me. He marched right up and got in my face.

"What ideas have you been putting in her head? It's not right, giving her hope like that." His face was reddening as he shouted.

"Why did she have to come and ask me, a complete stranger? At least I was as honest as I could be."

"And when she finds out her momma's dead?"

I could see the small, hesitant figure of Ava outside the door, chewing on her hair.

"I don't believe she is dead. I think they're keeping them alive."

From nowhere, Connor appeared in the small space between us. "You need to back the hell off, Chad, and calm down."

"Chad," said Vanessa, "I'll come and speak with you shortly."

Chad peered around Connor.

"You stay the hell away from my niece." He marched away with Connor behind him. Ava took a last look at me before she turned to follow them.

Vanessa and I were alone again.

"Why do you believe they keep the faders alive?" she asked.

"The agents don't kill; they incapacitate and take the faders up to the mountain complex. I'm not saying I think it's a good thing that the agents keep them alive. What they might be doing to them up there, it gives me nightmares. I think we should be trying to find out what's going on in there."

"Well, that's the plan," Vanessa confirmed.

"I don't understand. What do ley lines have to do with the mountain?"

"I should say, that's what the new plan is. The ley line plan itself depends on us getting into that mountain."

"Why?" This was news to me. All I'd heard about was the Network.

"David, the boy from the Washington State Academy, had an ability. He was able to communicate telepathically with other faders, but they needed to be fairly close by."

"Was?" I was getting a bad feeling.

"David was captured and taken to the Cheyenne mountain facility. It was my fault. I had people keeping an eye on the base after you moved there. David's ability was greatly increased with his proximity to the ley lines. Our plan was for him to send out a telepathic alert to faders everywhere, to warn them they were being hunted."

"Why wait so long? Why didn't you do this years ago?"

"It's only been in the last couple of years that we've understood the importance of the ley lines. Also, it was never my intention to actually take on the agency. They're too big, too well equipped. They are everywhere, you know that. I run a group of safe houses. Places like this, to protect faders."

"So what changed?" I asked.

"You. When I heard that you had awakened, and so violently, I knew the agency would want you for their collection. I sat by while my daughter hunted down her own people; I couldn't let that be your future too. I still didn't intend to take them on directly, just to get the message beyond their ability to control it."

"Why not send people out to tell the other faders what's going on? Surely if enough people know, we could find some way to safely get word to the trackers."

"There isn't a fader club, we don't have a Facebook page. We couldn't possibly find them all. There aren't many of us in the Network. Most of the others aren't trained to fight the Agents; they're too frightened to put themselves out there. We've all lost people."

"But now that David is in the mountain?"

"We have to find a way to get him out of there, if he's still alive. The mountainside is crawling with military trackers, and we certainly can't get anyone through the front door. People have tried fading into the mountain from various points, but no one has ever made it out alive. So, the ley lines plan can't move forward until we can get David out of the mountain, unless we can find some other way to utilize them."

"What's the current plan for the mountain?" I asked.

"There isn't one. Every idea has been shot down for one reason or another."

"Well, I broke out of the base. I'm sure I'm capable of doing something as stupid as breaking back in." I smiled. "I'll give it some thought."

"I'd be happy if you would. I've wound myself in circles thinking about it. We all have."

I got up and limped towards the door.

"Jenna?" said Vanessa. I turned around to face her. "Could you do me a personal favor?"

"What's that?" I asked.

"Could you cut Connor some slack? He's not Marcus."

Her words stung. I turned away without responding and left the room.

LATER THAT DAY, considering what Vanessa had said about me locking myself away, I made my way into the kitchen. There were a few women working on lunch. Sofia was there, I recognized a girl called Dorothy, and there was another young woman who had never spoken to me.

I knew Orla and Hannah were down at the winery, and Dad and Jason were helping with the vines. I figured I was on my own, but I might as well start trying to fit in.

I perched on a stool at the breakfast bar and lifted my leg onto the seat next to it.

"Can I help?" I asked.

"You should be resting your leg, *chica*," said Sofia.

"My leg's resting here." I knocked the air walker. "It's my hands that need to be busy."

She smiled and placed a knife and a bag of potatoes in front of me. I got to work.

"So, I guess this is different from England," said Sofia.

"You could say that." I wanted to make conversation, but all I could think to say was, "I love my hair, by the way. Dad says I look like my mum."

"Ah, another famous tracker," said a pretty young woman, bitterly.

"She didn't know," I said quietly. "None of us did."

"Great excuse," she replied. Slamming down her knife, she walked out.

"Anna!" said Sofia. To me, she added, "She doesn't mean it."

"Of course she does. I know I've got a lot to prove; I suppose we all have."

The back door swung open, and Zoe walked in with a box full of beets and onions. She placed the box on the counter and sagged with exhaustion.

"There you go, Dorothy," she said.

"Thank you, you're a little angel," said Dorothy, giving Zoe a brief hug.

Zoe came over to sit by me.

"You really fit in here," I said, trying not to sound as jealous as I felt.

"I think it's my general luminescence. The people here pity me." She put her head on the counter and closed her eyes.

"Don't knock it. At least you're not a pariah."

"Well, you're making a start. It's not good for you to spend so much time alone, and no one likes a freeloader."

I laughed. "How about you? You look tired," I said.

"I'm always tired. Twenty-four-seven emitting will do that to a girl."

Anna came back in and picked up the beets. "Thank you, Zoe." She smiled, then got back to work without looking at me.

"No problem, Anna," said Zoe.

I tried to think of some small talk so I could engage with the women. Felix wandered through the room, and it reminded me of something.

"I used to think faders could all turn into dogs."

All the noises in the kitchen ceased: no dishwashing, no chopping, no stirring. The three women turned to me and stared.

Zoe looked at me with her mouth hanging open. "I'm tired, I need a lie-down. Are you tired too, Jenna? You look tired." She shuffled me off the stool and out of the kitchen.

Back in the bedroom, she said, "That's what you decided to go with?"

"I assumed they'd find it funny that I ever thought such a thing. I thought…"

"You didn't think, though. You basically just called them a bunch of dogs."

"I did not. That's not what I did… Oh! I panicked." I put my head in my hands and rubbed my face.

"Okay." Zoe propped up her pillow and sat on her bed. "Tell me how, in that deranged mind of yours, you thought that conversation would proceed."

"I hoped they'd understand that the agency lied to us. That we didn't really know anything about them. I thought they'd cut us some slack."

"What's all this 'we'? I get on fine with them."

"That's because you're emitting all over the place and they can relate to that."

"Are you kidding me?" Zoe looked perplexed. "You really don't know why they don't like you?"

"Just me? It's personal?"

"They've all got the hots for Connor."

"But he's nineteen. Sofia's got to be in her thirties."

"Not Sofia. She likes... someone else."

"So, what's it got to do with me, anyway?"

"He follows you around like a puppy."

"Is that some kind of dog joke? Because I think they're falling flat these days." I folded my arms, thinking about what she'd said. "But I'm not interested in Connor."

"They don't know that. Those women like having him around. Have you noticed how often they ask him to fade them so they won't lose their clothes?"

I had noticed it.

"Oh, Connor," I said in a breathy Southern accent, "I have this basket of washing, and the line is just the other side of this wall. Would you mind awfully fadin' me through?" I fluttered my eyelashes. We laughed. "That's it, then. I'll just be mean to Connor in front of those women, then everything will be okay."

"So, you're going to be mean to someone who does like you, to make the green-eyed monsters who don't, happy?"

I stared into the middle distance for a few seconds.

"Hello?" Zoe waved her hand at me. I blinked and looked at her. "I said 'green eyes' and you started thinking about his green eyes, didn't you?"

"Green-hazel," I corrected her. "No... well, yes, but not like that. Just... they're a nice color, aren't they?"

"If you like him, go for it, and screw the jealous, mean girls."

"I'm not interested."

"He's not Marcus."

"Why do people keep saying that to me?" I asked. "I just need to get a grip on this ability. I can't risk hurting people again with this power, or any other way. And I've got a lot to make amends for."

"You're not alone. Don't forget I kicked Connor in the knackers when he was unconscious. I still haven't admitted to that."

"I mean the girl on the cosmetics counter in that mall, and this David guy who was trying to keep an eye on me when he was caught."

"Who? Which David?"

"Vanessa just told me about him," I said. The hair on my neck prickled. I blinked in to find someone had faded by the door.

"I see," said Zoe. "That girl wasn't an evil monster. She was just a person, trying to get through a day's work on a cosmetics counter. She could have had a family. I think about stuff like that a lot these days."

The faded person stood there in the room, seeming transfixed.

"Get out!" I shouted. Zoe jumped.

It was infuriating that I couldn't work out who people were when they were faded. Yellow shapes floated through the house day and night, and I hadn't a clue who they were. Okay, I didn't know who most of them were, but I knew Connor. Maybe I just had to spend more time with faded people to recognize their size, shape and stance. This, however, was not Connor.

Zoe had blinked in too. "Who is that?"

We just kept staring until they left.

"No idea. Everyone looks the same faded," I said.

"Maybe it was Connor."

"It wasn't him." I bit my tongue. That was careless.

Zoe said nothing, but a small smile played briefly on her lips, before she scowled at the intrusion.

"That's just so rude," she said. "Anyway, Hannah says I shouldn't keep brooding over the past."

"How are things going with Hannah?" I asked.

"It's great. She really saved me. The only thing we disagree about is that she wants to take her inhibitor out."

"I can see why she'd want that."

"I can't," she said. "We need as many people as we can find who can go off the property without emitting all over the place. Other than that, we're good. We both just stumbled into this thing, but it really works."

"It's good to see you so happy. Orla with Jason too."

"We just need to sort you out."

"That's okay," I said, "I'm not quite there yet. I'm no expert, but I think I'm going to need more than a few weeks to get over Marcus."

3

───────

The next morning, there was a knock at the bedroom door. Vanessa popped her head around it and asked me to join her in the kitchen.

When I hobbled in, only Vanessa was there. Five crock pots were lined up along the counter, simmering away with food for the evening meal.

"I'm making pancakes. Would you like to help?" she asked.

"I'll give it a go, but I can't really cook very well," I said, feeling that honesty was the best policy.

"That's alright, I'd be happy to teach you."

Vanessa measured out ingredients and we chatted as we went along.

"These are as good as Connor's pancakes," I said when we sat down to eat.

"Who do you think taught him?" she asked.

"He's been with you for a few years, hasn't he?"

"Oh yes. He had quite an attitude when we met, but he's grown into a good man. He's like a son to me."

I had the idea this was going to turn into a matchmaking session. It was time to nip that in the bud.

"You know I killed my last boyfriend, right?"

"Yes. Thank you for that. I know it was terrible, but if Marcus had succeeded in murdering Connor, it would have broken my heart."

It occurred to me in that moment and for the first time, that even if it didn't feel like I had done the right thing, the alternative would have been much worse.

"It must have been awful, having to give up my mum."

"It was. But when I look at the man she married and the child he raised, I'm so proud of her. Even though I never really knew her." Vanessa was quiet for a moment. "I did meet her once," she said.

"You did?" I nearly choked on my food.

"She spent her twenty-first birthday at an Italian restaurant with friends before going to a nightclub to dance. It was arranged for a staff member to take a birthday cake to the table. I gave the waitress twenty pounds to let me take the cake over. The candles were lit, the lights were dimmed, and I brought the cake. I sang *Happy Birthday* to my baby along with everyone else, and for just a moment, our eyes met as she blew out the candles. It was enough. I left the restaurant and the country, and I never saw her again."

Vanessa's eyes were bright, and mine stung with tears. I had no words.

AFTER A FEW MORE WEEKS, my leg was pretty much healed. Leg day was a dim and distant memory. Keen to start exercising again properly, I made my way down to the gym. I could hear people working out as I changed in the locker room, and I walked out to find Connor spotting Chad on the weights. They both looked up. Connor smiled, and Chad eyed me suspiciously. I put my ear pods in, switched on my music, ignored them both and started pedaling.

After a few minutes, I felt eyes on me and looked up. Connor had left the gym, and Chad was staring at me, his expression hostile. Looking away, I carried on with my routine. I felt uncomfortable, but I'd be damned if this guy was going to make me run away.

When I glanced over again, he was still looking at me, but his lips were moving. I carried on cycling, but focused my energy on my iPod, muting the sound.

"...think you're so special, but how many people did you help to kill? If it were up to me, you'd be dropped down a ravine, agency bitch".

I looked at him again and smiled, taking the ear pods out.

"Sorry, my music was loud. Were you saying something?" I asked.

"No, I was just saying a prayer for my fallen fader comrades," he said.

Connor walked back into the gym with a few bottles of water. Looking from Chad to me and back again, sensing the atmosphere, he passed one of the containers to Chad.

"Here you go." Connor slapped him on the shoulder and walked towards me. "And one for you too, Beautiful."

"Thanks," I said. Taking the bottle, I climbed off the bike and took a draw on it as I walked toward the ladies' locker room.

"Hey, that must be the shortest workout in history," said Connor.

"Well, you know how it is with us agency bitches," I said without turning around.

When I left the locker room, Connor was waiting for me.

"What did Chad say?" he asked.

"Nothing to my face. Forget it."

I tried to walk around him, but he stepped across my path.

"Jenna, look at me."

I looked up into his green-hazel eyes.

"This is your home now. Neither he nor anyone else has the right to mistreat you. You've been through enough. Way more than enough."

"You don't have to fight my battles for me," I said.

"You saved my life. I'm in your corner, whether you want me there or not, Beautiful."

"And stop calling me that," I said.

"No can do, Beautiful."

I groaned and walked away.

WE WERE STILL NO CLOSER to a coherent plan for getting David out of the mountain. Everything I suggested had already been thought of and rejected. I left another fruitless meeting and headed into the kitchen. The usual girls were there, but the atmosphere was no longer hostile. They still didn't seem to have warmed to me much, but they weren't rude anymore.

"Can I help with anything?" I asked.

Ava and her sister, Milly, were playing with Felix and the ping-pong ball again. They were rolling the ball from one to the other while Felix leapt at it. As I watched, the cat was tensing to jump when Milly grabbed the ball to pull it out of the way. Felix scratched her hand in a simple case of bad timing. The little girl squealed and started to cry.

"Oh dear, did you get a boo-boo? Let me see," I said, walking to her as she wailed.

"Get away," shouted Chad from the doorway behind me.

Before I could respond or even turn, he'd pushed me, hard. I couldn't get my balance and fell towards the door of the kitchen storage room. I put my arms up to protect my face, but instead of hitting the door, I found myself falling to the floor of the storage room. My leg hurt like hell.

Enraged, I got up, turned and threw open the door. Dorothy was shepherding the girls out of the room, and Connor was marching towards Chad.

"Get out of my way," I shouted at Connor. He turned towards me and snapped his face back around to Chad, but didn't move any closer to him.

Chad was smirking at me.

"You!" I pointed a finger at him, and a bolt of energy shot out of my hand and flung him backwards. He crashed into the stools at the breakfast bar, sending them flying, and slid to the floor.

I stared in shock at my hand and the fading stream of energy around it, noticing for the first time that my arm was bare. I looked down. My *everything* was exposed; I was completely naked. I screamed. Anna and Collette were gawking at me with their mouths hanging open. Connor was crouching down with the unconscious Chad, checking his pulse.

I began to shake. Sofia rushed in, pulling a throw from the back of a dining chair and covering me while leading me back into the storeroom, closing the door behind us and switching on the light. She removed the mop from the bucket and placed the bucket before me.

I looked at the bucket and back up to her face.

"Are you going to throw up?" she asked. "People usually throw up when they fade for the first time."

I went over what had happened in my mind: falling towards the door, but not hitting it. I was still shaking, but my stomach felt okay—probably because Connor had faded me in the past.

"Did... did?" I couldn't get my words out.

"It doesn't sound like he's dead." As though to emphasize her words, a howl came from the kitchen. "But I don't think he'll pick on you again. I don't know what's gotten into him; he's been angry for weeks. He's lucky he's got those girls or Vanessa would kick him out."

I stared at my hands and burst into tears. Sofia hugged me.

A few minutes later, the door flew open and Dad came in. His hands and shirt were stained purple from working with the grapes. He put his arms around me.

"I lost my clothes," I cried.

"Orla's bringing some clothes for you," he said.

"You faded!" said Orla, coming in thirty seconds behind Dad.

"You were fast," he said to her.

"I met Connor on the stairs coming down with some sweats for her."

"I shot Chad," I wailed.

"What?" asked Dad.

"Who's Chad?" asked Orla.

"Ava's uncle."

"Oh, the douche."

"I shot him with my finger." I stared at my index finger. It still tingled.

"Is this, by any chance, where they store the booze?" asked Orla.

My sobs turned into sniffs. I took the clothes from Orla and smelled them. Orla looked at me with an eyebrow raised.

"They're clean enough."

I nodded, embarrassed.

Everyone left the little storage room, and I smelled the sweatshirt again. I shook my head. Why did I do that?

I got dressed. When I left the room, Chad was gone, and the women were back working at dinner. They surreptitiously glanced at me as I walked through the room.

"Good for you," said Anna. "Chad's such a jerk, and he's so mean to those girls."

Collette and Dorothy nodded their agreement.

So I only had to almost kill someone to get them to like me. I shook my head.

Sofia took the throw out of my hands and smiled at me. I was so grateful for that smile, I thought I'd cry again.

Back upstairs, I sat in the room with Orla, Jason, Zoe and Hannah.

"It's not fair," said Zoe. "I've been emitting for months and haven't faded yet."

"Believe me, it's not all it's cracked up to be," I said.

There was a knock at the door.

"Hello?" said Orla.

The door opened and Connor stood in the doorway. "Someone wanted to make sure you were okay, Jenna."

Ava's head popped around Connor. She was chewing her hair again.

"Are you alright?" she asked.

"I'm okay, Ava. How are you and your sister?"

"We're fine. Uncle Chad was mad, but Vanessa shouted at him."

"I'm so sorry, Ava."

"It's okay. Did you really zap him with your finger?"

"Kinda."

"That is so cool."

"It's not cool, Ava. I could have really hurt him. Who would look after you if I'd done something serious to him?"

"Mom will look after us after you get her back," she said confidently.

"Okay, Munchkin, off you go," said Connor.

Ava disappeared down the hallway, and Connor stood there awkwardly.

"It's good to see you're okay," he said as he started to close the door.

"Connor?" I said.

"Yes?" He paused in the doorway.

"Are you busy right now?"

"No, not really. What do you need?"

"Why don't you come and sit with us for a while? We're just talking."

A lot went on in his face right then. It settled on an embarrassed smile.

"I've got it!" said Zoe.

"Well don't spread it around," said Orla.

"Got what?" asked Jason.

"I've been trying to work out what Jenna's superhero name should be."

"Oh, God!" I said.

"Ladies and gentlemen, I give you... TASER!"

I face palmed.

"That's great! Do you all have one?" asked Connor, laughing.

"Just the people with abilities, so only Jenna so far. But that means you should have one too, Connor," said Zoe. Connor looked around nervously. "I'll think about it."

It had been a long time coming. After everything Connor had done for us, we should have made space for him weeks ago. I knew it was my fault. I hadn't wanted to acknowledge that there was a space—the space that Marcus had left.

"So, what are you going to do with your blasty powers next?" asked Orla.

"I don't know. I didn't mean to do the thing I did today."

"Maybe you should practice with it for a while, so it doesn't surprise you again," said Connor.

"I guess that's a good idea."

I STOOD at the doorway to the gym. It was empty. I entered and pulled out a yoga mat, staring at my hands for a few minutes.

"I can't even think how to begin," I said to myself.

"Are you sure about that?" asked Jason from the doorway.

I glanced up at him. "Sorry, did you want to use the gym?" I asked.

"No. Connor told me what you were doing. I thought I'd come down with a fire extinguisher and a defibrillator, just in case."

"You appear to have forgotten both."

He shrugged.

"Where's Orla?" I asked.

"She's down with the horses. God, she loves those things," he said, shaking his head.

"Tell me about it. Her walls at the Academy were covered in pictures of them."

I looked at Jason. He'd compromised his position and

risked his life to help get us away from the Agency, and yet I didn't really know anything about him.

"How did you end up working with Vanessa?" I asked.

"I watched the Agents take out a fader back when I was a Spotter. It sort of changed my outlook on things."

"What happened?"

He sat down and got comfortable.

"We were at a shopping center in Manchester. We'd done our part and were moved to the other end of the shops while the takedown was going on. I was desperate to see the action, so I said I had to go to the bathroom, but I sneaked out through the fire doors onto the back staircase. I could see through the windows, down onto the delivery area. A naked girl of about twelve came running out of a back door and headed towards another door. Four Agents burst out of the door behind her. She veered off in another direction, but they shot her with darts. She dropped to the ground, and they threw her into a car and pulled away."

"Why wasn't she faded?" I asked.

"That's what I wondered. I went down the stairs, out of the fire door and over to the door I thought she'd been heading for. It was a storage area which had belonged to a shop that had closed down. I opened the door to find a little boy in there. If she'd faded, she would have led a trail straight to him. He was four or five and terrified—he'd probably heard what had happened outside. He had a mobile phone in his hand, and he held it out to me in tears and said, 'Charlotte's gone. I don't know how.'"

"I crouched down and said, 'My name's Jason, what's yours?' He said he was called Matthew. I asked who he needed to phone. He was trying to contact his uncle, Adam. I found the name in the contact list and called it. I just said, 'There's a little boy here called Matthew. Something's happened to his big sister. I can't get involved; you shouldn't use this shopping center again.' I took a Snickers bar out of my pocket and gave it to him. Then I told him to stay there until his uncle came.

"I did my best to forget about it. I was confused about what I'd done and whether it had been right or wrong. It was nearly a year before I was back at that shopping center. I couldn't help myself; I wandered down to that door and looked inside. The words 'Thank you, Jason' were written on the wall with a phone number. I thought about it for at least another month. Then I bought a cheap phone and texted the number."

"What did you say?" I was engrossed.

"'How's Matthew?'" said Jason. "I received back, 'Matthew's okay, he misses Charlotte.' I felt Adam was using the names like with hostages, so I'd see them as people. My problem was that I already did. I said there was nothing I could do about her. I didn't know anything, which I realized was true—I didn't.

"Over the months, I communicated with Adam. What clinched it was when he told me that he'd awakened at puberty. He used that exact word, 'awakened', like we do. I knew then. I told him I was transferring to an academy down south, but that I'd try to let him know anything I thought might help.

"One day, when I was off duty, I was mooching around a charity shop. This kid just shoved his basket into my hand as he walked past. There were clothes in it and a book. I knew. I went into the changing room and opened the book. It said 'Get changed. Leave everything that could be bugged,' so I did. The next thing I knew, he was there. He faded me through the back wall of the changing rooms into a storage area. It was Connor.

"He told me about you. Obviously, I'd already heard about what had supposedly happened to your dad. Connor told me the truth about a lot of things while I was throwing up. He asked me to get close to you, which was easy because I already had a massive crush on Orla. Before he left, he gave me a Snickers bar and said, 'That's from Matthew.' Then he faded me back through the wall, and I got changed again."

"Why did you take the military route?" I asked.

"I figured out early on that the Agents can't actually tell when you're blinking in. I would make a big deal about learning to blink in for hours, and they were so impressed they put me on guard duty most of the time. The faders don't come near the place, so I was never going to have to kill one."

"That's genius!" I barked a laugh.

"Now, you've got something to do here, haven't you?"

"I'm guessing you think I should be doing Tai-Chi."

"You seem to be able to affect things beyond you. You learned that through your tests with Dr. Philipson. Now you need to draw out what's inside you. And if you want to discover what comes from inside you, it won't hurt to center yourself."

We practiced the forms for twenty minutes, and during that time, I pushed away what I'd just learned about Jason. I drove away my confusing feelings about Connor, my worry over Zoe, my despair over Marcus, even my joy at being with Dad. All that was left was me and what was inside me. I wanted to see the energy. I wanted to see it in the palm of my hand.

I began to feel the flow of energy moving around me as I continued the forms. A light lifted from my palm and grew in my hand. I froze. Jason froze. My peripheral vision told me that he was as mesmerized as I.

After I had remained still for a few moments, the ball of energy began to shrink, but I wasn't ready to see it go yet. I tried to continue the forms, but as I moved my arm out, the ball shot out and ignited a pile of towels. I panicked and ripped off my t-shirt to smother the flames, but my t-shirt caught fire too.

"Out of the way," said Jason, running towards the fire with a thick yoga mat. I jumped back, and Jason dropped the mat onto the fire. We both dived onto the mat to smother the flames.

"Turns out that extinguisher would have been a good idea," said Jason. We creased up with laughter.

"Erm..."

We looked up to see Orla had entered the room to find me in my bra, lying on a mat with her boyfriend.

Jason tried to say, "It's not what it looks like," but with tears of laughter streaming down his face, his words were rendered unintelligible.

We rolled off the mat and pulled it back to reveal the smoldering mess. Jason picked up what was left of my t-shirt and handed it to me. Orla looked at us and shook her head.

"Didn't one of you loons think to bring an extinguisher?" she asked.

We howled with laughter again.

4

___

I woke to shouts of "Left a bit, right a bit" outside our room.

"What the hell's going on out there?" asked Orla.

We threw on some sweats and wandered out of the room. Facing us was the top of a Christmas tree and my dad shouting instructions down to two other guys.

"How big is this thing?" I asked.

"Not a clue. It's a whopper, though," said Dad. "I'm just glad I'm not decorating it."

"Who's doing that?" I asked, noticing a box of baubles next to our bedroom door. "Never mind, I've figured it out."

"I'll project manage," said Zoe, dropping into an armchair in the hallway.

It took the best part of a day to finish the decorating with everyone's help. Baubles dressed the tree, sashes of greenery wound along the staircase, and the big fireplace held stockings for Ava and Milly.

When Christmas Day came around, even Chad seemed to be in a good mood, which was a Christmas miracle all by itself. Many people in the house, including

Orla, Zoe, Hannah, Ava and Milly, were melancholy, missing family. I savored every moment of spending Christmas with my dad. I had spent the previous Christmas believing him to be dead, and none of my friends resented me for it.

We took tables and chairs from all over the house and put them together in the family room. With people from so many walks of life, the Christmas meal included turkey, fajitas, gumbo and lasagna. Dad gave me books, and I gave him a bottle of wine from the vineyard, which he thought was hilarious after he'd spent the whole previous day sticking the labels on them.

On New Year's Eve, we headed down to the winery's warehouse, which was now mostly empty. A few of the workers took out fiddles and guitars. The acoustics in the vast building were excellent, and of course, Orla flew in circles and seemed tethered to the earth only by Jason. We had a barbecue inside the warehouse and a campfire just outside it. People took turns to blink in and ensure no one was emitting. Unfortunately, Zoe had to stay inside the warehouse for the duration of the party, but almost everyone delivered a steady stream of s'mores to her throughout the night.

On a cold evening in February, Vanessa called us together to announce it was time to take our field trip to the ley lines. We were going the next morning.

As we left the office, I realized that Zoe still hadn't had a makeover.

"Aren't you getting a disguise?" I asked.

"I'm not coming," she said.

"Why not?" I asked, although I knew why.

"Have you blinked in around me lately?"

I didn't need to blink in, but did anyway.

"Ahh!" I said. "Very festive. We needn't have bothered with the Christmas tree."

"I'm emitting pretty much twenty-four-seven, and it's exhausting," Zoe said. "They're worried that if I get anywhere near a ley line, I'll turn Northern California into a tracker beacon."

"That sucks," I said. I couldn't bring myself to admit that I'd been using her for a nightlight when I got up to go to the bathroom in the middle of the night.

"The doc's looking to see if he can get the inhibitor back into me," Zoe said.

That did sound like a painful procedure. "I hope he knows what he's doing."

"Thanks. I'm feeling super-confident. Great talk," said Zoe with a thumbs up.

"Sorry." I gave her a brief hug and made my way up to the room I shared with the girls to prepare my clothes for our trip out the next day.

THE NEXT MORNING, I went down to the kitchen, picked up an apple and went out onto the deck. I glanced at a biker-type sitting at a table, drinking coffee and reading a newspaper. He had a bald head with tribal tattoos down the sides, a goatee and little round sunglasses. I looked at him again to make sure it wasn't Jason in disguise. It wasn't. I chuckled to myself.

I looked out at the grapevines which went all the way to the mountains in the distance. They were bare now, the last of the grapes having been picked months before.

"Morning, Little Duck," said Dad.

I turned to the kitchen door with a smile on my face, but

it was empty. I stuck my head into the kitchen and couldn't see him. I glanced again at the biker, in his AC/DC t-shirt and leather gilet. He was now looking up at me. I looked closer and let out a tiny scream.

Half an hour later, Orla wandered onto the deck. Dad cracked a tiny smile into his newspaper, and I said nothing.

"Morning, Jenna. Are you ready for our field trip?" she asked.

"Yes. Is Jason coming?"

"He'll be along in a few minutes. He went down to the gym." As she spoke, she gave me a look which asked who the stranger was as she shifted her eyes to the biker. He lifted his face and removed his sunglasses, looking directly at Orla.

"Holy Mother of God and all the saints and angels," she said as realization dawned on her.

Dad put his sunglasses back on and chuckled.

Finally, Zoe and Hannah joined us. Zoe glanced briefly towards the table. "Oh hi, Mr. B. Looking good."

Dad looked disappointed.

With breakfast over, Orla, Zoe and I sat in a little huddle, staring at Dad. Keeping my eyes off him was hard. Every few seconds, I'd find myself staring back at him again.

"They're not real, though, right?" asked Orla.

"No. They're drawn on with semi-permanent ink. It's the stuff they use in movies," I said.

"He looks scary as hell," said Zoe, walking over to Dad and shoving her face right up to the side of his head. "Those tattoos look so real. It even looks like they've been there a few years. Mr. B, you look awesome."

"Thank you, Zoe," said Dad, putting away his newspaper. "Is everyone ready to hit the road?"

"Can I ride on the back of your Hog?" I asked.

No, Jenna. There is no Hog. There is an SUV. Now, go and hop in."

We went down to the car. Connor was sitting at the wheel, and Vanessa was riding shotgun. Dad and I were in the back row, and Orla sat in the middle seat with Jason and Hannah.

The car idled for a couple of minutes.

"What are we waiting for?" I asked.

"You're waiting for me," said a little voice from outside the car. I looked up to see Ava opening the door next to me. She threw a bag on the floor at my feet and smiled at me as she climbed in.

Dad and I shuffled across the seat to make room. I looked up to see Connor staring at me through the rearview mirror. I returned my eyes to Ava, who had taken out a notepad and started drawing.

"Does your uncle know you're with us?" I didn't want to have to face off with him again.

"He's running an errand. He'll be back in a few days," said Ava, looking happier than I'd ever seen her.

"Have you come along for the ride?" I asked.

"Aunty Nessa asked me to come. I have to show you what I can do."

"Aunt... oh, Vanessa." I realized then that Ava must be like me: have an extra ability. "What is it that you do?" I asked her.

"You've already seen it," she said.

"I have?" I couldn't remember ever witnessing anything unusual.

"I moved the ball for the cat," she said as she tried to draw within the lines on her coloring pad.

"Oh! Was that telekinesis? I thought it was a breeze."

"It was. I made the breeze."

"Oh, I see. How big a breeze can you make?"

"Usually, just a little one. Maybe enough to pick up some dust, or move the bedsheets on the washing line, but with time, I can make it bigger."

"Well, that's quite something!" I said.

"Uncle Chad says we're not allowed to play with Felix anymore."

I turned to Dad who had been listening and muttered, "Uncle Chad's such a jerk."

"I know. I told him if my daughter ever has reason to electrocute him again, I'd have no problem burying the body."

I looked out of the window and watched the Californian landscape going by. It was cold. I glanced forward to see Connor looking at me again. It was annoying. He was always looking at me with those green-hazel eyes like he expected something. I just smiled and looked away.

As the miles rolled by, I began to feel the hairs rising on the back of my neck. I rubbed at it and shuddered. The feeling was powerful.

"You feel it, don't you?" said Connor who had, again, been looking at me through the rearview mirror.

"Are we there?" I asked.

"About ten miles out," said Vanessa.

"I can feel it too," said Ava.

When we got to within a couple of miles of the destination, Vanessa announced that she could feel it too.

We turned off the road, drove for a while down a narrow track, and finally parked by a lake. Dad and Ava climbed out. The lake was big and calm and beautiful, but the prickly feeling at the base of my neck was almost unbearable. As I climbed out of the car, I looked over at the others, who were all rubbing the backs of their necks.

"We must look like we've got fleas," I said.

Ava and Orla laughed.

I zipped my coat up to my neck and pulled my hood up. Watching my breath vaporize in the cold, I hadn't realized California could get this cold, and wondered aloud how long this would take.

"Oh, suck it up, you daisy. It's beautiful and brisk," said Orla.

"Okay, boys and girls," said Vanessa, "this place is a picnic ground used by a campsite further down the shore. It's closed out-of-season, so we've got the place to ourselves. It's time to play."

Dad, Orla, Jason, Hannah and I all stood in a group. Ava had walked over to Vanessa, and Connor had wandered a little further away. Vanessa looked at Ava, who appeared to be concentrating.

A light breeze began to stir the grass and the leaves on the trees. After a few moments, there was a wind whistling through the trees, and halfway out into the lake, waves appeared on the previously calm waters.

"Okay, Ava, don't exhaust yourself," said Vanessa.

The young girl smiled at me, sat at a picnic bench and continued her drawings.

"Well, that was something," said Orla.

"Connor," said Vanessa.

I looked over at Connor, who was now standing about fifteen feet away. He began to fade, which was not unusual, but as I watched, Orla, Hannah, Jason and Dad began to disappear, too. I blinked in to watch them. Sure enough, they were as yellow as faders. Then I realized I was also fading. After a few moments, we materialized again.

Orla said to Hannah, "Oh my God, that was amazing. Can you believe it?"

Hannah leaned forward and vomited on the ground.

"What do you want me to do?" I asked Vanessa. "I don't see anything electronic here".

"Do you see that little hut on the other side of the lake?"

I squinted. "Just about. What is it?"

"It belongs to the quarry mining company on the other side of that hill behind it. There's a light outside."

"You've got good eyesight. I'm still trying to confirm it's a hut."

As I looked out, she nudged my arm. I looked around to see she was handing me a pair of binoculars.

"Oh. Thanks." I looked through and turned the little dial to focus them.

"There's a lightbulb over the door. Do you see it?" Vanessa asked.

"I see it," I said. I was getting nervous. That was some distance.

"See if you can turn the light on." She stepped away.

I concentrated and pushed out the energy across the lake. I remembered how pointing my finger at Chad had helped to direct the power, so I raised my arm and pointed at the hut.

The hut exploded. I saw it before I heard it.

We all stood and stared. We were too far away to feel the blast, but I'd been looking at it through the binoculars, and I had black dots in my vision.

Orla looked at Dad. "Could that have been a coincidence?" she asked.

"Well, I think it might be prudent to make good our escape," said Vanessa. "Jenna, don't forget to pick up your water bottle."

"Yes," said Orla. "Fingerprints."

Vanessa stopped to look at her. "Environmental responsibility."

"Sure, that too."

I grabbed the bottle and walked quickly back up to the car, getting in with the others. Ava immediately took out a packet of crayons and drew flowers in her pad. She was completely unfazed. I was horrified.

"What if there was someone in it?" I asked.

"It was empty," said Jason. "I put a new padlock on it last night after I placed the explosives."

"The what?" I asked, leaving my jaw hanging down. "You did what?"

"Blowing a bulb wouldn't have been much of a display," he said.

"We were there for, like, ten minutes, and now we're back in the car for hours. This sucks, and it's your fault." Orla punched Jason's arm. Jason took the end of her long white plait and tickled her nose with it. She giggled.

"Get out of here, you eejit!"

After an hour, Connor pulled off the road and into the carpark of a large Target store. There were a couple of other stores at the same location and a fast food restaurant.

"We need to pick up a few things for the house," said Vanessa. "Jenna, I think you need to build up your wardrobe. I recommend lots of cheap sweats and tees, slip-on shoes and underwear."

We hadn't been to a store in months. Orla and I spent a fortune on clothes and CDs, and Hannah bought a whole heap of gifts for Zoe. My clothes were pretty basic; I didn't want to lose anything I liked.

As we drove up to the house, it was late, and everything seemed quiet.

"What the hell?" said Connor.

"What?" asked Dad.

I blinked in and saw a bright yellow glow around the upper floor.

"The house is lit up. The whole upstairs is glowing," said Connor.

We parked up and raced in. The house was quiet, everyone asleep. We split up to search for the source of the glow. Hannah ran straight for the room we all shared, and I followed.

"Zoe, honey, wake up. Can you wake up now?" Hannah was gently shaking Zoe, who seemed to be at the center of the bright emission.

Conner and Dad arrived at the bedroom door.

"She won't wake up," said Hannah, her voice shaking.

Dad walked in and checked Zoe's forehead and pulse. He pulled back her covers and picked up her unconscious form from the bed.

"Connor, grab the mattress. Girls, get the bedding," he said.

Dad carried her down to the first floor, then on to the basement and into the gym. Connor dropped the mattress on the floor and Dad lay Zoe on top of it. Hannah covered Zoe with the quilt and sat down beside her.

Sofia and Vanessa walked in with a first-aid kit. Sofia checked Zoe's vitals, and after a few minutes, stood up.

"I've never seen anything like this. I don't think there's anything I can do. There's certainly nothing in here." Sofia waved at the green box of bandages and safety pins.

Milly padded in with her favorite toy, Mr. Bobble, in her hand. She took hold of Vanessa's hand.

"Sweetie, you should be in bed," said Vanessa.

Milly walked to Hannah, who was crying, and sat on the floor beside her.

"Shh, she's sleeping," said Milly. Stroking Zoe's hair, she added, "She's special."

Milly yawned and walked back to Vanessa.

"Come on, then, we'll let her sleep," said Vanessa.

Back on the first floor, Jason was walking in through the front door. "The house is okay from the outside now. It was a good call, moving her. How is she?"

"She's asleep," said Connor. "We don't know what's caused it. There's no sign that she's fallen or hit her head."

Connor and I walked into the kitchen.

"Zoe's been exhausted for weeks. It's all this emitting, isn't it?" I said.

"Probably, but I don't understand why. Is it exhausting you?" Connor asked as he checked out the filter jug. He sniffed at the contents and threw the liquid down the sink.

I blinked in and looked down at myself. Sure enough, I was emitting a yellow haze.

"Oh! It's a good job that didn't happen in Target," I said, taking out a bag of coffee and a filter while Connor filled the reservoir in the machine.

"You've all been through a lot. Maybe it's just been too much for her," said Connor. He flicked on the machine and reached up for a couple of mugs from the cupboard.

"Perhaps you're right. I don't know. This constant emitting is getting her down. Have you ever heard of anything like it?"

"I've seen something similar with people before they fade for the first time, but never so extreme."

We sat on the stools next to the coffee machine in companionable silence as we watched the coffee dribble down into the jug. When it gave its last steamy gasp, Connor poured two coffees.

"I'm going to stay up for a while," he said. "We don't know how long the house was glowing, or if anyone saw it."

"I'll stay up with you," I said, leaning out into the hallway at a noise. Jason, Dad and Orla were carrying Hannah's mattress and bedding down to the basement.

We moved over to the family room.

"How have you been getting on with the fading?" asked Connor.

"I've not done it since that first time, except today when you faded me at the picnic ground, but you were driving it, so I guess that doesn't count. Otherwise, I haven't even tried."

"You should get into the habit of doing it. Spend some time on it every day for a week or so. Then it's like riding a bike."

We talked for a couple more hours. Eventually, I fell asleep on the sofa, and woke up a few hours later under a blanket. I gathered the blanket around me and padded into the kitchen, yawning. Hannah was sitting at the breakfast bar, staring into space.

"Did you get any sleep?" I asked.

"A couple of hours. Zoe's still out, and she's still emitting a radius of about three yards."

I blinked in and looked at the yellow haze covering the floor.

"Do you want something to eat?" I asked.

"I just had a bagel," said Hannah.

"I can see that, it's still on the plate with one bite in it."

"Oh!"

"How about I make you a fresh coffee to go with that?" I took away her cold coffee and started a fresh pot. After toasting a bagel for myself, I sat next to Hannah, and we both stared into space while the food and coffee went cold again.

"Why did I wake up in the gym?"

Zoe's voice at the door behind us made us both jump. Hannah flew off the bar stool and hugged Zoe. I blinked in to find we were awash with yellow.

"Do you want a bagel and coffee?" I asked.

"Yes, and other stuff too. I'm starving," said Zoe.

"Okay. Hannah, you take Zoe back downstairs and fill her in. I'll get food and come down."

I was toasting the bagels when Sofia came in. "Any news?"

"She's awake and hungry. Hannah's taken her back downstairs, and she's talking to her now."

"You take the coffee, I'll bring the food," said Sofia.

I took three coffees and two barely-touched bagels downstairs. Fifteen minutes later, Sofia showed up with an omelet for Zoe, which she demolished. We were all relieved that whatever had happened to Zoe, apart from the emitting, there seemed to be no side-effects.

5

Zoe spent her time in self-imposed exile in the basement. A room was cleared out for her, and Hannah moved into it immediately. Zoe wasn't the only one who was frustrated. The plan to get David out was going nowhere, and we were all feeling helpless and restless.

As Connor had suggested, I spent a few days alone in my room, fading in and out. After a few days, I left the room and faded around the house. It was unreal. The feeling of wandering around naked was just plain icky. I wasn't sure I'd ever get used to it. I knew that no one could see me unless they blinked in, and even then they could only see a yellow haze, but it still felt wrong.

I wandered into the living room to see Hannah biting her fingernails. She stood from the chair, walked to the sofa and sat, once more chewing on her nails. I went back to my room, dressed and went to find out what was going on.

"She'll be okay," said Orla as I walked in. "It won't be long."

"They're putting Zoe's capsule back in now?" I asked.

"Yes. And Hannah's working herself into a frenzy."

"They said you could sit with her, Hannah," said Jason.

"I don't do well with blood. I'd throw up all over her," said Hannah.

"Probably best you don't go in then. It shouldn't take long, and it's not like she's unconscious. She's only had a local."

"Maybe you could sit somewhere you won't see the blood," I said.

"She knows what I'm like. She said I couldn't go in," said Hannah, returning to her nails.

"Hannah," said Sofia from the door, "if you keep biting your nails, I'll chop your fingers off. Then what will you think of all that blood?"

"How is she?" asked Hannah, launching herself off the sofa.

"She's fine. The doc's just sewing up the incision."

Hannah swayed, and Orla led her back to the sofa. "Oh my God, you are a real daisy, aren't you?" said Orla.

"I told you."

"Hey, hands off my girl!" Zoe walked in and sat next to Hannah. "Did you faint?"

"Not yet," said Hannah. "Does it hurt?"

"No, but the local hasn't worn off yet."

"Did it work?" I blinked in.

"I wouldn't bother yet. It could take a couple of hours," said Zoe. Sure enough, she was still emitting. "I'm going to bed. Let's see in the morning."

"I'll be down in a minute," said Hannah.

Zoe walked out of the room and down the stairs with Sofia.

"I hope this works," said Orla.

"The capsule came out of her, so maybe it will work

back inside her," said Hannah. "You know, this is a situation we're all going to have to face eventually. The capsules need to be replaced every few years. We're all going to be emitting one day. Then we'll all be in danger."

"Jenna's dad will figure something out. He worked on the formula for years and tweaked those pills for you—didn't he, Jenna?" said Orla.

I nodded.

"What if it comes down to having the gland removed by surgery?" said Hannah. "Now that I know what I am, I don't want that."

"I don't think that's much of an issue for now," said Jason. "We don't know enough for someone to go blundering in there. They might pull out the wrong part."

Hannah shuddered. "I'm going downstairs," she said.

"Goodnight," said Orla.

The next morning, Zoe awoke to find that Hannah and I were watching her. No one was smiling.

"Oh!" said Zoe. She didn't need to blink in, but I could see she had anyway and had spotted the yellow haze around the room. "Well, never mind," she said. "We knew it might not work." She sat up and swung her legs over the side of the bed, dropping her head onto Hannah's shoulder. "Ah, nuts!"

Orla walked in with a cup of coffee, took one look at Zoe and sighed.

"It's okay. I'm okay. I feel quite good," said Zoe, looking anything but good. "I think it's time I got my makeover. So what if I'm never going to leave this place again. I don't care. I want my spa day."

Later that day, Zoe left the room Sofia had been using as a hairdressing salon. We all looked up.

"Oh my God, you look fantastic," said Hannah.

Zoe flicked her head left and right, watching the long black braided extensions fly about her face—a face that wore a grin none of us had seen in weeks.

"Sofia has outdone herself. You look like a completely different human." Orla lifted a braid, looking closely at the beads threaded through Zoe's extensions.

"I told you to keep away from that cat," came a shout from the deck.

"But the cat's funny," said a little giggly voice.

We walked out onto the deck to find Chad standing over Milly.

"If you don't keep away from that filthy animal, you'll be sorry. I'll make you sorry."

The little girl's face crumpled into floods of tears, and she ran into the house.

"What are you looking at?" asked Chad.

"You really are a piece of work," said Zoe.

Chad marched towards her and stared her down. Orla and I stepped up into his face.

"She's a liability," he said, pointing at Zoe before storming off.

"What a grade-A dickhead," said Zoe. "Let's check on Milly."

The next morning, Hannah and Zoe were sitting in the kitchen with huge smiles on their faces.

"Last night was eventful," said Hannah. "I heard a loud thud and looked around the room, trying to work out what I'd heard. Zoe wasn't asleep in her bed, but when I blinked in, I could see yellow everywhere. I called out her name, and in response, there was a loud yawn. I flicked on the light, crawled across the bed, and looked down to the side—no Zoe. I looked under the bed. There she was, butt naked with the most confused look on her face.

"'What are you doing under there?' I asked, and she just shrugged."

"It looks like I faded through the bed and missed the whole thing," said Zoe.

"Hang on, if you'd been sleeping on the floor in the bedroom, would you have faded through the floor? That's a worrying thought."

Hannah and Zoe both looked at me. The thought had evidently not occurred to them.

ZOE GOT on with fading a lot better than I did. She didn't seem to mind wandering around naked, but she remained exhausted.

A month after Zoe faded for the first time, I was sitting in another futile planning meeting with Vanessa, Dad, Connor, Orla and Jason, when the door opened and in walked Zoe and Hannah.

"Is it okay if we join you for a few minutes?" asked Hannah.

"Of course. Come and sit," said Vanessa.

Zoe took a chair by the door, as far from the window as possible.

"We've exhausted every avenue. That mountain is impregnable."

"But..."

"I'm not risking anyone else walking into that mountain from the side, so don't offer again," said Vanessa, cutting Connor off.

"Can't we use the ley lines without David?" asked Hannah.

"If only there were some way to do that, but it just won't

work. His ability is the only way we're going to communicate the message."

I looked over to Zoe to see her sleepily gazing into space, paying no attention to the conversation around her. Blinking in, I saw the whole room was yellow. I stared at Zoe while fine spider webs of thought danced across my mind and threatened to drift away.

"Zoe emits, all the time," I said grasping at the threads of the thought.

Zoe looked up at the mention of her name. Hannah looked at me as though I'd lost my mind.

"Yes?" said Vanessa, recognizing that something was turning over in my head.

"If Zoe emits twenty-four-seven, could there be faders who don't emit at all? Like, the opposite end of the spectrum?"

"I suppose it's possible, but I don't know of one," said Vanessa.

"I do," said Connor, sitting bolt upright. We all turned to look at him. "There's a magician in Las Vegas. He fades during his act."

"How has the Agency not caught him?" I asked.

"They showed an interest in him, of course. They turned up with a few trackers and watched his act, but because he doesn't emit, they assumed it was showbiz and went away."

"He could walk straight through the big metal doors in that mountain, and the trackers wouldn't see him," said Vanessa.

"That's where I come in," said Connor, warming to the idea. "While I can share my ability and fade others, I can also make use of their talents when I fade them. We could both go in there and get David."

We all looked at each other.

"Is this the beginnings of a plan?" asked Dad.

"I think we do have the beginnings of a plan," said Vanessa.

"I have to warn you, he's ornery…"

"I won't do it!" said the Great Shadow, looking at us in his dressing-room mirror. "Seriously, Connor. You and your friend fade into my dressing room ten minutes before I'm due to go on stage and drop this shit on me? It's never going to happen—never!"

He spun around in his seat to face us.

"They still watch me, you know. The Agents pop in fairly regularly, and here you are lighting up my dressing room like it's the Fourth of July."

"Sorry, dude," said Connor. "But this is kind of important."

"I don't care. I don't want anything to do with it. I get on with my life, and I don't get involved. You know that."

"But this is huge, Vince. We're trying to save lives."

"I've got a job here. The fans buy tickets months in advance. I'm doing two shows, six days a week."

"Yes, and we'll tip the waitress, but seriously, man, think about it."

"You need to get out, and use the door like fucking humans!"

Connor opened the dressing-room door just as a young man raised his hand to knock. He stepped back and blinked, looking surprised.

"Sorry, guys, I didn't see you go in." He stepped aside to let us leave. We stood outside the door, unsure of which way to go since we'd entered through the wall.

"Everything okay here, Vince?"

"Fine, Barry."

"Five minutes," said Barry, closing the door.

We walked down the hallway, changed our minds, and walked in the opposite direction. We passed the assistant, Barry, on his phone in a quiet corner.

"It's me." He listened. "Yes... I'm not sure. They could've been."

He disconnected and turned to see us standing near. "He's gonna go ape-shit when he finds out his purple M&M delivery has gone missing. Can I help?"

"Which way out?" Connor asked.

"Back the way you came."

"Which time?" I asked, looking around hopelessly.

He pointed. "Down the hall. Left at the drag act—careful, she's a bitch—right at the sequined thongs, and the exit's at the end of the hall."

We followed the directions and came to a junction in the hallway. I glanced into a room where a man was sitting at a mirror, drawing eyebrows halfway up his forehead. He saw me in the mirror, snarled, kicked out a long stockinged leg, slamming the door.

"That would be the bitch," said Connor.

We turned left. At the next junction was a hanging rail filled with sparkly sequined thongs. Connor reached out to touch one, and I slapped his hand.

"Right here, I think," I said.

We exited at the end of the hallway into a back alley, making our way towards three golden high-rise buildings. We had borrowed a room where Vanessa and Dad were waiting.

As we entered a casino, Connor took a leaflet from a pile by the door and passed it to me.

"Look at this," he said.

It was a list of shows in the hotel.

"Are we going to see a show?" I asked.

"Keep your head down, like you're looking at it. There are cameras everywhere, and our faces have probably been circulated around the country now."

As we walked, Connor put his arm around me and angled his face towards the leaflet. I stiffened. I couldn't help it.

"Sorry," he said. He removed his arm and reached out to snag another leaflet from a concierge desk as we walked by.

"No, it's okay. You surprised me."

He didn't try again. I could have kicked myself.

"I'm not comfortable being on the Strip," said Connor.

"Why not?" I asked as we made our way through a labyrinth of a casino with so many twists and turns, I was utterly lost.

"The Agency usually has trackers here. They think it's a good place to catch us. I guess it is. There's a lot of money floating around this place."

"You're the only fader I've heard of who could get away with robbing a casino. You haven't robbed a casino, have you?"

"No, I've never robbed a casino." Connor laughed, then sighed. "I do have a confession, though."

We made our way to the food court, and Connor ordered two large pizzas to go. We shared a Sprite and sat at one of the tables to wait for the food. While we sat, we put the leaflets on the table between us and kept our heads down.

"You remember I told you I'd only stolen enough to survive?" he said.

"Yes, I remember," I said, wondering what was coming.

"That was sort of true. That's all I stole for myself. Until I met your grandma."

I stayed silent.

"Where do you think the money for the safe houses comes from?"

"I hadn't thought about it. Vanessa looks… I don't know, like a rich old lady. But I guess now I think about it, she had to leave her life behind when she joined the faders. She left everything to start again. Where does it come from?"

"My main role over the last few years has been to source financing for our activities."

"Well, that doesn't sound suspicious," I said with my eyebrow raised.

"It doesn't?"

I punched his arm. "I'm being sarcastic," I said.

"Okay. Mostly, I fade into drug dens and arms dealers' homes and steal money straight out of the safe."

I glanced up at him to find him blushing. "Good for you!" I said.

"It's still stealing." It was like he wanted me to think he was doing wrong. I couldn't see it myself. I thought it was great. "There are consequences," he said. "People usually end up shooting each other when they find the money's gone."

"Drug dealers shooting each other? Nope, still not getting it. Are you even at the bit where I should be disappointed?"

"You're an ethical person, Jenna. I thought you would be disappointed."

"Nope."

"You confuse me."

The server came with the pizzas in boxes, and we headed back to the room. To avoid leaving a fade trail straight down the hallway to the room, Connor faded us at the other end of the hallway, and we made our way through the walls of several rooms before we reached the one where Vanessa and Neil were waiting.

"How did it go?" asked Vanessa.

"Well, I think I just grew up, really fast. Two rooms along from here..."

"Jenna, it was bad enough walking past that stuff. Please don't talk about it." Connor screwed up his face and shook his head. "It went about as well as I expected. The guy's a real dick. I'm leaving him to think about it. I'll go back and see if I can change his mind."

Later, Connor and I once again made our way across the Strip.

"I think it might be best if I try to talk to him alone," said Connor.

"If you think so, I'll head to the pharmacy to pick a few things up. Call me when you're ready to meet up."

"Okay. Keep your head down," he said.

We had an awkward moment where neither of us was sure what to do. I smiled, turned around and walked away.

I crossed a pedestrian bridge and went back down to sidewalk level. It was warm—for a Brit, anyway; the locals were in sweaters and jackets, I was in a t-shirt, but the sky was darkening slightly, and it smelled like rain might be in the air. I tried to remember to keep my head down, but it was difficult. Vegas was a spectacle. Something caught my eye in every direction.

As I walked along, gazing around me, I almost missed it. I wished I had. I finally remembered to dip my head down and saw Zoe staring back at me. It was her face, her hair, with the purple spikes, every detail, correct in chalk as it would have been a year ago. For a moment, I was confused, then I understood what it meant.

At that moment, the artist looked around, and I spun my head away. I walked quickly, putting some distance between us, then broke out into a run. I ran down a side street and through an open gate which led to the garbage area of one of the hotels. I wasn't even sure which hotel it was.

I slowed. Thinking I'd lost him, wondering if he'd even seen me, I took my phone out and called Connor.

"They're here. Someone might have spotted me. I don't know," I said.

A few steps sounded behind me. I disconnected the phone and looked around. There was nowhere left to run without fading. I turned.

"Jenna?" Alejandro looked confused. "Is Zoe okay? Where is she? Why did you leave the ...."

His body stiffened, his eyes flew wide open, and the light just went out of them. He dropped down. He was dead before he hit the ground.

WHEN CONNOR FOUND ME, I was on the ground with the wind blowing strands of my dyed-black hair into my face. Tears fell from my eyes and mixed with the first few splotches of rain. I cradled Alejandro's head in my lap. If only he hadn't seen my face.

Blood ran in rivulets from his eyes, ears and nose onto the ground, and I watched as it ran away like one of his chalk drawings in the rain.

"Jenna! Did you have to...?"

"No. It wasn't me."

"We've got to go," Connor said.

"I know."

I didn't want to leave Alejandro there on the ground, by the garbage bins.

"Where's the magician?" I asked.

"He's with your pop. They're waiting for us."

"He agreed to come?"

"In the end, he didn't have a choice. All hell broke loose, and we ran. He's not happy."

"Poor him," I said.

"Your warning came just in time. I was in with Vince when you called. He faded out into the hallway and saw the Agents coming. We faded out together. Thanks to him, we didn't emit. We just went past them."

By the time we reached the car, the rain had already stopped, and the sky was clear. I climbed into the car to face a shocked Vince.

"What happened in the alley?" asked Connor.

"It was Al, a student from the academy. He saw my face. I'm not sure what happened, but I think I can guess. He said my name and just died." I squeaked out that last word.

I needed to get a hold of myself.

We drove through the streets. I was dazed and unaware of what we were driving past until I noticed that Vince seemed very interested in the route.

"Oh, the Pinball Hall of Fame, I've been there a few times," he said, looking out of the window.

We all looked at him. His comment seemed inappropriate while we were running for our lives.

I pulled myself together and continued.

"Here's what I think. The Agents were somehow listening, and I think they've upgraded the inhibitors like the one they used in me. But maybe there was a kill-switch in it. I think they just flicked that switch and murdered him."

"What?" Vince recoiled. "But that's horrific." He wiped his forehead with his scarf. When he looked back up, the color had drained from his face.

"Now you know why we need to stop them," I said.

"Are we heading to your base of operations? It's been a long time since I've seen other faders. How many of you are there?" Vince fidgeted with his white silk scarf. Absently, I wondered if he was keeping a rabbit or a dove in there. As he repeatedly repositioned it, I saw a small spot of red at the back.

"There's a few of us," I said.

Vanessa was driving. I looked into her eyes through the rear view mirror, wishing I was telepathic. I desperately needed to convey something to her. Then, she very slightly nodded. I wasn't sure if I'd imagined it.

"The car feels sluggish, I think we've got a flat," she said, pulling off the road and parking up. Getting out, she said, "Stay where you are, everyone, I might be imagining things."

She walked to the curb and kicked a front tire.

"Jenna, honey, can you get the compressor from the trunk for me?"

I climbed out and went into the trunk. Taking the compressor round to the front, I crouched down next to Vanessa.

"The thing they used to kill Al, I think they've put one in Vince, and I think he's bugged," I said.

"I see. Go back to the trunk." Vanessa stood and opened the car door. "Okay, this will inflate faster if you all get out," she said.

"What can I do?" Dad asked Vanessa.

"We've got it covered," she said. "Vince?" He walked over to her. "I know something about having your life ruined by agents. I'm sorry all this has happened."

"That's okay," said Vince. "Who knows, what you're planning might mean there's no need to hide from them ever again."

"I hope so," said Vanessa as she disconnected the compressor. "Would you mind returning this to the trunk?"

Vince made to pass the compressor to me, but I pointed into the trunk.

"It goes at the back there," I said.

He leaned into the trunk. I brought up the crowbar and hit him on the head with it. He flopped half inside. I'd never knocked anyone out before; I hoped I hadn't killed him, or given him brain damage.

I realized that the noise could have been picked up by someone listening.

"Ow! Dude, are you okay? That looks so sore. I recommend avoiding the lid of the boot with your head next time."

Vanessa was at the front of the car, bringing Dad and Connor up to date. I checked for a pulse, and then removed Vince's scarf. Connor and Dad came to look as I brushed his hair out of the way with my fingers to show a fresh wound at the bottom of his head, smeared with glue.

We checked that no one was watching and put Vince into the back of the car. I taped his mouth, but he was entirely out.

We kept the chatter up for the sake of the bug while Connor went through Vince's pockets, looking for a tracking device as he lay unconscious, face down on the floor. There wasn't one. I guessed Vince was supposed to continue the random comments, giving the Agents directions.

Vanessa started up the car again and drove in the opposite direction. We'd have to leave Vegas via another route. As we talked, Connor crouched over Vince with a penknife.

Gripping Vince's head with his knees, he scraped off the glue across the incision point, carefully poked in with his little finger, felt where the inhibitor was and teased it out with a pair of Vanessa's tweezers. I remembered gouging out my inhibitor when Marcus was killing Connor, shoving my fingers into my soft flesh to pull it out. I shuddered, thinking about what Connor had said about being able to use other faders' abilities when they were fading together. I wondered why he hadn't faded Marcus, then taken all of his energy. I would have to ask him.

I half expected Vince to wake up and struggle—I think we all did—so I still held the crowbar, just in case. But he lay there, completely out. I then wondered if maybe I had killed him.

Connor removed a cloth from the back pocket of a car seat and wrapped up the little device immediately. Dad wiped the wound with a tissue and glued up the cut with the glue from the car's first-aid kit. I took the tape off Vince's mouth. The inhibitor was small. It couldn't have much explosive in it; just enough to kill a person, I supposed.

"I'm going to pull into this Walmart to pick up supplies," said Vanessa. There was no Walmart.

We stopped the car and dumped the inhibitor, still wrapped up, into a trash can, and drove on. Hopefully, the Agents would now be searching for us at a supermarket.

"Where to now?" asked Dad.

"We need to get off the road," said Vanessa.

Connor picked up his cell phone and began muttering into it. "A friend of mine is going to fly us to the Grand Canyon." He gave Vanessa directions, and she turned towards the airport.

After about ten minutes, Vince began to wake up. I was a little relieved.

He clutched his head. "What the hell happened to me?"

"Sorry, Man," said Connor. "We were heading to the local base and didn't want you to see where it was, so Jenna popped you on the head."

Vince looked at me, and I gave him a smile and a little finger wave.

"Seriously? I have no options now. I'm in this, and you don't trust me?" Vince was doing an excellent job at being indignant.

He reached back and felt his head where I'd hit it. I noticed his hand slide down to his neck. He seemed not to realize we'd done anything. It must have been hurting already.

"So what's happening now? Are we nearly there?"

"We've been. We're heading to the main base now," said Connor.

Main Base? I nearly snorted.

6

———

As we pulled into the little airstrip, Vince looked out of the window.

"Oh, Henderson Executive Airport, I haven't been here before," he said.

It seemed that he thought the bug was still working.

We parked by the hangar and boarded a little white plane. The seats were cream leather. This was a top-end ride.

Connor introduced us to Martin, the pilot. We strapped in and took off.

"Have you all seen the Grand Canyon before?" asked Martin from his seat in front.

Everyone said yes, except me.

"Your main base is at the Grand Canyon?" asked Vince, much too loudly, apparently trying to make sure the mic picked his words up over the sound of the plane's engines as it climbed.

"Okay, Vince, you can knock it off. We've removed your explosive little hitchhiker."

Vince looked angry and scared, and finally relieved.

"After you left, I did my show, then Barry came in and shot me with a dart. Son of a bitch, he's been with me for five years. When I woke up, they told me they'd inserted an organic explosive bug. They said if I tried to fade while it was switched on, it would explode. They promised me if I helped them catch you, they'd let me go back to my life. Then they told me they'd know if I tried to run or warn you because they were listening."

"Vince, we need to know if you're on board with helping us now. No one's going to force you to do this, but you need to know we can't do it without you," said Vanessa.

"Can I decide after you tell me what 'this' is?" he asked.

Vanessa leaned forward. "We need to break into the mountain."

Vince's eyes darted about as though reflexively looking for an escape route.

"The mountain? Cheyenne Mountain?" His voice had gone incredibly high. "What the hell do you need to go poking around in there for?"

"They've got David," said Connor.

"David? When?" He turned white.

"Months ago."

"Why didn't you tell me before?" Vince's voice cracked.

Connor shrugged.

"Honestly, I wasn't sure whether telling you would make you less likely to help."

"Are you sure he hasn't already…?"

He didn't need to finish the sentence.

"We don't know. But we've been trying to think of a way in for months. There isn't another way."

"Our end game depends on having David out of there. I'm not even sure it will work, but we need to try."

"David's a good guy. He's been through a lot, and irrespective of what happened in the past, I care about him," said Vince. "Of course I'm in."

The plane landed on a small airstrip near the Canyon, and we hired a car to take us the rest of the way. Connor had booked two rooms at a lodge in the park. We were lucky it was out of season.

By the time we reached the lodge, it was dark. The restaurant was still open, so we had a basic dinner and retired to the rooms. Vanessa and I were in one room, and the three men were next door.

As we lay in the dark in our beds, Vanessa spoke.

"You made a good call earlier. You have good observational skills."

"Do you have abilities? How did you know something was wrong?"

"Your eyes were almost out on stalks. You have no poker face."

I dropped into sleep straight away, and was awakened by a knock on the door at 5 a.m.

"Jenna?" It was Connor.

I opened the door. It was dark outside, and the air was thin and cold.

"Yes?"

"Do you want to come and see the sun rise over the Canyon?"

"Erm..."

"Jenna, you can't come to the Grand Canyon and not see the sun rise over it," said Vanessa from under her covers.

"Okay. Ten minutes," I said.

I had a quick wash, pulled fresh clothes out of my kitbag and went out to meet Connor, zipping up my coat as I left. It was a ten-minute walk to the edge from the lodge. Connor had scared up a couple of coffees, which I appreciated in the cold.

As we walked, I remembered I had a question to ask him.

"Connor, you told me you can share other faders' abilities when you fade with them."

"You want to know why I didn't do it with Marcus."

"Yes."

Traces of the sun were playing along the horizon, making the top of the Canyon visible, but that was about it.

"At that moment, I'd rather have died than draw the essence of that kid into me. When you shouted your warning, I had a moment where I considered it, but the idea disgusted me so much, I thought it would be better to let him kill me. I would have felt polluted. Look."

He pointed out across the Canyon. The dark, muted greys before us began to turn into rich browns and oranges. As the sun rose, layers of red and gold filled in the landscape like it was being painted before my eyes. The vastness and beauty of the Grand Canyon, or the part I could see, was revealed to me inch by inch, and I felt insignificant next to its majesty.

"It's beautiful," I said, barely above a whisper.

"I've never seen anything as beautiful," he replied.

I looked at him. He wasn't looking at the view; he was looking at me. Finally, I knew that in this place, I could let go of the pain and anger and guilt over Marcus. As I turned to Connor and watched the sun illuminate his green-hazel eyes, he took my face into his hands and kissed me, and I kissed him right back.

We sat together with our arms around each other, and had been gazing out at the vista for another half hour when Dad, Vince and Vanessa joined us. Connor made to step away from me a little, but I held him close. He settled into me.

"It never gets old," said Vince.

"A wonderful sight indeed," said Dad. He was talking about Connor and me, I knew that.

"Let's go save David," said Vanessa.

"Now?" I asked.

"The sooner, the better," said Vince.

"We can have breakfast first, though, right?" asked Connor.

As we walked back to the lodge for breakfast, I nodded my head towards Vince. "Was I wrong about him?" I said to Connor.

"As long as I've known him, he has always been out for himself. He'll be working some angle. We have to be ready for it."

After breakfast, Connor spent some time planning our trip. He called Martin and booked a flight from the local airport to a private landing field outside Denver. We piled into the car and began the journey.

A DAY LATER, in a Denver motel room, Connor and Vince planned their trip to the Cheyenne Mountain facility. Vanessa's laptop was open, showing a map of the area.

"How does Vince's ability work?" I asked.

"Come over here, I'll show you," said Vince.

I walked to his side and waited for instructions. Connor reached out and touched Vince's arm.

"Vince, fade and stay exactly where you are."

Vince and Connor both faded. I blinked in, but there was no yellow mist at all; they were both gone, totally invisible. Then Connor came back. He reached towards me and faded me.

"That's incredible," said Dad. "How do you know when you're connecting with Vince? Can you see him?"

"Do you want to try?" asked Connor.

"Sure," said Dad, being the curious scientist.

Connor faded Dad. I blinked in again and watched Dad reach out to where we thought Vince was standing.

A few seconds later, he was visible again.

"It's like a magnetic resistance."

"Vince, dear. Would you mind coalescing?" asked Vanessa.

Vince and Connor returned.

"Coalesce. That's a good word," I said. "At the Academy, we always called it 'fading back'."

"That doesn't even make sense."

"I see that now."

"It's interesting how most faders I've known use the word 'fade', but they use all kinds of words for materializing," said Vince.

"Another good one," I said.

"So, how are we getting in there?"

"If you just walk in through the gates, it will still take you the best part of a day to get up to the mountain entrance," said Dad.

"There are several regular visitors to the base," I said. "Some get through the gate; some don't. Laundry services and produce deliveries come into the base camp. I've never seen Amazon get past the gate. The only vehicles I've seen going up there are the ones bringing in faders. They sometimes used to go to the doc's office at the base first, but that stopped after Connor got away."

"I need to make a call," said Vanessa, stepping outside.

She came back in after a few minutes.

"We have someone willing to act as bait," she said.

"Why would anyone do that?" I asked.

"Many people are committed to what we're doing here. They know there's a chance they won't be coming back."

The plan was set. The next day, someone was going to put their life on the line for us. Connor and Vince were going to be waiting by the gates for their chance to get up the mountain.

We prepared the gear in the morning, but something had been bothering me, and finally, I spoke.

"I want to go with you."

"I don't think it's a good idea for you to go into that place," said Vince. "We're probably going to see some things... Well, if I had the choice, I wouldn't be seeing them."

"Do you have any abilities to defend yourselves?" I asked.

"Ouch! That hit me straight in the guy-pride," said Connor.

"Are you saying that you do?" asked Vince.

I stared straight at him while the TV rolled and the lights flickered. He looked at his arm as the hairs along it rose. I pointed my two index fingers at each other, and a spark jumped between them. I'd been practicing that.

"I could give you a more direct demonstration if you like," I said.

"Nope, I'm good." To Connor, Vince said, "I think she should come."

I looked at Dad, expecting an argument.

"I spent the best years of my life with a woman who knew twenty ways to kill a person without getting out of her chair. I've learned to trust and respect the women I love."

"Are you crazy?" asked Connor.

Vanessa was looking at Dad with shining eyes.

"Tessa was so lucky to have you," she said. "Also, I have girlfriends who would pay good money for an introduction to you."

"Hey, no pimping my dad out." I shook my head.

"But, on this occasion, I don't think you should be on the team, Jenna," said Dad.

"What? But you just said…"

"I'm sorry. I'm not ready to lose you."

"I'm trained. I can protect myself, and I can protect them." I pointed at Connor and Vince.

"Maybe next time," said Dad, signaling an end to the conversation.

I couldn't believe it.

"This is ridiculous. It's unfair." I allowed the energy to flare up with my temper, taking out the TV, the lamp and everyone's phones. I stormed to the door.

"Where are you going?" called Dad.

"To buy a new phone," I said as I slammed the door behind me. But there was nothing wrong with my phone, just theirs.

I was not planning to sit this one out.

MAJOR TOMOWSKI SAT in the observation booth and gazed down into the clinical white room. Four Agents stood in the corners of the room, each behind a metal post with a flashing amber light at the top.

In the center of the room, an unconscious man in a hospital gown lay on a gurney.

After a few minutes, the man began to awaken. The

Major nodded to the Agent next to him who flicked on the video camera and nodded back.

"Initiate," said the Major. The Agents each pressed a button on the posts, and the amber lights flicked to red. A persistent humming filled the enclosed space.

The man on the gurney sat up, rubbing his face. Unaware that he had been unconscious for several weeks, he lifted his head, took one look at the Agents and faded.

The Agents looked around and shifted uncomfortably.

The humming turned to a squeal, and the fader reappeared, dropping naked to the ground. He shook as though in a fit and a puddle of urine spread beneath him on the floor.

The Agents looked up to the Major, who nodded. One of the Agents stepped into the middle of the room, unaffected by the energy field coming from the posts, and shot the man with a dart. The other Agents switched off the posts, and the humming ceased.

The Major nodded to the camera operator, who switched off the device.

"How many is that now?" asked the Major.

"Forty-two," said a white-coated Agent behind him.

"They all fade immediately. Every single fader." The major stood. "I think we can call this a success."

Then he made his way to the door.

"I'm heading down to the base. Write the experiment up and put it in the file," he said, and left.

7
———

Vanessa started the car. "When Jenna returns, take a cab to the Strip. Martin will take you back to California, and then he'll come back for us."

She drove away, unaware that I was in the trunk of the car. When she got near to the base, she slowed and pulled over. Connor and Vince were sitting on the back seat, fading. I slipped my hand through the gap between the seats to stay in contact with Vince. He moved slightly, but didn't say anything. I knew he had felt me.

Vanessa dropped us at the side of the road. Anyone watching would have seen an old lady stop her car, consult a map and continue. Connor, Vince and I had faded out of the car with our gear and walked to the gate. As yet, Connor had no idea I had tagged along.

Vince and Connor spoke in hushed tones, even though they knew that the guards in their hut, a few feet away, were oblivious.

"It's been over two hours. Could something have gone wrong?" Vince asked.

"The fader will have been wandering around the mall, being sure to be spotted."

As he spoke, the gates opened and an SUV flew out.

"I think things are going as planned," Connor said as we settled down to wait.

After two more hours, the SUV was back. We faded into it as it idled, waiting for the gates to open, sitting unseen among the Agents in the vehicle and staring down at the body under the blanket on the floor. As the SUV drove over the bumpy road up the mountain, the body rolled on the floor and the cover slipped, revealing the unconscious face of my grandmother, Vanessa. I gasped in horror and felt the presence of Vince at my side, reminding me to stay silent. Connor didn't know I was there and finding out here could throw him enough that he might make a mistake.

After the long ride up the mountain, we arrived at the door to the complex. A team was waiting with a gurney and Vanessa was transferred from the car. Before she was taken away, an Agent shot her with another dart.

"Just in case." He laughed as he climbed back into the car.

Vanessa's gurney was pushed into the mountain, and we followed close behind. We entered an elevator, which plunged through many levels of the base. The doors then opened to a brightly lit corridor that ran forwards from the elevator.

The Agents reached a door and pushed Vanessa through. We followed into a sparse room with computers, a hospital bed with a clear plastic covering over it, and some machines.

"Any ID?" asked a female Agent.

"Nope, nothing in her clothes."

"I'll print her to see if anything comes up." The female

Agent lifted Vanessa's limp hand and laid it against an electronic tablet. The word 'searching' appeared on the screen and an icon began to spin as it counted up slowly.

"We'll get a coffee. When will she be ready to move?" one of the male Agents asked.

"Come back in twenty minutes," she replied.

I could sense Connor trying to choose whether to stay with Vanessa or follow the men. Vince pushed him in the direction of the men. It made sense as we knew Vanessa would be here for at least twenty minutes, and we could do with getting a view of the layout.

We moved to follow the men. They left the room and continued down the corridor, ducking into a small break room with a coffee machine. We carried on along the hallway to a door at the end, walked through it, and were met with a vision of horror. It was like something from a science fiction movie.

We were standing on what looked like a large balcony overlooking a vast space. To the sides were gates in the balcony railings that led to long rooms containing rows and rows of beds with translucent bags on top. Each bag had tubes coming from it, respirators and computers next to the bed, and each bag had a person inside. In the corner of the balcony were numbered buttons. There were seventy buttons—the balcony was an elevator with seventy levels, each potentially holding hundreds of unconscious faders.

A red light began to flash, and a voice came over the public address system. It was the female Agent.

"Agents Richards and Ford, please return to the induction suite."

We moved back into the corridor where the two Agents were walking quickly back. We entered the room directly behind them.

"She's a tracker," the female Agent said. "At least, she was. Her prints came up on the third database check. Vanessa Harvey. She went missing in 1979. There's a flag on her file. I've set up the anesthetic, but not the tubes. The bosses are going to be all over this. Keep her on this floor. Move someone if you have to."

"Oh shit!" said one of the Agents. "I hate it when the bosses get involved."

We moved around to the computer as the female Agent tapped at the screen. She then put down the tablet and led the Agents out of the room, along with the gurney. I watched as the tablet disappeared from the desk—Connor had picked it up.

We headed out as they wheeled Vanessa, now hooked up to the anesthetic and monitor, back into the room. Connor walked us into the little kitchen. I looked at the security camera in the corner of the room, surged some energy towards it and heard a soft pop. We reappeared.

"What the hell?" Connor stared at me in horror.

"Hi," I said.

"You must have known she was there," he accused Vince.

"I'm as shocked as you are," said Vince, who didn't look the least bit shocked.

"Focus, Connor, we've got a job to do," I said, but then I drew in deep breaths and leaned against the wall.

Connor looked at me. "Are you okay?"

"I thought I was going to faint when I saw it was her."

He shook his head and looked at the tablet. "I'm trying to work out where David would be," he said, scrolling through screens.

"Wouldn't his prints be in the system too?" I asked.

"His name's not here. They would have printed him

when he came in but unless he was already in the system, that wouldn't give them his name.

What about when he was a kid with the agency? asked Vince.

They might not have printed him so young back then," said Connor.

"But if they did?" asked Vince.

"If they did. His name might not be here because they already interrogated him," said Connor.

"You mean, killed," I said, feeling a stone in my chest.

"Or, they just don't know who he is. He could still be here," Said Connor

"His name's not here." Connor passed the tablet to me, still shaking his head. "Your dad must be freaking out."

"Can you search by date? When did they get him?" asked Vince.

Connor told me the date David had been captured, and I started to type it under the search bar, but stopped, my finger hovering over the tablet.

"What?" asked Connor.

"That date is familiar." I couldn't say why, so I dismissed the thought. "Maybe it's someone's birthday. Okay, there were two brought in on that day. Level 19 EW413 and Level 22 EM179."

"What do we do about Vanessa?" asked Vince.

"They're keeping her on this floor, so we know where to find her," said Connor.

We returned the tablet to the nurse's station and headed towards the balcony elevator. Connor began to walk through the door, and then jerked us back. I looked through the door myself to see the balcony was no longer there.

Vince pulled us towards a door on the right. It led to the stairs. I looked at the number fourteen painted on the wall.

Was it up to floor nineteen, or down? Connor led us down. As we turned on the staircase, I saw fifteen painted onto the wall. We were only a few floors away and heading in the right direction.

When we reached nineteen, we went through a door and passed hundreds of beds in linked rooms along a long tunnel. We arrived at a section called EW and started to check bed numbers as we walked, but I was getting the feeling we'd selected the wrong option. All of the beds were occupied by women. That must have been what the W in EW meant. We had to be sure, though, so when we reached bed 413, I looked through the translucent plastic at the body inside. It *was* a woman, but to my shock, I recognized her. It was the woman from the cosmetics store in the mall. That's why I remembered the date. She may have been taken the same day as David, but this one was my fault.

I looked around the room and saw a camera. I stared at it, willing it to move, pointing away from us. We reappeared.

I began unzipping the bag and pulling at the wires. Connor's hand grabbed mine to stop me. I looked at him.

"She's here because of me," I said.

"You're going to set alarms off if you free her without taking precautions."

"I can take care of the alarms, but you're right. We can't take her with us yet. She might freak out." I pulled back my hands and stopped to think.

"We have a mission here. We have to get David," said Vince.

"I'm coming back for her," I said as I zipped up the bag.

We retraced our steps to the central staircase and continued down three more floors. Assuming that the E in EM meant East, we moved off in the same direction.

A much shorter journey led us to EM179.

Connor unzipped the translucent body bag to reveal the face of a thin, balding man. The little I knew about David was that he was in his fifties and had some mental health issues. This could have been him, I supposed. His face was slack with a breathing tube in his mouth, taped to the side of his face and exiting the bag from a hole at the top. He didn't smell very good. I turned to ask if this was David when a loud gulp came from Vince. I turned to see his face contorted with grief.

"How can they do this to people?" he asked.

I looked around at the other beds and thought of the hundreds we'd already passed.

"You're just getting that now?" I asked.

"I know David. He's a good guy."

"They're probably all good guys."

Connor shook his head discreetly, warning me to leave Vince alone.

"Come on," I said. "Let's get your friend out of here."

We assessed the situation, taking in the sensors, the tubes and the cables.

"Could we disconnect the anesthetic and let him fade out of everything when he wakes up?"

"He won't fade out," said Vince.

"I'll have to do it for him," added Connor.

I didn't understand, but there wasn't much time to discuss it.

"I know this is horrible, but when I give you the nod, start transferring the wires to the guy on the bed next to him."

I glanced at the next bed as Vince unzipped the bag. Inside was an elderly man. I felt sick, but I promised myself that all of these people would be free one day.

I watched the monitor feeling the signal from David's

pulse through the wires to produce the visual representation of his life signs.

"What about the breathing tube?" asked Connor. "Is it alarmed?"

"It doesn't seem to be. I think the oxygen levels are read through this thing on his finger. You will need to move that too."

"Monitor wires first, then anesthetic," I said.

I pushed out the energy from myself. It was like being in the lab with the professor again. The reminder that the makeshift lab was very close by made me shiver. I synced myself with the rhythms of the machine, then nodded. Vince removed the wires and hooked them up to the elderly gentleman in the bed next to him. I slowly released my control of the signal. The old man's rhythm was slightly different, but didn't set off any alarms.

Vince swapped the oximeter to the old man without incident. Connor gently removed the needle from David's arm and unzipped the bag down enough to get his arms under the unconscious man. He faded them both, and the catheters dropped down into the bag. Vince swept the bag onto the floor and ripped off the sheet before Connor reappeared and laid David on the bed. Vince put the sheet over him.

We waited.

Vince looked around the long room.

"Don't go too far in either direction. I've adjusted the cameras on this section, but they're everywhere." I pointed out the cameras.

"I was looking for something to stuff into the bag so it won't be so obvious he's missing," said Vince, glancing around.

After ten minutes, David still hadn't stirred.

"Should we tap his face or something?" I asked.

"No!" both Connor and Vince said together.

"He's a little skittish," Vince explained.

"What if he doesn't wake up? Can you carry him?" I was getting nervous.

"We'll have to. But we might not be able to get Vanessa out if we have to do that."

"She knew the risks," said Vince.

I looked at Vince in disgust.

Connor took my hand. "Vince's right," he said.

A groan came from the bed.

"David?" said Vince.

David's eyes flew open but remained unfocused. He opened his mouth in what was clearly about to be a scream. Connor grabbed him and faded them both, and the room fell silent. A few seconds later, they reappeared.

"Hey, man, how are you? We're busting you out," said Vince with a huge smile.

"I don't remember them catching me." David's eyes fell onto me, and he looked suspicious.

"This is Jenna. Vanessa's granddaughter. Remember? We were working on getting her out of the base," said Connor.

"Where are we?" asked David as he rubbed at his throat.

'The base," said Connor with a smile and a shrug. "We're actually in the mountain."

David shook his head. "My throat hurts." He looked up at Vince. "You lost your job?"

"Hey, dude, I thought we had rules about that." Vince took a bottle of water from his pack and passed it over. David drank deeply and coughed. "You've been fed by tubes for a while. We should have thought about this. You might be too weak to walk." Vince took out a small carton containing a meal replacement liquid and passed it to David. "Do you think you can walk?" he added.

"How long have I been here?" asked David, still appearing to be shaking off his confusion.

"Not as long as some of these poor sods," I said.

"How long?" he asked again.

"A few months," said Connor. "They caught me too. Jenna saved me."

David nodded.

"But my balls still hurt," said Connor.

I froze, thinking that was months ago. Zoe must have delivered one hard kick to Connor's unconscious form. I decided that Connor must never know it was Zoe who'd performed that run-up kick.

"Who's Zoe?" asked David, looking at me.

"A friend of mine. You'll meet her soon."

"I'm not sure I'd like that."

"I forgot about your ability."

Connor looked puzzled, so I smiled at him, praying he wouldn't ask.

We heard a door swing open along the corridor.

"We need to fade," I said.

"No!" David shrank away from us and stared around as though looking for somewhere to hide. The terror on his face was alarming.

"He won't fade. I'll do it," said Connor. We held hands and faded together.

After a few minutes, a man in white trousers and tunic appeared with a clipboard, looking around the room and tapping on his tablet. He observed the mess of David's bed with a puzzled face. Walking to the bed, he looked more annoyed than suspicious as he reached towards his radio.

At that moment, Vince appeared and punched him hard

in the face. The man reacted quickly, hitting Vince in the stomach and winding him.

He went for his radio again, but I appeared and sent an overload of energy onto the device, which sizzled and popped. I pointed out my arm at him. Nothing happened. He looked at me like I was demented. Embarrassed, I tried it again, and a ball of energy flew from my hand and threw him across the room. The man was out cold.

I stared at my hand and the mass of energy surrounding it. I didn't know how to make it go away, so I shook my hand, and a burst of energy flew over Vince's head, busting the security camera on the wall.

"Oops," I said as Vince eyed me suspiciously.

"Don't think about it. It will go on its own," said David, reappearing with Connor.

"This is a problem," said Connor, looking at the unconscious man.

"This is an opportunity," said Vince. "Okay, Dave, we need to find out if you can walk because this man needs a bed."

Vince unbuttoned the man's tunic and pulled his t-shirt off, then flipped off his shoes, stuffing the clothes into his backpack. I helped David to stand. He was frail and naked; I expected him to hit the floor. He wobbled, but surprisingly, stayed on his feet.

Connor and Vince moved the unconscious man onto the bed, swept off his trousers, laid him on top of the catheter tubes and half zipped up the bag. Vince took the needle attached to the anesthetic and waved it over the guy's arm, looking unsure. He gave it to Connor who slipped it into the man's vein. The man began to rouse, but slumped straight back into oblivion. The breathing tube was stuffed back into the bag, which was zipped up around it.

"He won't suffocate in there, will he?" I asked.

"You care?" asked Vince.

"I'm not a killer," I said. For a moment, I thought of Marcus. *Yes I am*.

David was looking at me, I could feel it. I turned to face him. He had such a look of sadness and empathy, I nearly burst into tears. I shook my head and focused.

"When we get Vanessa, they'll be searching the place. They'll find him," said Connor.

"Vanessa? What's happened to Vanessa?" asked David.

"Nothing, if we're lucky," said Vince.

"How are we all going to get out of here without breaking contact?" I asked. "This is getting difficult."

"I've been thinking about that. Have you ever known a tracker to come up to this facility?" asked Vince.

"Not past the entrance. Only Agents get inside," I said.

"We should be able to separate. Being faded should be enough until we get to the exit. I'll go with you, Jenna, to get your girl. Connor, you take David and get Vanessa."

"I'm not sure that's a good idea," said Connor. He clearly didn't want Vince going off with me alone. I didn't blame him; Vince didn't seem very invested in rescuing the girl.

"It's okay," said David to Connor.

"We'll see you back on Vanessa's floor."

Vince passed his backpack over to Connor, knowing that he would lose everything when he faded.

"Are you ready, buddy?" Connor asked David.

David nodded, but his eyes looked haunted. He grabbed Connor's arm, and they faded.

Vince and I faded and headed for the stairs—or I hoped we both did. It was disconcerting to be unable to see the tell-tale yellow outline and mist that usually accompanied a fader. I peeled off at level nineteen, watching the bright yellow shapes of David and Connor continue slowly up.

At floor nineteen, we made our way back to the woman's bed. I felt uncomfortable appearing naked in front of Vince, but it seemed there was nothing else for it. As I began to appear, Vince turned and pulled the sheet from under the person on the bed next to her. He ripped it and passed half of it to me, covering himself with the other half. I wrapped the sheet around myself, surprised that he had been so considerate, and we set about detaching her from the cables and tubes.

She awoke, sluggish and confused.

"Stay calm, this is a jailbreak," said Vince.

She took in her surroundings, and her eyes fell on me. She screamed, faded and bolted in the opposite direction to the exit.

"Shit!" said Vince, and ran after her.

I stayed where I was and tried to keep it together, tidying up the bed as well as I could and hiding the tubes under the mattress. I looked at the bag of fluid hanging up on the other end of the tube from the needle, disappointed not to be with Connor. It would have been useful to keep a hold of his ability.

After what was probably fewer than ten minutes, but felt like a year, Vince appeared with the woman.

"This is Jodi," he said. "I've explained that you're going to apologize to her for what happened, but we're not going to deal with it now."

I pulled the sheet off her bed and handed it to her.

She looked at me like I was an alien. "You haven't been doing this for long, have you?"

"Not really, no," I said.

"You get over the naked thing pretty fast when your life is in danger twenty-four-seven."

We faded and walked towards the stairs and up to level fourteen. As we moved along the hallway, a doctor came out of a door behind us and walked quickly through us to another room. As he opened the door, I heard a familiar voice that sent chills through me.

We faded into a room to find the base commander, Major Tomowski, standing over Vanessa. The breathing tubes and catheters weren't attached, but she was anesthetized, and I could hear the beeps of the machines monitoring her vitals.

I looked around the room to see a nurse at a desk and Merv standing with his hand, as always, resting on his gun. Seeing his nasty face reminded me that I hadn't missed him one bit. Next to Vanessa stood the faded figures of Connor and David. I no longer knew where Vince was.

"Doctor Marvolo, thank you for joining us," said the Major, looking at his watch.

"Sorry, I was in surgery, and please, call me Tony," said the doctor.

"We need to know what this means," said the Major.

"I'm sorry?" The doctor took the pad and read. "Oh, I see. Interesting. Could it just be a coincidence?"

"I don't believe in coincidences. Vanessa Harvey has been off the grid for nearly forty years. She's the grandmother of the Banks girl—the one who escaped thanks to the ineptitude of your predecessor." He turned to Merv. "And they are definitely up to something with the Vegas freak."

The anesthetic bag was dripping about once every ten seconds. I watched Connor's arm move up to it.

"Marvolo. That would have been a great stage name. I

wish I'd thought of it," said Vince. It was good to know he was there.

"That Vegas guy can fade without leaving a trail. He could be in here with us, and a tracker wouldn't be able to see him." The Major looked around. He then drew back his arm and slapped Vanessa hard across the face. She didn't respond. I wanted to rip his heart out.

The Major looked around again, as though expecting someone to appear. I stood still, and I could see Connor freeze for a second. I knew he was looking at me to see what I'd to. His yellow shape nodded, then he continued his work.

As he worked the little plastic tap, there was a slight fluttering around it, the very ends of his fingertips becoming visible. I glanced around the room to see if anyone had noticed, but with everyone's eyes on Vanessa, no one had.

The drops ceased.

The Major continued as though he hadn't stopped speaking. "But if there are other faders in this facility, a tracker will see them. Merv, what's the ETA on the tracker coming up here to sweep the place?"

"Are you sure that's a good idea?" asked the doctor.

"It's someone dispensable. Once the tracker has confirmed it's clear, they won't be going back. They'll be joining the Agency for a mystery mission."

"Monster!" I said in disgust.

"I'll check the ETA," said Merv, and he left the room.

"What do you want doing with this one? I could try my new project on her," said Doctor Marvolo, pointing at a shiny metal tray on the nurse's desk.

"No, I don't want her dead," said Tomowski. "Prep her. I want the gland out. I need information out of this one."

The doctor looked sadly at the tray as Tomowski glanced up.

"Use it on another one. God knows, there's enough of them in here for you to play with."

"I'll get my equipment set up. I'll need some things from my clinic down at the base," said Doctor Marvolo, sounding so excited I wanted to vomit.

"Yes, yes." Major Tomowski waved his hand in a gesture of dismissal.

Vanessa's monitor beeped slightly faster. The nurse looked up from her desk. I was on it instantly, returning it to its slow and steady pace, and the nurse looked back to her screen.

The Major was watching Vanessa. "Where have you been all these years?"

8

———

The Major exited the room, leaving the nurse with Vanessa—and us, of course. We needed to get the nurse out of the way. I didn't know where Vince was and I was worried he might do something terrible to her.

Connor and David moved towards the nurse. I could see Connor was doing something. My best guess was that he was taking something out of a backpack. He bent down by the wall, and when he moved away, the bag was resting against the wall. He and David stepped behind the nurse. My heart began hammering.

Everything happened at once. The bag slid down the wall; the nurse looked up and made to turn, but froze and turned immediately back when she realized Vanessa's eyes were open. Before she could make a sound, Connor and David appeared. Connor put his hand over her mouth while jamming a needle into her neck. She struggled for a few moments, but in seconds she'd slumped down in her chair.

Vanessa faded and the cables dropped to the floor.

"Are you okay, David?" she asked.

I looked over to see David had an expression of confusion and consternation on his face.

"That man, he seemed familiar. I don't know."

Connor wrenched the nurse's lab coat from the back of her chair and threw it onto the gurney for Vanessa.

"Thank you, dear. It's chilly in here."

As she buttoned it up, the door opened.

"The tracker's coming down in the elevat..."

Merv took one look at Vanessa, Connor and David, and reached for his gun. When he discovered a hand already on his sidearm, the shock was evident on his face. He looked into the materializing face of Vince, who head-butted him.

They began a tussle for the gun, and both went down as they grabbed for it.

Connor picked up a chair and faded. I could see his silhouette moving around the room towards the fight, but I couldn't work out his intention.

Merv punched Vince in the nose, stunning him and probably breaking it. When Vince was slow to react, Merv took hold of the gun by the barrel and was in the process of turning it around to shoot Vince when a chair appeared in Merv's chest. Connor was standing behind him, holding the seat. The wheeled base was still attached to the hydraulic post that was going through Merv, who stared at it like he couldn't quite believe it was there before coughing up blood all over the wheels. He died in a second with the same incredulous look on his face, dropping to the floor, chair and all.

I spun away from the gruesome image. Things were moving quickly around me.

"You two stay faded," Vanessa said to Jodi and me.

Vince and Vanessa put the nurse on the gurney and rolled it to the back of the room. Connor faded Merv and dragged him out. A small pool of blood sat on the floor where Merv had been lying. Vanessa took a towel from a trolley and mopped it up, shoving the towel in one of the desk drawers.

Connor reappeared.

"What did you do with him?" asked Vince.

"Lift shaft."

"Was it loud?" asked Vanessa.

"Surprisingly, no. Not up here anyway. This place must go down real far." Connor shuddered, picked up the backpack and took something from the nurse's desk. "We need to get to that elevator."

"You need to learn how to insert a needle," said the nurse. She was crouching behind David with a scalpel to his throat.

"It would be best for you to leave him alone," said Vanessa.

"If your friend here shakes any more, he'll cut his own throat."

I panicked, scared I'd kill David if I tried to send a shot of energy at the nurse. As I searched for options in the brief seconds I had, I realized I could manipulate electrical signals. How could that help me?

I sent out my thoughts to the electrical impulses flowing through the nurse's body; I could feel them. I waved my arm out, and her arm flew away from David. The scalpel skittered across the floor, and David crawled away while she stared in shock at her arm. I thrust a shot of energy into her, and she slumped, unconscious, behind the desk.

A minute later, out in the hallway, the elevator door opened as we all stood along the opposite wall: Connor, Vanessa, Jodi, David, Vince and I, all holding hands, all completely invisible with no yellow trail. The tracker stepped out of the elevator. I recognized him and caught my breath. He hadn't been one of the students, but I'd seen him on guard duty a few times.

"We can't save them all, Jenna," said Vanessa, next to me.

The Major was with him. "Anything?"

"Nothing, sir."

"Right, we'll sweep this level then work our way down." The Major opened the door of the nurse's room and the tracker peeked in, looked around and shook his head. They moved on down the hallway.

"This place is so cool," said the tracker.

"It sure is," said the Major. "You know, I've had my eye on you for some time. You do good work. Tell me, would you be interested in joining the Agency?"

"No way! The guys are going to be jealous." The tracker looked like he could hardly contain himself.

"I'm sure they will. As soon as we've finished the sweep, you can call them, while I sort the paperwork out."

"Sir, you won't be disappointed."

"I know that, son. I know," said the Major, disappearing with the young man.

The area sounded clear, and Connor reached out to close the elevator. The doors were beginning to slide shut when we heard running footsteps.

"Hold the elevator," called a familiar voice. Before the doors could close, Dr. Marvolo appeared. "Oh, just me then," he said to the apparently empty elevator.

He stepped in and pressed the button for the ground level, took out his phone and scrolled through his pictures. From where I stood, I could see the screen. They were photos of naked women, unconscious, with tubes coming out of them. In some of the pictures, he had his hands on their breasts. The more he scrolled, the more depraved the images became.

"I'm going to be sick," I said.

"I'm going to kill him," said Jodi. She was right beside me, and even though we were faded, I could feel her vibrating with anger. I realized he might have done this to her as she lay defenseless.

"We have to get out of here. Keep it together, dear," said Vanessa.

Finally, at ground level, the doctor put away his phone. Outside, he climbed into a jeep, gunned the engine and started driving down the mountain. We went with him.

"We need this car to stop before he heads for the base," said Connor.

When we got close to the bottom of the mountain, I pushed an energy pulse out to the engine and the car glided to a stop.

"What the f...?" began the doctor before lurching forward with a guttural moan.

"Hi," said Connor, appearing behind him. "You're in pain because I have my fist around your intestines."

The doctor froze, but continued to groan.

"I know—disgusting, right?" said Connor. "Next, I'm going to put my hand around your heart. Then you and I are going to drive us off the base. If you give any indication to the guards that anything is wrong, the last thing you will see is your heart sitting on the dashboard. Have I made myself clear?"

A moan indicated that Connor had given the doctor another reminder.

"Yes. I understand. Please, don't hurt me," the doctor said.

I tried not to imagine what it might be like to touch someone else's guts.

A few minutes later, we approached the gates.

"Hey, Doc," called one of the guards. "Are you okay? You don't look so hot."

"Heartburn," the doctor replied.

"You didn't eat at the diner, did you? That place will kill you."

The guard laughed. Dr. Marvolo tried a smile.

"Maybe that's it."

"Well, I hope it clears up. You have a good day, now."

We drove through the gate and on down the road.

After about twenty miles, we pulled off the road at a sign which read "Crop dusting" and headed down a single track with an old building and a hangar at the end. There was a small, familiar plane parked next to a runway.

As we pulled up, Martin came out of the plane.

"Spare clothes onboard," he said.

We ladies climbed onto the plane first, leaving Connor, Martin and Vince with the doctor. After a few minutes, I came out, dressed in shorts and a vest top.

"Hello, Doctor," I called. "May I call you Tony?"

"Hello," he said nervously, "I hope we can come to some agreement here."

"Well, I don't know. Let's talk about what happened to Alejandro."

"Oh! You must be Jenna Banks. You're talking about the upgraded inhibitors—that happened before I arrived. I've only been here a few months."

"And haven't you been busy?" I said.

"What's this?" asked Connor, holding up the little device he'd taken from the nurse's station.

"I think I'd like some assurances that I'm going to get out

of here alive," said Tony as beads of sweat began to appear on his forehead.

"Let's talk about it." I directed him to board the plane. He looked around, probably hoping for the cavalry to arrive. That wasn't going to happen.

We buckled in, and the plane took off. I watched Tony as he sat there, casting furtive glances at me and looking sorry for himself. I wasn't buying it for a minute. Unable to look at him anymore, I walked past Vince who was in a world of his own, sitting next to David.

"You have to accept it's all gone," David was saying to Vince. "Like Kim. I lost Kim, that was my fault. It was all my fault."

Vince was an odd one. He'd been so arrogant and dismissive when I'd first met him, but he seemed to care for David. I wondered what their history was.

"May I sit here?" I asked Jodi.

She nodded.

"I'm sorry. I didn't know..."

"I figured that out," she said. "You didn't have to get me out, but you did, so thank you. Where is this thing going?" she asked, looking around her. "I need to get to my kids."

"You have kids?" My eyes stung.

"Nearly a year has passed. I don't even know if they're still alive. What if they're back in that place?"

She was getting worked up.

"Tell me about them," I said.

"Ava-Jean would have had a birthday by now. She'd be twelve."

My jaw dropped.

"And my little one..."

"Milly?" I asked.

She looked at me. I looked at her.

"They're staying with us at the vineyard in California." I grinned. I couldn't believe the coincidence. Belatedly, I wondered how loudly I'd said that last bit and glanced towards Tony. He didn't seem to have heard.

"They're okay?" Jodi gulped in air and tears cascaded down her face.

"Yes. Your girls are obsessed with my cat. They won't leave him alone. Your brother's okay too. He's there with them." I didn't add that I thought he was a total shit.

"Who? What?" She looked genuinely puzzled. "I haven't got a brother."

"I'm sorry, I assumed he was your brother. Your husband's, I guess. They call him Uncle Chad."

"Chad's got my kids?" Her voice had risen to a squeak.

Vanessa was with us in a moment. "What's wrong?"

"Jodi is Ava and Milly's mother," I told her.

"Chad isn't my brother. He's my loser abusive ex-boyfriend. And no, he's not their dad." Jodi was beginning to look very distressed.

"It's okay. We'll be back there soon. I'll call ahead." Vanessa went up to the front of the plane.

"I'm sorry to interrupt," called Tony from a few seats up, "I need to go to the bathroom."

"Sure, Tony. Just unbelt yourself. We trust you," said Connor.

I raised my eyebrows at Connor, and he winked at me. Having us use his first name was obviously unnerving Tony.

After Tony had been in the bathroom for a few seconds, Connor walked to the door and took a cell phone out of his pocket. He faded his hand through the door and called, "Are you looking for this?" Then he pulled it back quickly, chuckled and pocketed the phone.

After a minute, Tony came back out of the bathroom

and took his seat silently without making eye contact with anyone.

"I'm sorry, Jodi, I need to speak to this guy," I said.

I stood, and David stood abruptly and took my place.

"It's okay," said David to Jodi. "I'm sure that won't happen."

"What?" she asked.

I left them to it.

Connor and I took the seats across from Tony.

"So, are you ready to talk?" asked Connor.

Tony ignored him. He looked at me. "It looks like Marcus surprised you all."

"Excuse me?"

"His energy leeching ability. They never had a clue. I wonder how he managed to hide it for so long, or how it worked so well regardless of his inhibitor. I wish I'd had the chance to experiment on him."

"How do you know?" I asked.

"The Agents were listening. The inhibitor Doctor Philipson inserted at the lab when he was running your tests contained a listening device. It wasn't perfect—an earlier version. I've improved it since. So, what did you do to him?" he asked Connor. "I've heard the fight on the recordings, but then it just goes dead."

"Are we over a populated area?" Conner asked Vince.

"No. Desert." Vince, who had been looking out of the window, now looked at Connor, and then at Tony. "You need to start talking, now."

"If you kill me, you're not going to know anything," Tony said to Connor.

"If you're not going to talk, I might as well fade you through the walls and drop you." Connor was pushing up his sleeves.

"Tony, you have my word. If you tell us what we want to know, I won't let him do it." I didn't want to see another person die today.

"I'm not sure what your word is worth, Jenna…"

"Okay, I'm done here," said Connor, leaning forward and grabbing the odious little man by his jacket. Connor began to fade slowly enough to let Tony understand what was going to happen.

"No… I'll tell you… Please don't," he stuttered.

Connor released his hold and sat back in his seat.

"So. You were going to tell us what this is." Connor held up the little device.

"It's an inhibitor, for faders," Tony finally admitted.

"It looks like mine, but bigger," I said. "What does it do?"

"We can sometimes inhibit a fader's abilities with the hormone implant, but that doesn't always work. Up to now, the only sure way to stop a fader from fading was to surgically remove the gland, which takes time and effort and is irreversible. This device works differently. The capsule is metal, so it disappears when you fade, but the contents can be any one of a selection of organically based drugs—a sedative or a fast-acting neurotoxin, which spreads once the capsule has gone."

"And if they fade while it's in?" I asked.

"Unconsciousness, death, something like that." Tony shrugged.

"This is sickening." I turned away.

"Truthfully, it's not going well. I'll have to end my trials soon. The first thing a fader does when they wake up is panic and fade. We haven't yet been able to explain quickly enough what a bad idea that is."

"What's the point of it?" I asked.

"They don't tell me everything, but I believe the Agency

was going to try to turn some faders .... it doesn't matter. There are other projects in the works."

Vanessa returned with a troubled look on her face.

"We've got a problem," she said. "Chad and the girls have gone."

9

W e landed on a private landing strip. After we'd exited the plane, Martin flew immediately out towards a small airport a few miles away.

The strip had a trailer which doubled as someone's home and office. Connor took Tony over to it. He faded his arm through the door, unlocked it and shoved Tony in.

"Where are we?" asked Vince.

"California. Our place is a couple of hundred miles from here," said Connor.

David walked over to Vince. "You're coming with us, right?"

"Sure, I've got nowhere else to go."

There was a cry of pain from the trailer.

"Where's Jodi?" asked Vanessa.

I blinked in and saw a trail of yellow leading to the trailer. We ran for it. Connor got there first and faded through the side of the trailer at a pace. I pulled at the door, but it had been re-locked from the inside. I could have faded in, but I didn't want to lose my clothes again.

"We're around the other side," called Connor.

On rounding the corner, I barked a laugh at the sight of Tony hanging from the little bathroom window with one arm out and one arm stuck inside. As I came to stand in front of him, the scene was not so funny. He was bleeding from holes in the cheek on one side of his face. I blinked in to see Jodi standing in front of him, her hand reaching out to his face and occupying the same space. Then as she appeared naked before him, five holes appeared in his cheek, and he screamed. Blood poured down his face, and he struggled to free himself like a demented, trapped animal.

"Look, Doctor, I'm naked. You like us naked, don't you? I've seen your pictures. Except I'm awake. You don't like that, do you?"

Tony howled.

Vanessa put her arm out to Jodi. "Don't do this. We need to get your kids."

Jodi burst into tears and allowed Vanessa to envelop her in a hug before being led away.

Tony continued to struggle and scream.

"Alright, you disgusting weasel, I'll get you out." Connor gripped the man's ear and faded his hand.

Still blinking in, I watched Tony turn into a yellow misty shadow of himself and drop down to the floor level of the trailer. Tony's other arm came out of the trailer, holding a knife. He plunged it towards Connor. The sudden action made Connor jump back in fright, letting go of the doctor's ear. Tony materialized naked. Connor and I both stared in horror as the upper half of his torso landed on the ground with a sickening thud.

My stomach churned and I turned, vomiting into the scrub.

"Oops! He didn't think that through, did he?" I looked up

to see Vince had peeked around the corner and was staring bug-eyed at the half-corpse.

"We need to get the other half from inside the trailer," said Connor.

I vomited again.

Vince removed his t-shirt and began to pull down his jogging pants. I spun around to give him privacy, only to find myself facing the body. I stood still, closed my eyes and tried not to listen as Connor dragged the top half of Tony a few feet away.

"This is gross," muttered Connor.

"Erm, dude?" called Vince. "I'm gonna need a little help here."

Connor sighed, picked up Vince's clothes and faded through the wall into the trailer. I walked around to the front, knocked and waited for the door to be unlocked. I decided that the bottom half of Tony couldn't look as bad as the half with a face on it. As I entered the trailer, I realized I was wrong.

I found Connor and Vince standing at the door to the bathroom, both scratching their heads. The floor was awash with blood. Most of Tony's stomach was either on the floor or inside the waste pipe, and his butt was sticking out of the toilet bowl. His legs were lying disconnected on the floor under the toilet bowl with one leg bent at the knee. The kneecap itself was probably inside the wall. Three pieces of soft flesh lay on the floor in front of the bowl.

"Oh man!" said Vince. "Is that his junk?"

"Oh!" I said. Something rose from my chest and burst out as a giggle. I slapped my hand over my mouth, horrified.

After a few moments of silence, Vince turned to Connor. "I say we burn this whole fucking thing down."

"Oh yeah! Burn it," said Connor, backing out.

Silently I agreed with them, but I still had my hand over my mouth, half afraid I'd burst into hysterical guffaws.

Connor put the top half of the body into the trailer as I watched Vince pouring a liquid into the air humidifier.

"Dude, we want fire, not water," said Connor.

"Oh, I think it'll burn," said Vince with a wink as he flicked the machine on.

Our lift arrived and the driver climbed out. It was my dad. I ran to him and burst into tears. I'd seen such horrific things, and all I wanted was to hug him.

He hugged me back and said, "You are grounded for the rest of your life."

We climbed into the SUV and stopped a safe distance away. I sent a pulse of energy out towards the trailer to spark a light switch and start the fire. There was a loud "Whomp!" and a second later the whole thing exploded.

"Bloody hell!" said Dad. "What did you use in there?"

"I put aviation gasoline in the humidifier," said Vince. Everyone looked at him. "It's all I could find."

We raced away, slowing down to a more sedate pace to join the main road and begin our journey back to the vineyard.

"Can you find somewhere with a bathroom?" asked David.

"Again?" Vince was shaking his head.

"You've given me about eight pints of water. It's your fault."

Dad pulled into a gas station and I got out to stretch my legs in the direction of the Cheetos.

"No more than five minutes. We're on the clock here," called Vanessa, reminding us that we still had to find Jodi's girls.

As I left the store with my giant bag of Cheetos, I passed

Vince who was also holding a giant bag of Cheetos. I smiled at him, thinking anyone who likes Cheetos couldn't be all bad.

"You'll turn into a bloody Cheeto," said Dad as I climbed back in with the snacks.

David quickly followed me into the car. Then I watched Vince leave the store a minute later. He stopped and threw his trademark white silk scarf into the trash bin.

He saw me watching and smiled sadly. Climbing in, he said, "I guess I'm not the Great Shadow anymore."

We carried on to the vineyard and didn't stop again until we reached it. We walked into Vanessa's office to find Orla, Jason, Zoe, Hannah and Sofia looking at a map.

"Where are we?" asked Vanessa.

"He took one of the cars. There's no way to tell which direction he went. He had about an hour on us before we realized he was gone."

"This is Jodi. She's the girls' mum," I said.

"I recognize you. Your hair's different," Jodi said to Orla, frostily.

"We're doing everything we can to get your girls back to you. As for the other thing, I don't blame you for feeling the way you do," said Orla before turning back to the maps.

"Where is everyone?" asked David.

"Most of them have been moved out to other safe houses," said Sofia. "We don't know if Chad's going to give away this location. We can't consider it safe anymore."

MILLY SAT on a booster seat in the back of a car next to her sister, facing forward. Her eyes were red and her cheeks flushed from crying. She was tired—they both were. They'd been traveling for hours, and it was now the middle of the night.

"It's okay." Ava-Jean held Milly's hand as she sat looking at Chad, who was filling the gas tank.

"I'm hungry," said Milly, "and I can't chew on Mr. Bobble's hat."

"Mr. Bobble is back at home in your toy box. We'll be back there soon. We have to help Uncle Chad with his errand."

"I don't like Uncle Chad. What if Mom comes back and she can't find us?"

A loud knock on the window made them both jump.

"You stay still now. I have to make an important call," said Chad.

After a few minutes, he got into the car and passed back some candy bars.

"Okay, girls, we need to find a hotel room for tonight. We're going to meet someone very important in the morning, and he's going to give me a lot of money."

"Can I have some money, too?" asked Milly.

"Yeah, sure. Whatever," said Chad as he gunned the engine.

MAJOR TOMOWSKI BLINKED and turned from the piercing light. An overreaction perhaps, since it was he who had flicked the light switch. He did not need an alarm clock. A lifetime in the military had ensured that he would awaken at precisely 04:30 every day until the day he didn't wake up at all.

He stared into the mirror, recognizing that he looked every one of his sixty-five years, and perhaps a few more. He should have retired, but the President had extended his service until he was sixty-eight. He wondered what he would do then. He had no wife or kids; all he had was the job. Eat a bullet, probably. He didn't have any friends outside the Agency; he had been invited to join at a pretty young age. There had been no reunions with old buddies for him, not within the Agency. That kind of thing was discouraged.

He shaved, washed his face and patted it dry with a towel. He smiled into the mirror, invoking the spirit of Major Tom. The kids at the base loved Major Tom. He wrinkled his eyes—the smile must always reach the eyes, so it looked sincere.

His eyes fell to the scar on his shoulder: the three deep horizontal slices that resembled the Morse code symbol for the letter O, and the reason his comrades used to call him "O". When he returned his gaze to his face, the kindly smile had slipped away.

He headed back into the bedroom to dress for his ass-kicking at the Capitol. He hated being reprimanded by politicians who had never served a day in their lives. It wasn't that he didn't deserve it. A fader had escaped from his base. He'd lost four students, two of them with abilities they could have learned much more from, and worse, they had information that could bring the whole program down. The list of catastrophes was growing, and the buck stopped with him. No, he deserved this ass-kicking at the Capitol, but he still wanted to shoot them all in the face.

As he switched on the coffee machine, his phone rang. He noted the name.

"What have you got, Lieutenant?"

"There's been a development, sir."

"I know there's been a development. I told you to call me only in the event of a development. Spit it out."

"We've been contacted by someone with information about the erm... current situation. He wants to meet."

The Major thought that at least the idiot was careful on the phone.

"Call the Senator's office and cancel our meeting. I'm coming straight back."

Retrieving his shaving gear from the bathroom, he returned to the mirror to find a more gleeful smile on his face. "No ass-kicking today," he said to his reflection. Walking out of the room, he flicked off the light.

10

I walked into the kitchen at 6 a.m. Dad and Sofia were talking.

"Morning, Jenna," said Sofia, casually taking a step away from my dad.

"Morning, Sofia, Dad. Look, I'm cool with whatever this is," I said, waving my finger between the two of them. They looked at each other and Dad shrugged. "Now, what's the plan?"

"We'd been going to take David to the ley lines today, but we'll have to put that off to look for the girls." Dad took a drink of his coffee and smiled his thanks at Sofia.

"You're kidding, right?" said Vince as he walked in and headed for the coffee.

"We have to put the girls first."

"But you can do both things. If you take David to the ley lines, his ability to communicate will expand. He could reach out to the girls. Leave half the group ready to hit the road as soon as David can tell them where to go."

Dad stared at him. "You're a genius."

"He might just well be," said Vanessa from the doorway of her study. Jodi sat behind her, looking like she'd barely slept.

Zoe and Hannah walked in.

"I'll go with Jodi then," said Zoe.

"I think we need you at the ley lines," said Vanessa. "We can't let your emitting put the girls in danger, but if you're going to emit, it might work in our favor if you're by the ley lines. It might make you harder to pinpoint. But if you team up with Connor and Vince, you won't emit at all."

"Will the inhibitor affect that?" Hannah asked.

"I forgot about that. Could we get the doc in to remove it?" asked Zoe.

"What inhibitor? Do you mean the one that will have disappeared since you've been fading?" asked Orla.

"What? Oh! I didn't think of that. But are we sure it did go away?" Said Hannah.

"Not a clue," said Zoe, shrugging.

"Could someone waggle a little finger in there to see?" I asked.

Hannah swayed.

"Sorry, Hannah," I said.

"I'll go with Jodi," said Sofia. "A couple of the guys are shipping out the last delivery of bottles. They'll come along and help us with Chad if needed."

I looked over at Vince, who was sticking his finger into the pet carrier and wiggling it. Felix hissed at him and scratched his finger. Vince pulled back his hand.

"Cats hate me, always have. I still like to give it a try now and then."

I lifted Felix out of Vince's reach and went to Jodi, holding the pet carrier. "The girls love Felix. Would it be okay for them to look after him, until we...?" I asked, trying not to cry.

Jodi had been holding on to Milly's little stuffed animal. "You know, I only half believed you were telling the truth about them being here. When I saw Mr. Bobble, I couldn't believe I was this close," she said, wiping her eyes.

"You'll get them back," I said as she took the cage.

"Thank you, we'll look after him." She hugged me.

I went back into Vanessa's office to find her ripping down the ley line maps.

"Are you sad to be leaving this place?" I asked.

"Yes. But we have several other places like this; places Chad doesn't know about."

"Where are we going next?" I asked.

"To a horse ranch in Canada."

"Orla will be beside herself." I laughed.

"My ears are burning," said Orla, walking in. She came up to me and hugged me.

"What's that for?" I asked.

"Jason and I are going to find the girls. We want the chance to kick Chad in the goolies for what he's done."

"Okay. I'll see you in Canada, then," I said.

It felt weird being separated from Orla again. She was my best friend.

"Don't look sad. It'll only be a few days," she said.

We said our goodbyes and headed out in three cars and a delivery truck. We went in different directions when we got to the main road.

"Are we going to the same place as last time, by the lake?" I asked.

"About a hundred miles further east where more ley lines cross," Dad said.

"I saw that on the map. That's a lot of lines. This is going to be quite interesting," said Vince.

About twenty miles out from where we were due to stop, David said, "Can you pull over, please? I think I'm close enough to reach her."

"Surely it's best just to get it all done at the same time?" said Vince.

"The sooner we can send the others in the right direction, the better," David replied.

"Do you have, like, a helmet or anything?" asked Hannah.

"I'm not Professor X."

Hannah giggled.

David sat quietly with his eyes closed and a look of concentration on his face. He turned his head this way and that. Finally, he spoke.

"Hello, Ava. Don't be afraid. My name is David. I'm a friend of Vanessa's... Oh, you're not afraid. Well, that's good. Are you with Chad right now? Where did he go? Is your sister okay? Can you tell me where you are? Do you know the name of the nasty motel? No? What if you look outside the window, can you see any signs? Sometimes there's a little notepad by the bed with the name on it. Great! Did Chad say how long he'd be? Well, I've never met him, but yes, he does sound a lot like a douche."

I chuckled. That was Ava alright.

"Yes, Jenna found her and rescued her. She saved me too."

David turned to us and gave us the name and address of the motel. "I'm worried about the timing. I don't think Chad's going to be long. We could miss them."

Vanessa was on the phone to Sofia. "Tell Ava we need a distraction. A big one."

David communicated the message to Ava. He turned back to Vanessa and nodded, sighed and rubbed his temples.

"Are you okay, buddy?" asked Vince with concern in his voice.

"I'm fine."

"Maybe when we get there, you should rest in the car for a while to get your energy back."

"We can continue," said David. "I've done what I can for her. I think it's time you helped our little glow-worm."

I blinked in and was barely able to see past the illuminations coming from Zoe. Connor, Vince and Zoe held hands. They all faded and disappeared completely.

We parked at a small car park in a beauty spot and followed the path towards the top of the hill. As we entered a plateau marked out by several unusual poles, I heard David behind me, muttering to himself. I looked back to see him casting about distractedly.

"No, we have to go back. Something's wrong," he called, running towards us.

"David, stop." Vince appeared next to him, trying to grab his arm. I realized he must no longer be stopping Zoe from emitting—that wasn't good.

Zoe and Connor appeared next to me.

As David and Vince reached us, a high-pitched sound whistled uncomfortably in my ears, but just as quickly, it was gone. I looked around to see that lights had appeared on top of the poles.

"Miss Banks. What a pleasure to see you again."

I turned to see Major Tomowski and several Agents rounding the path from the other side.

"Are there any more?" The Major asked a young tracker, who would likely not live past the end of the day.

"No, sir, that's the lot of them."

"Vince, what have you done?" asked David in disgust.

"We'll be okay, Dave. I cut a deal. I can go back to my job, and you can come with me. It will be like before, you and me."

"Vincent, I'm going to have to alter the terms of our agreement," said Tomowski.

"What? No. You can't. You promised Dave would be okay."

Vince went running towards the Major and the Agents raised their guns.

"No, let him come," said the Major.

Vince faded as he ran full tilt. A loud clang sounded, and he suddenly appeared again, writhing and naked on the ground.

"What have you done to me? I can't fade. What have you done?"

"It'll wear off. It's something Dr. Marvolo was working on before his life—and indeed everything else—was cut in half." Leaving Vince writhing on the ground, Tomowski turned to me. "I wouldn't bother, Miss Banks. Your abilities will not affect the barrier or anything beyond it."

He was right. I'd been trying to interfere with the signal.

"Hello, Craig," said David.

Major Tom stopped speaking and stared at David. "Have we met?"

"I watched you murder the kids at Washington State Academy. I saw you with Chris at the armory." David's voice was shaking, but he continued. "I saw Chris stab you in the shoulder with something, before you shot him in the face." David's tears flowed as he spoke.

The tracker standing with Major Tom took a step back, a look of pure horror on his face. David looked at him with an expression of surprise, then sympathy. I looked at him too. The tracker was surrounded by Agents and was never destined to return from this mission.

"David? I wondered what happened to you. The years have been unkind. I think you're talking about this. A goddam spork. I still have the scar." The Major laughed as he pulled a little metal spork from his pocket, turning the shiny object around in his hand. "I keep it with me as a reminder to do everything right the first time. So, you've all learned that you can't fade out of here." The Major glanced down at Vince, who was shivering on the ground. "You could run, but my men will shoot you. So how about we don't waste any more time, and you stand there like good monsters while we tranquilize you?"

"I'm not making this easy for you." Connor began to fade. Being as he was so close to the others, they all faded too. The Major's face paled as my dad started to vanish.

"Come on, Dave. I'll fade you," Connor called.

"We'll all still be here when you eventually reappear," said the Major, smiling.

"Not this time," said David, walking towards us.

"Tag him," said Major Tom to one of the Agents.

"Why is he fading red?" said the tracker. I blinked in, and sure enough, the mist appearing around David was red.

"Tag him, now!" shouted the Major, seeming to sense that something wasn't right.

"You're being lied to, trackers are faders," David shouted as he ran towards us. It wasn't the message he was supposed to have delivered, but I heard it through my ears and screaming through my mind. The tracker with the Agents could clearly hear it in the same way. He put his hands over his ears, throwing himself into the Agent who was about to fire a dart at David. The shot went wide.

"No!" shouted the Major, throwing the little metal spork at David in frustration.

As David joined the group, we were surrounded in a bright red mist.

All the red, I thought.

11

"*You're being lied to. trackers are faders.*" David's voice reverberated around the heads of everyone in the car.

Vanessa pulled off the road and skidded to a halt.

"That wasn't the message we agreed," said Sofia.

"Should I have been able to hear that?" asked Orla.

"David? David?" Vanessa called.

"That close to the ley lines, he must be able to hear every thought for miles. He might be blocking them out," said Orla.

"Something's gone wrong," said Vanessa, gunning the engine.

"What do we do?" asked Jodi.

"We've got our mission. We're getting your kids back." Vanessa pulled back onto the road and continued to the town.

"WHAT IS GOING to stop her from just fading away after we've paid for her?" asked the large Russian.

Chad waited until the waitress had passed their table.

"You'll have her sister. She can't fade yet, and won't be able to for at least five years," he said.

"A twelve-year-old is bad enough, but dragging a six-year-old around with me won't do much for my reputation."

"If you feel that way, I'm sure the triad could make good use of her."

"Charles, my friend, we are just talking business, yes? There's no need to complicate negotiations." The Russian leaned forward.

Chad held up his phone again, showing the video of Ava creating a dust storm.

"Ilya, do you want her or not? I want to get on with my life, and I've spent enough time with these kids. She is talented." Chad looked out as a man raced by with the wind at his back, seemingly being chased by newspapers. He looked up at the bare trees bending in the wind. "It sure is picking up out there," he said.

"Could her sister be so talented when she awakens?" asked Ilya, uninterested in the weather.

"There's no way to tell for sure. I don't want to make promises I can't keep."

"You are an honorable businessman, Chad." Ilya laughed at his own joke. Chad was a cheap son-of-a-bitch, and they all knew it.

"Can we meet her?" asked the other Russian.

"You can meet her when you've paid for her. She's in a motel room nearby. We do business; I give you the room key; she's yours. You can do what you like with her."

"Let's talk about the price," said Ilya.

"We talked on the phone. It hasn't changed."

"Okay, my friend. You drive a hard bargain. Let's complete this out at the car." Ilya picked up his coat.

"Let's complete this here, or I fade, and the key and room number disappear for good." Chad eyed Ilya suspiciously while patting his jacket pocket.

"So little trust." Ilya turned to his partner. "Bring in the case from the car."

The other Russian stood and left.

"*You're being lied to. trackers are faders.*" The words screamed through Chad's mind.

"What the fuck?" He grabbed his head.

"What's wrong, my friend?" asked Ilya, looking more edgy than concerned.

"Nothing... migraine," said Chad. He guessed the others from the vineyard had done whatever nonsense they'd been planning, although he didn't see the significance of the words. He already knew trackers were faders.

"Let's have a refill of this terrible coffee while we wait." Ilya signaled the waitress.

The waitress, whose name badge said "Betty", bent to refill Chad's coffee, offering a view of her cleavage with a glimpse of a black bra. Chad gazed at the view as though hypnotized, utterly unaware of the silenced gun in her other hand, pointing at the back of his head. The weapon discharged, and Chad fell face first onto the table.

"Natalya, check his pockets, he's got the key on him," said Ilya as he pulled on his jacket to cover the blood spray on his sleeve.

Natalya pulled the key card from Chad's pocket and passed it to Ilya. It was in a little folder with the room number and motel name helpfully written on it.

The other Russian re-entered the diner. "My God, the weather is terrible out there."

"Ha! Maybe it's our new little superstar. Now, if she were capable of something like this…" Ilya laughed. "Ivan, help Natalya with our friend." He stepped out of the booth and stood while Natalya and Ivan dragged Chad's body around the counter to lie with the corpse of the real waitress. Natalya removed her apron and dropped it on top of the bodies. They left the diner and climbed into their car to claim their new prize.

"What the hell has happened here?" Natalya looked out from the passenger seat of the car. The devastation seemed to get worse the closer they got to the motel. Fire engines, ambulances and police cars littered the area. It looked like a tornado had passed through—which it had.

"Are you sure you want this kid?" asked Ivan. It was obvious now: the girl had done this. The motel was the epicenter of this disaster.

"I want this kid now more than ever." Ilya licked his lips in anticipation of having so much power at his command.

"We're not going to get anywhere close in the car. We'd be better off turning around, parking near the diner and walking the back way. That's probably what Chad did."

"Park in this side road, we'll walk from here," said Ilya.

The three of them walked to the back of the motel and over the ornamental lawn and rockery. Cars were parked haphazardly in the parking lot. At least half of them were upside down.

"You go in first," Ilya said. Natalya stared at him. "You're a woman. They'll trust you more."

Natalya walked up to the room and inserted the key.

"Girls? Don't be afraid. I've come to help you," she said.

"Where's Uncle Chad?" Ava stuck her head out of the bathroom door.

"Your uncle sent me to pick you up. He's ready to go home." Natalya smiled. Ava didn't.

"Did he sell us? That's what he was doing, isn't it?" she said.

Natalya sighed. She measured the girl up. She wasn't dealing with an idiot.

"Ilya will treat you like queens. You will want for nothing. As long as you do as you're told, life will be good."

"What's the holdup?" Ilya stood in the doorway. "We need to move."

The girls came out of the bathroom.

"They're coming," said Natalya, pushing Milly further into the bedroom so that she tripped into Ava. Ava held her little sister, but Natalya walked over and pulled them apart, holding Milly's hand so tightly the little girl whimpered and kicked out at her. Natalya brought her palm down in a slap across the little girl's face.

A sudden wind took a hold in the room.

"Cut it out or she'll get more," said Natalya to Ava. The wind ceased.

As they reached the front door, Ilya dangled Chad's keys. "Which piece of shit car is Chad's? I hope it's not upside down."

Ava guessed Chad wasn't going to be needing his car again.

"That one," said Milly, pointing to a car parked near the room. The car Milly was looking at didn't look anything like Chad's. Ava was about to correct her when she saw Mr. Bobble was sitting on the hood of the car.

Ilya looked around at the devastation, then at Ava. "You did this?"

Ava nodded.

"May I ask why?"

Ava shrugged in reply, but said, "I need to fasten her coat."

"Go to your *syestra*." Natalya let go of the little girl.

Ava sat on a chair and stood Milly in front of her.

"Close your eyes, keep them closed," Ava whispered as she leaned forward to zip up the little girl's coat, then she hugged Milly and snapped her own eyes shut.

"What was that? What did you say?" asked Ilya, looking suspiciously at the girls.

Natalya whined. Ilya turned to see her face crumpled in pain.

"What's wrong with you?" he asked.

She stood still, as though frozen to the spot, looking at Ilya with a panicked expression. Then she let loose a long howl as her body emitted cracking sounds. As Ilya watched, her jaw jutted out with a bang and blood began to ooze from splits in her skin. She screamed one last horrifying time before she burst apart before his eyes.

As the ruined remains of Natalya's body slid to the floor, standing there in her place was a woman, naked and covered in blood and gore, like something from hell.

"Why don't we talk about what you planned to do with my children?"

Ilya ran. He ran past Ivan, who had been waiting at the corner; he ran all the way back to the car with Ivan jogging and puffing behind him. Ilya didn't stop moving until he was several states away.

AVA COULD EASILY IMAGINE what condition her mother would be in. She kept her eyes closed and Milly's face tucked into her shoulder until she heard the bathroom door click.

"That was Mommy," whispered Milly, still keeping her own eyes closed.

"Let's get you two out of here," said Orla from the front door.

Ava opened her eyes to see Jason and Orla. Jason had already covered the remains on the floor with the quilt from the bed. There wasn't much he could do about the furniture and the walls and the ceiling. The girls left the room with Orla and walked to the car with Milly's favorite toy on the hood. Orla took it down and passed it to Milly.

Vanessa went in with clothes for Jodi and put them in the bathroom while Jodi showered, then waited outside the door while she vomited into the bowl before dressing. She left the bathroom, shaking.

"You know how dangerous that is?" said Vanessa. "It's a miracle you didn't both end up in a heap of body parts."

"I want to see my girls," said Jodi, shakily.

As soon as Ava saw her mother emerging from the motel room with Vanessa, she shot away from the car and flung herself into Jodi's open arms, her little sister hot on her heels. Struggling to hold her emotions in check, Jodi clung onto her daughters, whispering incoherent words of love into their hair until Vanessa gently patted her on the shoulder.

"We need to get going," said Vanessa.

Hoisting Milly into her arms and holding Ava tightly by the hand, Jodi nodded and made her way over to join the others in the car as Vanessa climbed into the driver's seat.

Orla looked out of the car window, tutted and shook her head.

"What's wrong?" asked Jason.

"I didn't get to kick Chad in the goolies." She slumped in her seat.

"I think they..." Ava looked across at Milly, who was falling asleep in her mother's arms. "They had his car keys. I'm guessing he didn't need them anymore. I think these were evil people."

Vanessa pulled down the front of her baseball cap and started the large black seven-seat SUV. It picked its way through the cars around to the front of the motel, passed the emergency services and media vehicles, and headed north.

"YOU'RE BEING LIED *to. trackers are faders*," howled the disembodied voice in Sean's head.

"What the hell?" He clapped his hands over his ears.

The fader he had been following had grabbed her head too. She stopped and looked around the Trenton mall, confused. Their eyes met. He knew she had heard it. He didn't pretend that he'd been looking at something else; he just stared at her and she at him. In that instant, he saw in her face that she knew he was a tracker and had been following her.

His radio buzzed.

"Team, we've been asked to assemble at meeting point two," said the Agent.

"Did anyone else hear that?" came a second voice.

"I did," said another.

"Assemble at the meeting point. We're under attack from the faders," said the Agent.

"On my way," said Sean.

He looked up, and the girl was gone. He turned around and started towards meeting point two, which he knew to be the stairwell at the back of the mall on ground level. He was at the other end of the building.

trackers are faders. It was ridiculous, thought Sean. But the girl had heard it too, he knew it.

He walked around a barrier with a sign reading "Closed, Cleaning in Progress" and headed through the door into the stairwell. Carl, his Agent, was waiting for him.

"Where is everyone? What the hell was that?" asked Sean.

"They're in the car already, we need to get back to base," said Carl.

"Am I the last?" asked Sean, walking past Carl to the exit.

"Yes, you are definitely the last," said Carl.

Something about his tone made Sean turn. Carl was holding his weapon. From his new vantage point at the top of the stairs down to the basement level, Sean saw his three friends slumped at the bottom.

Sean stared straight into Carl's eyes as Carl pointed his dart gun at him. It was essential to do this so that Carl remained unaware of the naked girl standing behind him with a fire extinguisher.

"We trusted you," said Sean.

"You're just freaks and monsters," said Carl, confirming the truth of what Sean has heard.

The girl grunted as she brought the extinguisher down onto Carl's head. The noise made Carl begin to turn, which was lucky for Sean because the gun was no longer pointing at him when the impact made Carl jerk the trigger. It went off, and a dart flew uselessly past him and exploded against the wall.

Sean flew into action. His jacket was off in a moment and he passed it to the girl. Picking up the dart gun, he shot four of the tranquilizing pellets into Carl's neck. He then pulled Carl's car keys out of his pocket, but the girl stopped him.

"They'll have a tracking device on the car. We can go to mine."

"What about my friends?"

"Are they alive?" she asked.

Sean ran down the stairs. Chester and Leroy were still breathing but unconscious. Jake had blood trails running from his eyes, ears and mouth. He was dead.

Sean looked at the stairs; he could get Chester up to the ground level, but Leroy was huge. The girl seemed to be making the same assessment.

"Okay, new plan. We'll drag him through to the service elevator and up to the car park level," she said.

They dragged Leroy together, grunting and gasping as they went. As they got him into the elevator, the girl collapsed onto the floor.

"What do they feed you people?" she asked.

Chester was a much easier job. Sean went back upstairs and shoved Carl's unconscious body unceremoniously down the stairs. He took the dart gun with him and headed back to the elevator.

The girl was dressed again in different clothes and held out his jacket to him.

"Hi, I'm Sam. I'm a fader," she said.

"Hi, I'm Sean, I'm a Tr... apparently, I'm a fader too." He shook his head at the idea.

Sam moved her car to the elevator, and after a few minutes of heaving, they got Leroy and Chester into the vehicle.

"I'm sorry about your other friend," said Sam as they pulled out onto the road.

"Thanks, but I didn't know him well. He was a transfer

from Colorado." There had been no visible wounds on Jake, so Sean wondered if his upgraded inhibitor had been the cause of his death. It seemed a ridiculous thought, though. That would mean any trackers and Spotters out there could have been murdered immediately upon hearing that message.

12

———

A bright light flashed before my eyes. We all collapsed, fully materialized, onto the ground. I kept my eyes closed and waited for the sting of the darts.

"Where are they?" asked Connor.

I sat up, and the world spun. The Major and his Agents were gone. The spork had missed David and landed harmlessly on the ground.

"Maybe Connor faded them," said Zoe.

I blinked in and looked around. There was no yellow. Something seemed wrong about that, but I didn't register what it might be.

"Did anyone see that red mist? What was that?" Hannah said.

"It came from David," said Connor.

"And the flash of white light? Jenna, did you smoke the Major?" asked Zoe.

"No, of course not."

"I'm not judging or anything."

"It wasn't me. Did we lose consciousness?" I felt the back

of my head for a fresh wound indicating the Agents had injected something into me.

Hannah was sitting in front of me, staring over our heads.

"What's that?" she asked.

We looked towards the top of the hill to see a white band of energy about fifteen feet high, going as far as could be seen towards the west and disappearing over the hill to the right. Pulses of yellow light flew along it.

"Did we do that?" asked Zoe.

I took stock of who was around me. Zoe and Hannah were still sitting on the ground, my dad had his head between his knees, hyperventilating, and Connor was checking on David, who had curled into a fetal position on the ground.

"Hey, look at this," I said. Walking over to something on the ground, I picked it up. It was a bundle of clothes.

"Are these Vince's clothes?" I asked. I passed the sweats to Zoe, but left the underpants on the ground.

"Vince was wearing this stuff before he faded, right?" Zoe asked Hannah.

Hannah nodded. "I wonder why they didn't disappear."

"Vanessa's stuff doesn't disappear. It just drops to the ground, like this," said Connor.

Zoe went through the pockets and pulled out a cell phone.

"The two-faced bastard, he was messaging them." She raised her arm in the air. "No signal."

"David, come on. We're all okay," Connor said, looking at the white energy field. "Maybe their stupid new tech wiped them all out."

"It was created by Doc Philipson. I'm pretty sure he didn't know his arse from his elbow," said Zoe.

"I suggest we get the hell out of here before more Agents turn up," said Dad.

I blinked in and took a last look around. Nothing. I realized what had seemed odd.

"Zoe, you're not emitting," I said.

We all looked at her, and she looked at herself with a huge smile.

"Hey, maybe their stupid new tech fixed me. I don't feel tired anymore," she said.

David reached down and picked up the little metal spork. He wiped his eyes and put it in his pocket. Looking out for Agents as we went, we walked down the way we had come. When we got to where the car should have been, it was gone.

"Damn it. They took the car," said Connor.

"It would appear they also took the road," said Dad.

We all looked across where the leveled off car park should have been, but it was an uneven pile of rocks.

"We've come down the wrong way," said Hannah.

"I don't think so," said Dad.

"Where the fuck, are we?" said Zoe.

I stared at Zoe. She'd used the F-word in front of my dad, which might have been the most shocking thing of the whole week.

"Or more to the point, *who* the fuck, are you?" said a voice from behind us.

We spun around to face three Agents: two men and a woman, pointing guns at us. Connor started to move slowly towards Dad and Hannah, but one of the Agents looked straight at him and faded, right before us. Connor froze.

"Agents can't fade. Who are you?" asked Hannah.

"Maybe they turned some faders to work for them," I said. "You must be pretty low to be working for the Agency."

The faded Agent returned with a puzzled look on her face. She had reappeared with her clothes still on. I looked at Connor, who seemed as shocked as I felt.

The female Agent moved forward and clicked a single cuff onto Connor's wrist, then did the same to Zoe, David and me, but not to Hannah or Dad. She stepped back and pressed a button on a wristband of her own. A high-pitched tone, similar to the one on the Major's poles, briefly sounded. We looked at the cuffs and each other. No one was going to attempt to fade now.

One of the uniformed men was waving what looked like a cell phone at us.

"They're not Broken, sir, but there are no tags," he said before putting it away.

"They're not Broken?" The commanding officer seemed surprised.

"No sir. Levels are normal. No sun sickness," said the officer.

"Good to know we're not broken," said Zoe. "I'm sorry. Would you mind helping us out with where we are? I mean, I can bloody well see it's not Kansas."

"No, Kansas is quite far from here," replied the woman.

"Heidi... erm, Officer Malone," said the commanding officer.

"Sorry, sir." The woman took a step back.

I smiled at the female officer, and she smiled back, shrugging slightly.

"So, it looks like we've got a group of domestic terrorists," said the commanding officer.

"I'm sorry, what?" My eyes swiveled to him.

"What are we going to do with the incs, Callan... sir? The travel would be a problem."

"I'll say!"

"What are incs?" I asked.

"We already know you're not Broken, so this game isn't going to help," said Callan.

"Pretend we're Broken," said Connor.

"Incompletes are people who can't fade. You've got two in your party," said Heidi. Callan looked at her. "They seem okay," she added, defensively.

He pressed an object in his ear. "California 77 reporting. No visible cause found for the spike in this sector, but the ribbon has raised above the ground, and it's almost white. We've got six unknowns, no tags. Status: mixed. We need transport."

About thirty seconds later, another ten uniformed individuals came running down the hill we'd just come down.

"Where were this lot hiding?" asked my dad. They didn't respond.

"This is starting to creep me out," said Zoe, stepping back and grabbing Hannah's hand.

"We need to get them back to L.A.," said Callan.

"Why not Colorado? Look, what happened to the Major and the other Agents?" asked Connor.

"Slow down. Why do you keep calling us Agents?" said the lead officer, who we now knew was called Callan. "We're police officers, not FBI. We're in California, not Colorado, that's why L.A."

"It looks like the ribbon's starting to settle. We'll take it, and the incs can follow on when we've located transport."

"The ribbon?" Dad asked.

Callan looked across to the vast energy field running across the landscape and looked back at Dad as if to say, "*Are you blind*?"

"I'm not leaving my dad," I said, holding Dad's arm.

The officers looked at each other.

"Your dad's an inc, but you're not? I've never heard of that. You can't be related."

"And I'm not leaving Hannah," said Zoe.

Callan and Heidi looked at each other again. Heidi took out a device which looked like a pen and stamped the back of our hands. A shiny pattern appeared for a moment, then disappeared.

"Here's the situation. It's not safe out here," said Heidi. "If you're as innocent as you're making out, we need to get you back to the city where it is safe. A huge energy spike appeared here a few minutes ago. Every second we spend here is making an attack more likely."

"An attack? From whom?" said Dad.

"When will I see Hannah again?" Zoe asked.

"A few hours, I expect. We have to get transport out here."

"A hopper's on the way, sir," said one of the other officers.

Dad looked at me and mouthed, "*Hopper?*"

I hugged Dad and Hannah and allowed some of the officers to walk us up the hill. These people weren't from the Agency, but I couldn't work out who or what they were.

I turned back to the officers standing with Dad and Hannah. "If anything happens to them..."

"They'll be fine. The officers are there to protect them."

We were each paired with an officer and walked to the energy field which was beginning to turn yellow. It was no longer as high, down to about eight feet. I took a step back. The energy coming off the thing felt lethal.

"It looks smaller than before," I said to Heidi.

"It's usually underground. What did you do to it?" she asked. "Is one of you a brightling?"

I looked back at her with an expression that was probably as confused as my mind at that point.

"We didn't do anything. It wasn't there, and then it was," I said.

Heidi clicked her cuff and the tone sounded again. She moved me closer to the ribbon of energy.

"You want us to step into that?" I asked.

"Well, it would be best if you faded first, unless you want it to shred you to pieces."

"I'm not... I can't go in that." David began to struggle.

"He's unwell. Let me go with him, it'll calm him down," said Connor.

The officer with David didn't look like he was going to comply.

"Let him help," said Heidi.

I blinked in as Connor linked his arm casually with David's and said, "It's okay, Dave, we'll fade together." Connor faded himself and David, and with their two officers, they stepped into the light. The yellow mist shot away along the ribbon of light, which followed the landscape into the distance.

I paired with Heidi, who said, "You need to fade now."

I gulped. I could have done with having Connor with me. I would be naked at the other end of whatever this thing was.

I didn't understand what was happening. Had we somehow traveled to the future? I had many questions. I suspected David had caused this with his red fade and I needed a very long talk with him.

I said a silent goodbye to my clothes and faded. We stepped into the energy field.

All I could see was the bright ribbon of light speeding by for a few seconds, then it slowed. It felt like the thing was ejecting me. I took a step, and we were standing on a platform.

I moved my hands to cover myself and discovered I was still clothed.

I heard the whine of the cuff activating again. After seeing how similar tech had affected Vince, I wasn't going to put it to the test.

Connor, David and Zoe were already there, looking around. I couldn't believe my eyes. Steps led down from the platform to a wide pedestrian pathway. People were appearing and disappearing in front of the ribbon and walking away in different directions. faders, everywhere. They just seemed busy with their day like this was normal. Zoe's Oz reference had been spot-on.

I looked up to see a vast glass dome above the city. I decided we had definitely traveled through time.

"Hey, I'm not naked," I said, surprised.

Heidi looked at me like I'd lost my mind.

"When we fade, we usually lose everything we have."

Heidi's eyebrows shot up. "Clothes, bags, glasses, every-thing?" she asked, sounding a little excited.

"Everything," I said.

"Callan?" Callan walked over. "We need to get them in. They're not Broken, I think they're from HE."

"No way! Are you sure?"

"Pretty sure. What's the right thing to do here? I don't think they're criminals. If we put them into the system, we might not be able to get them out again."

"I'll check." Callan took a few steps away and muttered into his communicator, then returned. "He still wants them in," he said, shrugging.

Heidi looked disappointed.

As we made to walk across the road to the station, I

became aware of people staring at us. Quite a few people. A crowd was gathering around us; people were popping out of nowhere to stand and stare and point.

Heidi grabbed Callan's arm. "Engage, now."

I could see he was blinking in, so I blinked in too. Zoe was emitting at maximum. So much for being fixed.

"I'm calling this in again," said Callan.

"Let me," said Heidi, pulling out a wafer-thin device that looked like a cell phone. "Yolanda, it's me. We've got some HE visitors; one is a brightling, and another is probably a red-mister. Can we bring them over to you?"

She repeated it. And again.

"You heard me all three times. We're gathering quite a crowd here. I need an answer."

She waited a few seconds.

"Okay, we'll be straight there." Heidi turned to Callan. "Yolanda said to take them over there. Back in the ribbon, folks. One more hop."

When we turned to face the ribbon, it looked different to what we had seen previously. The energy field didn't travel off into the distance; it traveled between two large pillars set about twenty feet apart. Heidi swiped her hand across a panel. As I took a step towards the ribbon, my cuff began to whine.

"Oops!" said Heidi, pressing a button to deactivate the cuffs.

"Really?" Callan stared at her.

Heidi blushed.

As we stepped out of the ribbon a moment later, I happily looked down at my clothed body.

"It looks like whatever it was that made us naked, you've fixed it in the future."

"The future?"

"What year is this anyway?"

"I'm sorry to disappoint you, but you're still in the same year. I'm going to let someone else explain it. It's way above my pay grade." Heidi laughed.

"How far have we traveled from where you found us?" asked Connor.

"About a hundred and fifty miles," said Callan.

"But that was in seconds," I said.

"It's the ribbon. It's how we get around," said Heidi.

"It's cool. But I'll be happier when I've got Hannah back," said Zoe.

We walked away from the platform and onto a large concourse. People stopped and gaped at Zoe.

"I'm doing it again, aren't I?" she asked.

David patted her shoulder.

"So, can I ask you something?" said Heidi.

"You can ask me anything. I am literally a captive audience." I indicated for her to continue.

"What's a tracker?"

"What?" I was at a loss how to answer.

"What was the whole 'trackers are faders' thing? The telecoms have been off the hook at the station. Everyone heard it. Everyone, everywhere, except the incs, I suppose."

"We should get into the building. There's a lot of people staring."

Callan was right. People were appearing before our eyes to gawk at Zoe. I blinked in to see that the town was a lot busier than it had first appeared. People were walking along faded, until they stopped and appeared before us.

We were being led to a large building across the road when a boy of about fourteen or fifteen ran out of the crowd and kissed Zoe's cheek before being dragged off by officers.

He ran back to his friends who cheered him, as did the whole group.

"Sorry about that," said Heidi. "It's good luck to kiss a brightling. I'm holding myself back. Let's get inside before there's a stampede."

Zoe was speechless, which was a new experience for the rest of us.

"Just think, Hannah is the luckiest girl in the world right now," Connor said.

"She was, anyway," said Zoe.

We entered the tall building and walked to the reception desk.

Callan's radio chirped. "Base to 77. Where are the prisoners?"

Callan winced. "I'd better get back to the station and explain this." He headed out the door.

The receptionist looked up at Heidi. "He's in San Francisco."

"No, I'm not, I'm here," called a voice from behind us.

I turned to see a man running towards us from the entrance.

"Have you seen what they're doing out there? It's like Mardi Gras." He laughed.

I looked outside. The street looked empty. I blinked in to see the shapes of faded people dancing and spinning around within the glow coming from Zoe. I turned to see her standing with her face in her hands.

"How are there so many faders?" asked Conner.

"I'm James. Let's get you out of here before there's a riot."

We walked to an elevator. Unusually, the floor numbers were on the outside wall. The numbers went up to forty with an M at the top. James pressed the button marked M.

"Thank you, Officer Malone," he said, dismissing Heidi.

"Can she come with us?" I asked.

"I'm not sure that…"

"This is all a bit much for us. Heidi's been really nice. I'd like it if she could come," said Zoe, testing the limits of how special these people thought she was.

"Of course. I understand how unnerving all this is. Thinking about it, you're really into artefacts too, aren't you, Heidi? I don't think you've seen my collection."

Heidi squeaked.

The doors opened, but instead of an elevator car, a ribbon of energy was shooting upwards.

We knew the drill. Following Heidi, we faded and stepped into it.

13

Craig Tomowski stood with his fists gripped onto the front of the tracker's jacket.

"What's red? What do you mean they've gone?" He pushed the man to the ground and stood over him. The tracker seemed to be having a personal crisis.

"We're faders? Am I a monster?" he was muttering.

Tomowski looked at the empty cordoned-off space before him. They'd gone. How? And along with his lucky spork—that was annoying. He couldn't believe the job had been screwed up so badly. He didn't seem able to catch a break.

"Maybe I should eat that bullet now," he said to the mumbling tracker.

"Sir?" asked one of the Agents.

Tomowski's phone rang and he held it to his ear.

"I see." He sighed. "Push the button... Yes, all of them."

He disconnected the phone. As he watched, the tracker before him stiffened, and then blood gushed from his eyes and nose as he collapsed lifeless to the ground. Tomowski had made an effort to remember the kid's name while he was alive, but now, it was gone. Irrelevant.

"Clean this up," he said to the Agents, then walked back to the car.

WE APPEARED in a hallway with a suite of offices either side. I couldn't shake the feeling of joy I had at seeing myself fully clothed yet again. Heads were poking out of every doorway, and as we walked along the hallway, people at desks gazed up through the glass walls to watch us pass.

"We're forty floors up in a second," said Connor.

We reached James's office door, the only one that wasn't transparent. It opened into a massive office with a desk ahead of us. Doors stood open to a conference room on the right, and a room with sofas and display cases on the left. James flicked a glance at Zoe, then led us to the left.

"You've got a nice office for a cop," said Zoe.

"Ha! A cop? I'm sorry, I didn't introduce myself properly. I'm James Dowser. I'm the Mayor."

Zoe dropped into the closest seat to her. She was beginning to look exhausted again. David sat in the corner-most seat, put his hands on his knees and stared at them.

"I'm Jenna. This is Connor, Zoe and David."

Heidi was gasping and cooing at the items in the cabinets. I glanced over to one of them. It contained an unopened can of Coke next to a Twinkie. James noticed me looking.

"The Coke can is one of my finest pieces. It's worth thousands. We're not sure of the value of the cake, though. I've only had it a couple of weeks. I don't know how long it will last."

"I think you're good," said Connor with a chuckle.

I'd seen enough. I turned to James and asked, "What is going on here? Where are we?"

"Yeah, man, I've been to L.A., and it wasn't a dome-topped city of faders," said Connor. "And the air is clean here. This is not L.A."

"This might be difficult to believe, but you're not on your earth anymore," said James.

"It's the multiverse," said David, still looking at his hands. "I suspected it. I'm sorry, it's my fault."

"The what?" asked Zoe, looking first at David, then at James. James directed his response to her.

"You are in the Full Earth. We think you are from what we call the Half Earth. As far as we can tell, the planet itself is pretty much the same. While we can fade—most of us anyway—previous asylum seekers have explained that your earth is pretty much all incs"

I sat down heavily. Connor came and sat next to me.

"Were you the bridge?" James asked David.

"I'm sorry?" I asked.

"As far as we know, travel across the Multiverse isn't possible without a red-mister."

"Yes, I guess that's me," said David.

"I've never heard of a red-mister being able to also fade yellow, like regular folks."

David glanced at Connor and opened his mouth to speak.

"David's a talented guy," I said, while mentally saying to David, *"Don't tell him too much. See if you can gauge his intentions."*

"I think I've been here before with my friend, Kim. It was a long time ago. I lost her," said David.

So that's what happened to Kim, I thought.

"We can look into that for you." James made a note on a pad.

"You've certainly got an eclectic taste in music," said Zoe, looking up at CDs in frames on the wall. "The Sex Pistols, Simon and Garfunkel. Ha! Look, Jenna, Glee. Hannah will be made up." Zoe smiled.

"Those are all artefacts from your earth," said Heidi.

"What artefacts do you have?" James asked Heidi.

"Nothing like this. Just a t-shirt and a book."

"A book? Fantastic! They're my favorites. What is it?"

"It's by Stephen King, called *Misery*. It scared the crap out of me," said Heidi, blushing at her unguarded language.

"I've got one of his books, called *It*. Want to swap?" asked James.

"Sure, that would be great." Heidi was smiling from ear to ear.

"Why is Zoe so important?" asked David.

The question had come out of nowhere, but we all looked at James.

"Apart from being lucky?"

James smiled. Zoe sighed. James perched himself on the arm of a chair.

"Since we lost the last brightling, the ribbon has begun to darken. It used to be pure white. Now it seems to be losing energy. We don't know how long it will sustain itself. It's the center of everything in this world. It's the way we move around. It powers everything. We're not the only earth to experience this. We are aware of a third earth. We call it BE, the Broken Earth. That earth has begun to collapse. There are terrible storms, uninhabitable areas, radiation sickness. The last we heard, most of the populations were moving to the equator—it will soon be the only safe place to live. So news of a new brightling is incredible. We haven't had one for years."

"What's that got to do with me?" asked Zoe.

"Brightlings are attenuated by the ribbon," said Heidi. "As the energy builds within you, the weight of it tires you. If you connect to the ribbon, it draws the excess energy from you."

"I'm not sure I like the sound of that. I've had something similar happen before, and it wasn't pleasant." Zoe glanced at me, and a vision of Marcus flashed before my eyes.

"When you arrived?" asked Heidi.

"No. What do you mean?"

"We think you've already transferred energy to the ribbon. There was a huge spike in the reading when you arrived. That's how we knew where you were."

"So you want to hook me up to that thing?"

"No!" said James. "Once the brightling aligns with the ribbon, they go about their life as usual. I don't understand the science of it. I'm sure someone can explain."

The door opened, and a man came in with a trolley carrying sandwiches and a coffee pot. As he arranged the cups, I looked absently at his hand and noticed a silver pattern on the back of it.

"We'll do that," said James, not even looking at him.

"Thank you," I said to the man. He didn't seem to realize I was speaking to him.

The man left, and Heidi began pouring coffees. We hovered around the sandwiches.

"At least that guy didn't gawk at me," said Zoe.

"He's an inc," said Heidi. "Even if he knows one of you is a brightling, he won't know which one. Looking around the room now, even I can't tell. The glow is everywhere."

Zoe looked at the artefacts on the wall while absently

rubbing at her cuff. The Mayor's eyes bulged, staring at it. I discreetly elbowed Heidi and nodded towards him.

"There's no need for these anymore, let me take them off you," said Heidi to me.

As I held out my wrist to her, I observed that a golden pattern had appeared on the back of my hand. She removed the cuff and made her way around the others. I could see they all had the same pattern.

"When will I see Hannah?" asked Zoe.

"I understand they're on the way back. Hoppers use the ribbon, but they are much slower."

"May I ask you a question?" asked James.

"Of course," I said, taking a cup.

"Obviously, I know what a fader is, but what's a tracker?"

"Ah, the message," I said. "Where we come from, as you know, there aren't many faders, but an organization is hunting us. They use people called trackers to find us. The Agents tell the trackers they can see monsters called faders and, from childhood, they are sent out to find them."

"That's barbaric. But what are these trackers?"

"We were," said Zoe. "They injected us with hormones, which they told us increased our abilities. What the hormones actually do is inhibit the fader gene from fully activating. We could see the faders, and that's all we knew.

"Then Jenna found out what was going on and we escaped. We've been hiding out from the Agency for months. The faders aren't an organized group for the most part. Some people don't realize they've awakened. There's a target on their back, and they don't even know it. We planned to send a message out via the ley lines using..."

Zoe stopped speaking for a moment.

"...someone with an ability to communicate with other

faders. We were betrayed and almost captured. The message was severely truncated, and we ended up here."

"Ley lines?" asked Heidi.

"Yes, the shadow-ribbon," said James. "This is why we call your earth the Half Earth. Your ribbon is not fully realized. So, who had the ability to send this message so far?"

"Vince," said Connor quickly, before anyone else could tell the truth. "He didn't make it to this side."

Heidi looked up at Connor with her eyebrows raised, but said nothing.

"So, they are using fader youngsters to kill other faders? It's monstrous."

"They don't kill them," I said. "The Agents keep faders in a drug-induced coma in a mountain in Colorado."

"To what end?" asked James.

"We know they remove the fader gland and interrogate them. God knows what else," said Connor.

Heidi gasped and sat down on one of the sofas.

A console beeped on the wall, and James walked to it. "I'm sorry, I should take this."

A woman's face appeared on the screen.

"Yolanda, I asked you to cancel my day."

"I'm sorry, sir, it's an emergency. I've got Sergeant Lawler for you."

A familiar face popped up onto the screen. It was Callan.

"I'm sorry, sir, we've had an incident. The hopper carrying the incs has been attacked."

"What?" said Zoe. We all moved to the screen.

"The visitors are safe. We're running them into the medical center to be checked out. The hopper came down with a bump. I don't think the attackers were expecting a hopper full of officers. The officers tagged a few of them of them and are bringing them in now."

"Put them in lockup and…"

"Sir, they're Broken. We're just waiting for transport."

"Oh, I see. Make sure your people get checked out immediately upon their return. Sergeant, I want you to head up a security detail for our visitors personally." James looked across the room to Heidi. "Officer Malone, I'd like you to act as the liaison for the visitors."

"Yes, sir," said Heidi.

The call ended.

"What does 'they're Broken' mean?" asked Connor.

"We've been having problems with criminal gangs from the Broken Earth making raids over here," said Heidi. "They're desperate people. We lost our last red-mister years ago. We can't get over there, but they can come here. The problem is, most of them have diseases that could wipe us out, and they all have sun sickness. That's how we knew you weren't from the Broken Earth."

"I want to go and see my dad," I said.

"He'll be checked out and brought straight to you. If the Broken are raiding again, it would be best for you to stay safe. Also, if anything happens to the brightling on my watch, no one will vote for me next year."

James smiled. Zoe huffed.

"You must all be very tired. It sounds like you've had a busy day. I want to meet with you tomorrow. We can't start an all-out war with another earth, but I think there might be some ways that we can assist you in your cause." James shook our hands, and when he came to Zoe, he said, "I sincerely hope that we can help each other."

As we walked back down the hallway, a woman came out of one of the offices. It was the woman who had called James.

"Heidi?"

"Hi, Yolanda." Heidi stopped, and we all stayed behind her. I could feel the stares of the people in the offices again.

"Go straight down to the Mayor's ribbon. It's heaving outside. We've had to switch the barriers on so they can't get up here. Reception is full of flowers, and we've had about five thousand offers of marriage for the brightling, and some proposals that weren't marriage." Yolanda shuddered. "You don't want to know about those."

Yolanda took out a pen-like device similar to Heidi's and stamped a shiny gold dot onto Heidi's hand. Heidi looked at it with a massive smile on her face.

"This will get you to the residence. Log the guests in, and give me some time to sort out security. I've sent a couple of guys out there already. I need to pop out—I'm going to the infirmary to pick up the incs and bring them to you."

"Thanks, Yolanda."

Yolanda moved to stamp the rest of us. I was hesitant, but David moved forward, holding out his hand to her, so the rest of us followed suit.

"Are we still on for Friday night?" Yolanda asked Heidi.

"I'm not sure. Let's see how it goes," said Heidi as she moved to the elevator doors and pressed the B button below all the numbered buttons.

We faded, and Connor faded David. We entered and came out in a bright room with no natural light, but a yellow ribbon was running the length of one wall. We all stayed faded. Heidi walked straight to the ribbon and waved her hand at a panel to the side. She stood while we entered the stream of light. When Zoe entered, it flashed white.

This time we stayed in for several seconds before being ejected.

We materialized in a high-walled garden. I turned to see that the ribbon we'd just stepped from was between two posts. Heidi waved the shiny pattern on the back of her hand up to a panel on one of the posts and the ribbon disappeared. Behind it, the wall continued around the garden.

"I've never been here before, but I've heard about it. Nice res," said Heidi.

"Who lives here?" I asked.

"You, for now."

I turned and looked at the large single-story home. It was indeed a beautiful place. The garden had water features and wind chimes; it all had a very calming vibe.

We entered the house through sliding glass doors into a living space with a light, fresh feel. I walked into the kitchen and looked in the cupboards and refrigerator. The brands were unrecognizable, but everything was there: bacon, eggs, bread, milk, coffee, tea.

"I've picked a room for Hannah and me," said Zoe, walking into the kitchen.

"Oh, your room will be downstairs," said Heidi, directing Zoe to a door. We followed stairs down to several more bedrooms and another vast living area.

"In the basement again," said Zoe, rolling her eyes.

"Why are there so many rooms?" I asked.

"For lots of guests? Parties, maybe?" said Heidi with a smile. "Here, Zoe, I think this would be yours."

We entered a room which must have been the size of half the house. It had the biggest bed I'd ever seen with beaded bedding, and a thick carpet. A chandelier hung from the ceiling, and a Victorian-looking bath stood in the corner. Although underground, the room did have natural lighting. Floor to ceiling windows and glass doors ran the length of one wall onto a patio area under a glass roof, which must have been at the front of the house.

"Oh yes. You're right. This room is mine and Hannah's, for sure."

Good for her—she was the brightling, after all. If not for her, we'd probably all be in jail.

"There are twelve rooms here, so you don't have to share," said Heidi.

Zoe looked at me. Then she looked at Heidi.

"Yeah, we do."

"Oh! Right. Is anyone else sharing?" asked Heidi.

Connor and I looked at each other.

"I'm sorry, Jenna, your dad would kill me. I don't want to die," he said. He was probably right. "Dude, you wanna share?" he asked David.

"I have nightmares. I should probably sleep alone."

"I sleep like the dead, but it's up to you."

We went for a stroll through the house, picking rooms. The bed in mine was huge too, just to keep my options open.

When I walked back into the living room, Heidi was in the kitchen.

"You have pizza over there, right?" Heidi asked.

"Sure, pizza would be great," I said.

"Okay, I'll order a selection." Heidi took out a tablet and began typing.

"I thought we could come and go as we please," shouted David from the front hallway.

"Oh shit!" said Heidi. "My fault, sorry. Just a moment." Heidi walked through to where David, Connor and Zoe were standing by the door. She waved the gold stamp on her hand at a panel next to the door, and a voice spoke.

"Accessing... Present."

"Okay, present your tags to the screen and wait," said Heidi.

David, who had been standing closest to the door, stepped back and Connor walked up to the panel. He placed the golden stamp before the panel and waited.

"Name," said the automated voice.

"Connor Delaney."

"Connor Delaney, confirm."

"Erm... yes, that's right."

A light moved along the bottom of the screen from left to right and back. Heidi leaned in towards the panel and said, "Confirm."

"Activated," said the machine.

The process was repeated for Zoe, David and me.

"Don't you have to do it?" I asked Heidi.

"No, I'm already entered as your host." She waved her tag across the panel and said, "Open."

The door clicked open. Heidi closed the door and turned to David. "Just swipe your tag across the panel and say, 'Open.'"

David walked to the door and said, "Open... sesame."

We all laughed.

The door unclicked and the disembodied voice said, "Ta-da!"

David stood in the open doorway and leaned his face to the panel, saying, "No one likes a smart ass," before walking through the door.

"Dude," said Connor, "don't piss off the house."

We stood on the porch. I was unimpressed, and I didn't seem to be the only one.

"Well honestly, I'd hoped for more," said Connor.

We were looking at the high wall which encircled the whole property. I glanced down to my right to see the raised glass area that would be above Zoe's little patio.

Heidi walked past us and up the long path to a door in

the wall. She looked back at us, waiting. We all jogged to catch up. Heidi moved out of the way and indicated another panel.

I waved my tag at the panel and said, "Open." The door clicked, and Heidi opened it.

David and I bustled through the door, ready for our first proper look at this new world.

"Well honestly, I'd hoped for more," said Connor again from behind us.

We appeared to be surrounded by desert. The only life outside was a vehicle with two officers leaning against it. Heidi waved to the officers, and they waved back.

"We've ordered pizza," she called. They both gave a thumbs up.

When Zoe walked through the gate, they jumped up and started looking around like they were expecting trouble.

"I get it, I get it," said Zoe, walking back in.

I wandered out into the road and looked back at the walls. The dome which was transparent from the inside was black and seemed visually impenetrable from the outside.

Back in the house, we sat in the living area and chatted for a while.

"Heidi, am I going to be able to leave this place?" asked Zoe.

"I don't understand. You mean the house?" Heidi looked confused.

"James made it pretty clear that he wants something from me."

"Oh, I see. Yes, he will always make his thoughts and feelings clear—we all do. We have faders here who can pick the thoughts right out of your head."

All of us made a concerted effort not to look at David.

"Well, there aren't many of them. It's a rare gift, but it is out there. There is utterly no point to deception in our society. Lying is redundant. If someone wanted to stop you from going, they could have separated you from your red-mister or stopped him from fading. You can fade out of this world anytime you choose."

"Could you do that? Stop me from fading?" asked David.

"Of course. As you know, you could have the gland removed, and you'd be an inc, but we usually only do that for medical reasons or to the worst criminals. You're not considering it, are you? Red misting is a wonderful talent, to see another world..."

Heidi's eyes glazed over.

14

A tone chimed, and Heidi launched herself off the chair.

"Food. Thank God, I'm starving." She headed to the front gate.

"I like her," I said.

"Well?" asked Connor, looking at David.

"They're very welcoming and genuine people, don't you think?" said David. If anyone was listening, the way he had phrased that wouldn't have given anything away about his abilities.

Heidi came back with five huge pizza boxes, and another box with a tap on the side.

"Wine! Outstanding," said Zoe.

"Wine? Good Lord, no. This is Dooley Cola."

Heidi headed to the open kitchen.

Zoe and I looked at each other and mouthed, "What?"

Connor followed Heidi and watched as she laid the boxes out on the worktop. "Lombardi's? How do you have a Lombardi's?" His mouth gaped as he opened the boxes.

"You have Lombardi's too? That's so cool," said Heidi.

"It's only in New York on our earth."

"Same here. That's where I ordered it from."

"This ribbon travel is immense. We need to get the others over here. I'm ready to move in."

Two of the pizza boxes had a slice missing.

"It looks like the boys out front have taken care of themselves already," said Heidi, rolling her eyes. She pressed the tap on the side of the Dooley box, and a dark fizzy liquid poured into the glasses below.

"Tastes like Pepsi," said David.

After eating, we took the remains of the pizza down to the basement living area, near to Zoe's palatial room.

"Zoe, I think there's something that hasn't been explained to you very well, although you've already experienced it," said Heidi.

Zoe sat up, giving Heidi her full attention.

"If you choose to stay here, once you have resonated with the ribbon, you won't be emitting like this anymore. Your life will be your own."

The door chimed again, and Heidi went up to answer it. She came back in, followed by Callan, my dad and Hannah. I walked across the room and hugged my dad. He kissed the top of my head and hugged me back. Zoe jumped up, and she and Hannah kissed and hugged.

"What happened to you all?" asked Connor.

Hannah pulled away from Zoe and said, "Can we go somewhere else?" To me, she said, "If I hear your dad say 'They really upset the applecart' one more time, I'm going to scream."

"Come with me, we've got the best room," said Zoe, pulling her through the door.

"Can I smell pizza?" asked Dad.

"We saved you some," I said, turning to the basement

kitchen area. We gathered around the countertop, and Dad picked up pizza and rammed it into his mouth.

"I am so hungry," he might have said. I couldn't quite work out the words, but the sentiment was there.

"So, what happened?" I asked.

"After you left, a message came in on their radio saying the hopper was a few hours away, so they diverted one bringing produce from a farm into the city. The hopper arrived in about forty minutes, and we set off. Have you seen those things? The science is incredible."

Dad stopped for another bite and a drink of Dooley.

"We'd been traveling for about ten minutes, in silence—honestly, they wouldn't say a word to us. Then a copper had some kind of communication and they started chatting quite animatedly among themselves about some bright thing. After that, they were really chatty with us.

"Then we were shot off course. The pilot landed the hopper a bit roughly, but the right way up. Half a dozen ruffians came running at us. The doors opened and about 400 apples piled out, followed by all the officers. They really upset the applecart."

Dad laughed to himself. A muffled scream came from the hallway.

"Sorry," called Zoe as she closed their door.

"So, they took us to the infirmary to check us over. Somehow, Hannah's inhibitor is gone and here we are. Oh, and Jenna—we're on another earth. Another bloody earth."

He looked like he wanted to hold hands and jump up and down. I stepped back.

We took a walk upstairs and out to the garden. I told him about our meeting with the Mayor and the offer Heidi had made to Zoe.

"Do you think she'll accept?" he asked.

"I don't know. This emitting problem saps her energy, makes her a huge target back home and, as things stand, an unwilling superstar over here. Hannah has family. I don't know what she'll do."

"What about you? Would you like to stay here?"

"We have a mission. We don't know how the message was received by the faders or the trackers back home. Honestly, I'm concerned."

"I thought David could communicate with the faders. Why do you think the trackers even heard it?"

"The tracker standing next to the Major quite clearly heard it. It must have been caused by David's proximity to the ley lines," I said.

"I realized I could hear his thoughts. I knew I wouldn't have time for the full message we'd discussed. I did what I could in the seconds I had. A message that would mean something to faders *and* trackers," said David, who had been sitting quietly on a bench under a tree in the garden.

"Did you know what would happen when you faded?" Dad asked.

"I suspected. It's why I don't fade. It terrifies me, but it was the only way out. I'm sorry."

"There's no need to apologize," I said. "You saved us. You're a hero. And wherever your friend Kim is, you saved her, too."

David shrugged and seemed to go back to his thoughts.

"The Mayor thinks they can help us. I'd like to hear him out first."

"Hey! Hey!" called Zoe, running out to us in the garden. "I found the coke."

She held up a medicine bottle, which said, "Coca-Cola. For upset stomachs."

"This place cracks me up," she said, laughing and wandering off into the house.

"Well she's happier than I've seen for weeks," said Dad.

"Let's get you and Hannah logged into the house," I said.

We walked in to find Heidi and Callan eating pizza in the kitchen.

"Hey, Jenna, some clothes and sleepwear have arrived for you," said Heidi. "Zoe's put them in the rooms. I'm afraid we couldn't find much that would be to your taste, Neil."

"That's okay. This is more of a disguise."

"Oh Neil, I asked about you getting access to the archive. It should be no problem," said Callan.

"The archive?" I asked.

"I want to learn as much as I can about this place before I wake up and find it was all a dream," said Dad.

"Thank you. You've all been incredibly kind. Whose house is this—I mean, before it was ours?"

"It belonged to the last brightling as a vacation home. She lived in the Citadel. She died a few years ago."

"I'm sorry," I said, wishing I hadn't asked.

"She was old." Heidi shrugged.

"The Mayor asked me if you wouldn't mind a visit tomorrow," said Callan. "He's been on calls all afternoon. He thinks we can help you with your tracker problem. If you want our help, that is."

"That's fine," I said.

"Great. I'll be back in the morning."

"Before you go to bed, you should show your tag to the panel and tell it to lock down," said Heidi. "That will stop anyone from fading into the residence. The officers will remain outside should you need them."

Heidi and Callan left.

I looked at Dad's shiny stamp. It seemed different to mine. I told him to hold it up to the panel by the door.

"Inc," the panel said.

"I think it's supposed to register you," I said.

He held it up a few more times. The panel just said "Inc" every time.

"It's okay, we'll sort it tomorrow," he said.

I put the house into lockdown, then Dad and I walked along the hallway.

"This is me," I said, then pointed to his room across the hall.

"Good to see you're not in with Connor," he said.

"He thought you'd kill him."

"I like that young man. Very astute. Night, Little Duck.

"Night, Dad."

THE NEXT MORNING, I awoke to the smell of breakfast.

I padded in my pajamas towards the kitchen, following my nose. Connor was cooking while Dad made coffee. I stopped still and just watched. My dad was alive, I had a boyfriend, and I realized I felt safe.

"Morning, Beautiful, breakfast will be five minutes," said Connor, walking over to me and kissing me.

"Coffee will be three," said Dad.

"David's in the garden; Zoe and Hannah haven't put in an appearance yet. Heidi called; she and the Mayor will be here in about an hour."

I walked back into the hall and called down the stairs, "Breakfast in five."

"Okay," called Zoe.

Connor opened the garden door. "David, breakfast."

We sat around the table. Zoe and Hannah walked in, smiling.

"I slept like a log last night," said Zoe.

"Oh! You're all asking yourselves the same question," said David, walking in from the garden.

"Dude, could you try to turn that thing off?" asked Connor.

"It's mostly off, but I afforded Vince that consideration. If I'd been listening, we wouldn't be a world away from our friends."

"And a world away from Major Tom," said Zoe. She and Hannah toasted with their pancake laden forks.

"I wonder what they did with Vince," I said.

"I wonder why you care," said David.

"He did a terrible thing, but he did it because he cared about you."

"He did it because he cared about his career. That's all he ever cared about."

I began to get an inkling about their history. I guessed David and Vince had once been a couple, Vince always putting his career first, but unable to let David go.

"That's about it, yes," said David, responding to my thoughts.

"I'm sorry, I shouldn't speculate."

"You can't help what pops into your mind."

I glanced automatically at Connor. David nearly choked on his food, and I blushed furiously.

"So, you're going to stay?" said David, turning to Zoe.

"Well, I'd have liked to announce it myself, but yes, that's the plan. Assuming some conditions are met, and everything is as it seems here."

"I haven't detected any subterfuge. All the Mayor was

thinking was how desperately he wanted you to stay. Also, I'm still alive."

"Sorry?" said Dad.

"I'm your only way out of here. If they want to force Zoe to stay, they only need to get rid of me."

"So you think you can cross back?"

"Yes, I'm sure I can, but if we try it, everyone who wants to go will need to be here. I don't want to risk leaving anyone behind."

"If you need to do it any time soon, I should get dressed. I don't want to appear on our earth in my PJs."

I headed to my room.

"It's better than butt naked," Zoe called from behind me.

About a half hour later, the doorbell sounded. I went to the door, flashed my tag and told it to open.

"You know, I'm right by the door. A handle would have worked just as well," I said to Dad.

"Safety first," he replied.

Standing outside was James with Heidi and Callan.

"Come on in." I stood back to let them walk through.

"Pastries," said James, waving a large white box.

"Look at that, the Mayor knows the password," said Zoe.

"None of that, call me James." He put the pastries down on the kitchen counter, and Connor poured coffees and refilled the machine. We all went to the sofas.

"How was your night?" asked Heidi.

"I slept like a log. I think we all did," I said.

"That's because you weren't being monitored all day and night," said David.

"Erm, maybe," I said, confused that he would bring that up.

"I'm just moving James's thoughts around so I can access

what I need to know. They're not bugging us," said David in my mind.

"The world you come from frightens me a little," said Heidi.

"A little? Really?" said Zoe. "Because it scares the crap out of me."

"I was in meetings half the night," said James. "We should have a full and frank discussion about your situation and ours."

"Excellent. I'm glad to hear it. Neil Banks," said Dad, offering his hand to James.

"Erm, Jenna's father, of course," said James, awkwardly taking his hand.

"Neil, would you like to visit the archive now?" asked Callan.

I'd had my suspicions, and seeing Callan try to shuffle my dad out of the room so the grown-ups could talk was the last straw.

"Okay," I said. "Here's the first thing on my agenda. I wonder if you might clarify for me what status incs have in your society?"

Heidi and Callan looked at each other and James blushed.

"Let me help," I said. "Every inc I've seen since I got here has been in a service role. The guy who brought the sandwiches to your office and people cleaning the pavement at the platform. Not even the house will recognize my dad."

"It's just how our society works," said James.

"Are they slaves?" I asked.

Heidi choked on her pastry.

"Jenna, I know you're new here, and things look very different, but you need to get out and have a proper look around. Incs aren't slaves, but they don't have the same opportunities because of their inability to fade. They can't get around as fast. They accept a slower way of life. When I hire an assistant, for example, I might need them to be in Singapore within ten minutes. I couldn't hire an inc for that role."

Zoe muttered something about Skype.

"Then why won't the house computer accept my dad on the security panel?" I asked.

"There is an element of dissatisfaction among some incs Some groups have moved off into their communities and won't even live with us. They've built a whole radical religion around faders being Satan's children. They have been known to come into the city and martyr themselves by walking into the ribbon in front of everyone. We assess incs before we give them access. We can sort your father's tag with the panel."

"How does it even know Dad's not a fader, and why won't these things wash off?" I asked.

"The tags are made with nanites. The first one you had read your DNA and transferred it into a unique code. It then assigned that code to everything you're carrying so that it all remains with you when you fade. Our scanners didn't recognize Hannah as a fader at first. I gather your military injected something to stop her from fully utilizing her fader gland. The nanites identified her at the medical facility and deactivated it. You'll see that her tag is the same as yours. She should be able to fade by now."

"I thought that took a year," said Zoe.

"She should have fully faded years ago. The nanites will have fixed that."

"She might be glowing now, but it's a little difficult to see," said Heidi with a glance at Zoe.

I blinked in, but Zoe was swamping everything out in yellow.

I looked at the back of Hannah's hand to see that her stamp was a gold pattern like mine, and Dad's was silver.

David, who was sitting on the sofa next to me, put his hand on mine.

"This is their society. It works differently to ours. We're not going to be able to change it. If we're going to stay here, we have to accept that."

In my mind, David said, "*They're good people. Different, but well-meaning, and they want to help us. Give them a chance.*"

"Dad?" I asked.

"As long as no one expects me to make sandwiches—I'm rubbish in the kitchen, as well you know. I'm more concerned about what might be going on at home."

"Which brings me on to last night's meetings," said James. "I've been authorized to offer you and your families asylum here on the Full Earth. I know you'll need to get back and assess the situation and organize bringing them over, and I'd like to send a small party with you. Callan, Heidi and a couple of others to support you and offer protection."

Heidi squeaked involuntarily and covered her mouth, blushing.

"This isn't an artefact shopping trip," said James, turning in his seat to face Heidi.

"No, sir, of course not."

"But I'll be disappointed if you don't bring something back for me." He winked at her.

"How does everyone feel about this?" I asked.

"It'll be great to see Orla again..."

James looked at Zoe and cleared his throat. Zoe looked back.

"I can't go, can I," she said. It wasn't a question.

"That would be a condition, I'm afraid. If I let you get killed…"

"No one will vote for you next year, I know." Zoe slumped in her seat.

"You can't ask that of her, it's not fair," said Hannah.

"He's right," said Zoe. "With this emitting thing, I'd put them all in danger. I'm okay with this, but if I'm staying, so are you. I don't want to be alone here."

"I wouldn't be anywhere else," said Hannah, putting her head on Zoe's shoulder.

"Okay, it's going to take a few days to organize. Are you okay with that?" asked James.

We all nodded.

"Right. Callan, sort out the panel before you take Neil to the archive. Make sure there's a dedicated hopper for his use. Heidi, you made a good point about them needing to get out. Organize a ribbon tour and I'll sort something social for tomorrow night." James stood and headed for the door. "If you need anything, let me know." With that, he left.

A few minutes later, Dad popped his head into the room.

"We're heading to the archive. I'll see you later," he said.

"Is the panel sorted?" I asked.

"Yes, I'm now 'Neil Banks, inc'."

I followed Dad down to the gate and caught my first view of a hopper. It was like a small bus without wheels or driver. All the edges and corners were curved, and the bottom side curved inwards along its length, leaving it standing on its side edges.

Dad entered the vehicle along with Callan and a couple of other officers. The ribbon appeared, and the hopper leapt up from the ground and settled a foot or so above the ribbon, which dropped back down under the ground. The hopper shot off, presumably following the ribbon's underground path.

With the ribbon gate gone, I found myself facing two officers who had been standing on the other side of it.

"Hi," I said, awkwardly.

"Ma'am."

"If you need anything, let us know," I said.

"Is the brightling okay? Does she need anything?"

"She's fine. I'll let her know you were asking after her."

I turned and closed the gate on their smiles. When I reentered the living room, Hannah had a panel in her hands and was waving her nanite stamp in front of it.

"Open stores."

"Unrecognized request," said the same voice as the security panel.

"View products for purchase."

"Unrecognized request," it repeated.

"Show me pretty things."

Heidi came in from the garden. Hannah flashed her tag at the panel and opened her mouth to ask again.

"Catalogues," said Heidi.

"Catalogues open. Please select a catalogue," said the panel.

"Yes!" said Hannah. "Wait, how do I pay for stuff?"

"I think there's a stipend on the house, but I don't know how much so don't buy a hopper," said Heidi. "Why do you want to buy from the catalogue anyway? I've been ordered to take you on a tour. I can take you on a tour of the stores."

For a moment, Hannah looked excited, but then remembered Zoe's emitting problem.

"I don't want to go without Zoe."

"You go ahead. I'll give you a list, if that's okay?" Zoe called from the kitchen.

"Are you sure? What are you going to do?"

"I'm going to have a bath for at least half the day. Then I'm going to find out what passes for good music around here." It was clear that Zoe was putting on a brave face.

"This is not a problem," said Heidi, pulling a little white cube out of her pocket and throwing it over to Zoe. Zoe caught it and turned it over in her hands.

"Press the white button," Heidi said.

Zoe pressed the button, and a light appeared.

"Is it a night light?" she asked, staring as the light grew a little brighter.

"Have you engaged?" asked Heidi.

"Sorry?"

"Blink in," I said.

I blinked in too and watched Zoe's yellow mist getting smaller and smaller.

"Hey, you're emitting," Zoe said to Hannah.

"Why can't Zoe use one of these and go home?" I asked.

"Well, two reasons. Firstly, each one only lasts for an hour. I've got six on me. That'll do us for a day out, but not an extended trip. Secondly, they won't stop you from getting shot."

"That's fair," said Zoe.

"It will probably take a few days for Hannah to get the hang of fading, though, so we'll have to send for a hopper and shop locally," said Heidi.

"Can I get information on this pad thing? Like the news, movies, that kind of thing?" David asked Heidi.

"Oh yes, you can just ask it to list commands, and it will help you find what you want."

Zoe and Hannah headed out of the room.

"Connor?" called Zoe.

Connor stood and left the room too. I watched while Heidi showed David how to do a few things on the pad.

Five minutes later, Connor, Zoe and Hannah returned.

"Okay, I'm ready for an adventure," said Hannah. I looked up to see her fade and return.

"I've never seen anyone get the hang of fading so fast," said Heidi.

"It must have been those nanites. They're amazing," said Hannah.

Connor winked at me. He'd been fading her to help her get the hang of it.

"I'm going to stay here," said David.

"Don't you want to come and soak up the atmosphere, Dave?" asked Connor. I guessed by 'soak up the atmosphere' he meant read minds.

"No, I can soak up the atmosphere from here, in Zoe's fancy bathtub. Then I'm going to have a nap."

"Dude, you slept for months."

"I don't think I'd call that quality sleep."

"You slept for months? Were you sick?" asked Heidi.

"No. The Agency captured me and kept me in a drug-induced coma." David lifted another pastry and walked into the garden. Heidi watched him go as her jaw dropped.

"He likes that garden, doesn't he?" said Connor.

"It's very calming with the wind chimes and everything. He needs calm," I said.

"We're ready," said Hannah, standing with Zoe by the garden door.

We wandered into the back garden and said goodbye to David before calling the private ribbon. After a few minutes, as we walked out into a shopping mall, Hannah squealed with delight.

15

Not one of the store or brand names was familiar, but the layout of the mall looked pretty much like any other back home. The people were different, though; how they interacted was a strange sight to behold. I watched two women walking directly towards each other, neither moving out of the way. They just faded and walked through each other, reappearing and continuing on seconds later.

It was interesting to see how incs dealt with it. They just put their eyes down and walked. It was a waste of time trying to jump out of a fader's way. Much easier to let faders go through you, I guessed. I wondered what the protocol was for incs walking towards each other—would they bump heads before realizing they were both incs? I chuckled at the thought.

"I can't get over how much it looks like our earth," I said as we stood at a balcony and looked down on several levels of stores.

"Really?" said Heidi. "Your description so far has been frightening. The Agency, the trackers, keeping people drugged. I was excited to get the opportunity to visit another world, but I'm also scared."

"All those things, they're under the surface," said Zoe. "We estimate that less than zero point zero one per cent of our society are faders. The Agency is a secret organization. The world doesn't know they or we exist."

"The rest of it is kids going to school, people going to work, shopping, watching TV," said Hannah.

"TV?"

"People acting in shows. It gets beamed to the house," I said.

"We have the pads for that—the little hand-size ones or the bigger wall-mounted ones. Oh, I should have mentioned that to David." Heidi took a pad out from her bag. "Play Beethoven on main pad with message: David, I hope you're having a great day. Sign, from Heidi."

Hannah looked up at the dome. "Hey, it's raining out there. Where did that come from?"

We all looked up.

"We were just outside Los Angeles before. We're in New York now."

"No shit!" said Connor, looking around.

"No, they keep all the cities clean," said Heidi, looking down.

"He means 'Are you telling the truth?'"

"Oh, like horse shit? No, I'm not talking horse shit."

As we walked past other unfaded shoppers, I gazed at them, expecting to see familiar faces. I figured if this earth and our earth were the same at some point, there must be some of the same people on both.

I noticed the stores all had similar signs in the windows.

"What's a Shine Sale?" I asked.

"Oh, this is embarrassing. The President declared a four-day weekend to celebrate the brightling. Sorry, Zoe," said Heidi.

"Happy brightling day, honey." Hannah threw her arms around Zoe.

"Happy   you'll-be-single-if-you-don't-cut-that-crap-out day," said Zoe.

Hannah laughed, and Zoe chuckled to herself.

"That reminds me," said Heidi, taking out another cube. Zoe made to hand hers back; there was a warm light growing within. "Would you mind clicking it off before handing it back? I don't have surplus energy; I'll probably faint if I touch it while it's on."

They swapped cubes.

"What is that thing? How does it work?" asked Connor.

Heidi turned the cube in her hand.

"I'm not sure. I'm not really into science. It somehow holds ribbon energy and draws in the brightling's energy. You can see it's full because of how bright it is. You can power your pad or comms from it, or as you said, Zoe, use it as a night light. If you had one big enough, you could power a hopper or a house."

"I'm so happy Major Tom doesn't know about this," I said.

We entered a clothes store and started throwing clothes into baskets. I wondered what size jeans David might wear.

"Twenty-eight waist, thirty-four leg."

"Oh!" I said out loud.

"What?" asked Connor.

"David," I said, tapping my head.

"Is everything okay?"

"He wants some jeans."

"Ha!" Connor barked a laugh.

"How are you doing this?" I asked David.

"I called the ribbon into the garden. It's just like being next to a ley line."

"Okay, well if you need anything else, let me know."

"I'm good. I'm listening to Beethoven."

"Don't forget we're going out tomorrow night. Party dresses!" said Heidi from a couple of racks away. She looked at Connor. "And boy stuff," she added, pointing vaguely in the direction of the menswear department.

"Twenty-eight waist, thirty-four leg," I called to Connor as he headed off.

Hannah picked a short metallic-bronze colored shift dress. Zoe picked some shiny black trousers with laces up the sides and a black spaghetti strap top. I found a standard halter-neck little black dress.

"Ah, the LBD. Indispensable on any earth," said Hannah.

Heidi was last to find what she wanted. She picked up a long red dress, looked at the price and put it back.

"I think you should expense it to the residence," I said. "You're seconded to the Mayor's office, you can't embarrass him at his party."

"You talked me into it. I'm trying this on."

"Wow, really? That was way easier than I expected."

I walked with her over to the changing cubicles.

"Can I leave this with you?" she asked, passing me her bag.

"Sure," I said.

I sat down in the hallway outside the cubicles and waited. I glanced at Heidi's bag, and then I started going through my shopping from previous stores. I took out the messenger-style bag I'd bought, took off the tags and put it across my shoulder. As I glanced at Heidi's bag again, finally, my curiosity got the better of me.

I looked up and down the little hallway and opened the

bag to see the small ribbon cubes. Four were dark, and one was glowing. Zoe had the sixth. I picked out a dark one and turned it around in my hand before switching the little button. Instantly, it shone a bright white light, illuminating the small, dark hallway as though it were outside. Feeling instantly dizzy, I clicked off the button and the draining feeling stopped, but the cube remained intensely bright—much brighter than the one Zoe had filled. I panicked and took out some socks I'd purchased and tucked it into them. By the time it had eight socks around it, the light was no longer visible. I tucked it into my messenger bag and closed the flap. Then I closed Heidi's bag and sat there with my heart hammering.

After a minute, Heidi came out and swirled around in the dress.

"That's stunning. You have to get it," I said.

"Are you okay? You look pale."

"I think I could do with something to eat."

With our purchases paid for, we headed over to a Chinese restaurant and ordered. While we waited for the food to come, I asked Heidi, "What's with all these domes?"

"About fifty years ago, we began to have terrible storms. The planet's protective layers thinned and people got sick. The decision was made to protect the populations by encasing the cities in these domes. The material they used is incredibly thick and mostly protected the cities from the awful storms."

"And the storms now?"

"Over the course of a couple of years, they gradually reduced and then just stopped. But by then, millions of people all over the world had sun-sickness and died."

"But you still have the domes," I said.

"We don't know why it just stopped. It could happen again, so we kept them."

It was incredible to see how one planet might change with a different set of circumstances.

The meal had been outstanding. The waiter, with his silver nanite tag, brought a pad over, and Heidi scanned it with her tag to pay.

"The ultimate in wearable tech. I love it," said Hannah.

"Doesn't the idea of tiny little computers running around your body creep you out?" asked Zoe.

"It does now," said Hannah with a shiver.

Heidi signaled to a couple of guys who were sitting two tables away. I hadn't even noticed them. One of them stood and walked over to us.

"Can you drop these back at the house? We're heading to the Museum of Artefacts," said Heidi.

"I'm supposed to be protecting the brightling."

"There's at least ten of you around. I think we'll be okay. We promise not to need saving until you return."

He gathered up the bags and left.

In my head, I said, "*Dave?*"

"*I heard. I guess I'm expecting a guest. I'll send this ribbon back, so I'll be out of contact.*"

We made our way back to the main ribbon in the mall, faded and stepped into it, coming out in a vast space. A sign ahead of us said "The Museum of Artefacts".

"This is my favorite place. Callan calls me a geek. It means..."

"We have that word too. It means Hannah," said Zoe, stepping out of the way of Hannah's hand.

"It's not very busy, is it," I said.

"It's a museum. Mostly school groups and me, although I've seen the Mayor in here a couple of times."

Heidi led us through the entrance of the most curious place I'd ever been—if I didn't count this entire planet. The artefacts were in different sections for clothes and accessories, books, art, technology, weapons, and tins of food. They were set out in each section by date and location. Mannequins were wearing 1930s style dresses with intricately beaded bags. Teddy boy outfits, records, cigarettes, spectacles, bowler hats, and huge collared shirts and flares from the 1970s. Everything that a person could wear or carry on them. The technology section had Dictaphones, cell phones, nose hair clippers. There was a collection of groceries and pictures of groceries, including a tin of Spam.

We followed the exhibition path into the next section: surgical implants. There were knees, hips, fillings and skull plates. As I watched a couple of people walking around the exhibits, I made an observation.

"Heidi, I have a question," I said.

"Go ahead."

"If the people with gold tags are faders and the people with silver tags are incs, who are the people with no tags?"

"Everyone has either a silver or gold tag."

"What about the two men with no tags on their hands, over by the toys, staring at us?"

Heidi led us across to a toy display. We discussed a model of the Starship Enterprise while Heidi looked through the display case to check out the men.

"Brian is going to make me regret sending him back with the bags if we run into trouble," she said.

I blinked in and noted there were eight other people in the room apart from us and the strangers. It wasn't looking good for those guys.

The men wandered through the exhibits away from us and out of the door.

I exhaled.

"This section is called Curiosities. I call it 'The Weird Stuff People Have In Their Pockets'," said Heidi.

"Oh my God! Look at this," said Zoe.

We wandered over to the display. It was a shelf of mostly stress balls, and two items that weren't stress balls.

"You'd be livid if you paid 10,000 dollars for those, and whoosh! They were just gone," said Zoe.

"Why would a fader even do that?" asked Hannah.

"What are they?" asked Heidi.

"They're breast implants," said Zoe.

"I'm sorry?"

"For women who want bigger..." Zoe cupped her hands in front of her.

"Oh... oh... I think they should be in the medical department."

After a brief chat with the curator, we left the section. Heidi reached into her bag.

"Oh, I thought I had six of these. Hell, this is the last one. I'm afraid we need to get back soon."

"It's okay. I'm shattered anyway. It's been a fantastic day," I said, feeling awful for my deception.

We entered the gift shop and bought Dad and David a keyring each with little models of a tin of Spam and a tin of Heinz beans. As we reached the ribbon, a few of the officers appeared around us, and Heidi flashed her tag at the panel. We faded and stepped in. A few seconds later, we stepped out into the garden.

"I'll come and get you at about seven for the party tomorrow night," said Heidi, picking up her shopping bags and leaving.

I hung up my dress in the room and took a shower.

After a couple of hours, Dad entered the house.

"Who's here?" he asked.

"We're all here, why?" I followed him through to the kitchen and we all gathered around, drawn by his nervous energy.

"What happened?" asked Connor.

"You won't believe the history of this place," he said.

"We will if you tell us," I said.

"It looks like the universe duplicated at the beginning of the last century. The differences are incredible. Neither the First nor Second World War happened on this earth, which explains so much."

"So what made that happen?" I asked.

"No one knows. It could have been something at the other end of the universe. It's possible that they're multiplying all the time, but they don't usually connect in this way. It may have been a comet hitting a moon or a butterfly fluttering its wings that caused the ribbon to appear and the fader gene to activate."

"But the ley lines have always been there, haven't they?"

"They were first identified in 1921. That's what Vanessa told me,"

"What did you mean about no wars explaining things?" Zoe asked.

"I wondered at first if I'd see people I knew from the other earth."

"I thought about that today too," I said.

"Roughly sixteen million people are thought to have died in World War One and over sixty million in World War Two. The population here today is completely different to what it is on our earth. Couples who met because of the wars didn't meet here. I met your mum at the Academy, but that wouldn't have happened because there's no Academy here. Vanessa and Tom met at the Academy, but they were from different parts of the country, so they probably wouldn't have met at all, if they'd even existed."

"So there was no Adolf Hitler?" I asked.

"I looked him up—nothing. There was someone like him, who blamed the faders for everything wrong in his life, but then, virtually all the kids were fading. No one's going to put their kids into concentration camps, so he disappeared into obscurity reasonably quickly.

"Then people with abilities began to appear. Mind readers turned the general population into a much more honest bunch. Good people were voted into office. Most of the scientific progress—travel, medical advances, nanotechnology advances—has involved fading and the ribbon. This whole earth is about moving forward. Even space travel is so much more advanced here. They haven't found life out there yet, but they're a hell of a lot further than us.

"The only problems they seem to have are overcrowding, and there are inc communities that refuse to integrate. There's just one religion on the American and European continents: a brotherhood that stays inside citadels. The main one is in Europe, and there's one in South America. They swear a vow of solidity, refusing to fade."

David said, "I have some news too. When the guy left after dropping your bags off, I opened the private ribbon again to speak to you. I could hear distant mutterings, so I just sat in front of the gate and made myself emit. The mist was sucked into the ribbon at first, and I could hear thousands of people all at once. It scared me, so I went to lie down."

"Wow! That must have been awful," said Hannah.

"Not so awful that I didn't try again. The next time, I didn't sit so close to the ribbon. I just sat in a red cloud, hovering on the edge of fading. The people I could hear this time weren't from this earth. I was connecting to our earth. I searched for Vanessa, found her, and we spoke."

"Is she okay? Is Orla okay? Did Jodi get the girls?"

"Yes, yes and yes," said David.

I blew out a lungful of pent-up nerves.

"They are at the ranch in Canada. There was some unpleasantness getting the girls back, but they're all safe for now. And, we were right to worry about the message I sent. trackers are on the run all over the world. Vanessa suspects that all of the trackers with the upgraded inhibitors are dead. I told Vanessa what happened and why the message changed. I told her where we are. She thinks I've completely snapped."

"At least we know they're alive and safe," I said.

"Well done, David, you've done remarkably well," said Dad. "I guess I'd better get a move on. It's going to take me a lot longer to get to the party than you. I might get there in time to go home."

"Neil, I've got a suggestion about that," said Connor, walking with my dad out into the hallway.

David went out to the garden, and I followed.

"How are you?" I asked.

"I'm okay. I'm still angry with Vince, and I'm worried about what's going on at home. I shouldn't have said what I did. The message. It was all wrong. I think I did it again."

"Did what again?"

"I didn't know your grandfather. But I watched him die, and it was my fault. They all died because of what I did."

"I've seen a video of the aftermath. I know the Agents did it. You don't have to tell me this."

But he was determined, so I listened.

16

David lay on his bed in the dorm as Chris and Mark prepared for their night out.

"Who else is going?" he asked.

"Just Kim and Alice. It was Alice who got the tickets; she's crazy about the lead singer," said Mark.

"How are you getting past security?"

"We got a four-hour pass out to the town," said Chris.

"I don't see you getting to Portland and back in four hours."

"It'll be too late by then, and we're going home tomorrow, so hopefully, they'll have forgotten about it by the start of next semester."

"And Craig's on the gate. He's cool," said Mark.

"You can hope. Are you going into the town?"

"No, we'll be picking up the bus to Portland at the crossroad."

The boys finished dressing, then stuffed piles of clothes under their covers to make the beds look occupied.

"Are you ready, Mark? If we miss this bus, we'll have to wait an hour," said Chris.

"Good to go, buddy."

"See you later, Dave."

David remained on his bed, but slipped his hand under the pillow to retrieve his pass out. He looked over at the overstuffed beds and considered making them look more realistic. Glancing at his watch, he figured there would be time for that when he returned. He sat up and got ready for his trip to the town; he planned to leave after the others had caught their bus.

Before David left the dorm, he blinked in and looked down at himself. Nothing yet, he thought.

David showed his pass to Craig at the security gate and headed to the bus stop. The stop was empty; the others had left. This was good. He didn't want to be questioned.

Sitting on the bus, David thought about the day he'd met the fader Cindy in a Vancouver, WA library. She had a list of books as long as her arm, and the librarian was running all over the building to collect them for her.

"I thought there was a limit on the number of books we could take out," said David.

"I'm home-schooled, so they let me take what I need for the semester."

She smiled, and his stomach flipped.

"I'm sorry, Cindy, four of the books you need are out," said the librarian. "I'll keep them for you. They should all be back this time next week."

"That's okay, I think I've got enough for now." She looked at the pile and sighed.

"Do you have far to carry those?" asked David, trying to think of something to say to keep the conversation going.

"No. My dad will be in to pick me up soon. He'll help."

David looked through the book titles. The pile consisted mostly of books he was studying himself.

"I don't remember seeing Isaac Asimov in the curriculum," he said.

"Shh! I'm hoping to get that one past my dad."

They laughed and began to wander through the stacks.

"Do you go to the local school?" asked Cindy.

"No, I'm at a kind of boarding school over in Ireland."

"I didn't know there was one out there."

"It's more of an academy. How come you get home-schooled?"

"We live quite a ways out. Mom and Dad say it's for the best."

"That must be lonely," said David, feeling a swell of empathy.

"Sometimes..."

"Cindy?" said a gruff voice from the doorway.

"Oh, that's my dad," she said, sounding disappointed.

"You're coming back next week, aren't you? I'll be here," said David, staying in the back of the stacks while Cindy walked out to her father.

David thought about Cindy for the whole week and waited several hours in the library for her to return. When she finally walked through the door, his face lit up at seeing her.

"I thought I might have missed you," she said.

"I only just got here myself," said David. Out of the corner of his eye, he saw the librarian's lips twitch into a brief smile.

"Dad's got some chores to do around town, so I'm here for about an hour."

"I can stay that long, if you'd like." David had never said anything so forward to a girl in his life; he held his breath.

"That would be nice," she said, taking the Asimov from

her bag. "I have to return this. Dad caught me with it. I was just a couple of chapters from the end." She shrugged.

"Finish it now. I'll read this." David held up his copy of *2001: A Space Odyssey*.

"You like science fiction too?" Cindy smiled.

"I've only really gotten into it lately, but I've read a few now." Lately being this week, thought David, who had been back to the library three times and was devouring its small science-fiction collection.

David and Cindy sat down together in companionable silence and read their books. Finally, Cindy closed the book and sat back.

"That was great. Have you read it?" she asked.

"Not yet. I'll read it next," he said, taking it from her and putting it under his Arthur C. Clark book.

When her father turned up, Cindy was waiting at the counter.

"Did you return the trash one?" her father asked.

"Yes, Daddy," said Cindy as the color rose in her cheeks.

"I'm sorry, one of those books you wanted hasn't returned yet. It should be back next week," said the librarian.

Cindy's father huffed, and they left.

The librarian looked over at David and winked. He floated out of the library and traveled back to the Academy with a dreamy look on his face.

The week went by slowly, but seven days later, he was back at the library. He'd read several more science-fiction books and had been devising scenarios which might result in Cindy's father letting him see more of her. He wondered if he could tutor her. He was quite good at math.

His daydream was interrupted by Cindy's approach. He was about to greet her, but she looked furious.

"So, are you going to kill me today, or were you waiting until you could take out my whole family?" She prodded him in the chest as she whispered the words.

"What?"

"I know what that Academy is now. They train you to kill people who are different—people like me." The outrage on her face was shocking. There were tears in her eyes.

"No, you've got it wrong. We catch monsters, not people." He blurted out the words, trying to make her understand.

"Monsters?" She drew in a breath and stepped back, then vanished. Right before his eyes, she was gone. She was a fader.

David was shaking. He couldn't believe she'd been a fader all along. He went home with a heart full of rocks.

The week went by. He told no one. He was conflicted. She wasn't a monster. She was a sweet girl. He could see that. Was it some trick? But she was nice.

The thoughts circled through his mind. He didn't want to go to the library, but by the end of the next week, he knew he had to see her. He didn't think she would be there. She wasn't.

More weeks went by; he returned to the library on the same day of every week, hoping to see her, feeling more discouraged, confused and conflicted every time. Each week he would sit down on a chair in the science-fiction stacks and wait.

Finally, something happened.

He was reading his third Asimov book when the hairs on the back of his neck raised. He looked up, but there was no one around him. He blinked in, and there she was. He couldn't recognize it was her, he just knew.

His heart hammered. She was his enemy in her alien

form. She just sat there, and so did he, lifting the book in his hands to show her the cover: *I, Robot*. She nodded, reached out her hand and stroked his face. He couldn't feel it.

She began to walk away; he stood to follow her, but she turned and motioned him to sit. He sat.

A few minutes later, she returned in human form.

"I didn't think you would come back," he said.

"I wasn't going to, but I've learned something you should know."

He expected her to tell him something, but instead, she asked a question.

"Why do you think I'm a monster?"

"That's what they teach us at the Academy. You take human form sometimes, but your natural form is this misty yellow shape."

She giggled. "I'm sorry. I know this is serious, but that's just funny." The smile left her face. "We're people. We're just different, and there aren't really that many of us. We're normal kids until we get to about eleven or twelve. Then we have the awakening, and we can see the yellow mist of other faders. Stop me when this sounds familiar."

"I don't understand. That's what happens to us," said David.

"I know. But they start to give you drugs, don't they?"

David thought about the little dark red pills.

"The pills are to help the Sight develop. To make us better trackers..." He stopped talking. The truth was finally bare and undeniable before him. "I'm a fader?" he asked, his voice tiny.

"Yes. And they use you to track down other faders," she said.

It was a lot to take in. He stood.

"I need to go." He raced through the stacks, stopped and

turned back. "See you next week." He turned again and left.

The next morning, when the Agents came around the tables, handing out the little red pills at breakfast time, David held his in his cheek and discreetly discarded it. Every morning for several weeks, he cheeked the pill. One way or another, he would know the truth.

DAVID'S BUS arrived in the town. Chris, Mark, Alice and Kim were on their way to the concert, his other friend Melissa was working on a project at the Academy, and he was planning to be undisturbed for several hours with Cindy at the library. When he walked in, he saw that Cindy was already there. She looked at him with wide eyes and dragged him into the stacks.

"You're emitting," she scolded him as though his zipper were down.

He blinked in. Sure enough, he was lit up.

"That's it then. It's all true." He sat heavily on a chair. He had wanted it to be true, except that he also hadn't wanted it to be true.

"You need to leave that place," said Cindy.

"I need to tell the others the truth."

"Not looking like that, you can't. You won't get near the place. They've been lying to hundreds of kids and their families for years. What do you think they'll do to you?"

"Cindy, what are you doing? We need to go," said her father from the end of the aisle.

"Dad, this boy needs our help," said Cindy.

Her dad blinked and looked at David. "Come with me," he said.

With no better idea of what to do, David followed him

and Cindy into their car.

"You shouldn't be out like that. It's dangerous around here. Where do you live?"

"I go to an Academy out of town," David said.

Cindy's father froze, looking at David through the rear-view mirror.

"The place north east of Fern Prarie?" he asked.

"Yes." David looked away, ashamed.

Cindy's father looked at her with disbelief.

"She told me. I didn't want to believe. I stopped taking the pills. It's not Cindy's fault, Mr..."

"Smith," said Cindy's father in a deadpan voice. He started the engine and drove out of the car park. "Lie down in the back. I don't want you to see where we live."

David curled up on his side across the back seat and covered his face with his arm.

They were in the car for about an hour, turning this way and that. David was pretty sure that Mr. Smith was driving randomly to confuse him, but he wasn't paying any attention to the route anyway.

After a bumpy ride on what seemed to be a long access road, the car pulled over.

"You come with me to the kitchen, and you go to your room, young lady," said Mr. Smith.

David walked into the kitchen and sat in a chair at the table.

"Marylou, can you feed this boy while I figure out what the hell we're going to do with him?" Mr. Smith picked up the telephone. "Hey, James. I'm having a card game tonight. Can you call the others? No, a card game. No, A. Card. Game. Yes."

Mr. Smith left the room. Halfway through a bowl of soup, David heard shouting upstairs.

"You risked your life even talking to him in the first place. That's no excuse. He can't stay here. They'll be looking for him. He's not safe here. Well, you should have thought about that before."

A door slammed.

Cindy's father walked back into the kitchen.

"I'm sorry, Mr. Smith," said David.

"It's not for you to apologize, son. Cindy dragged you into this mess."

"Mr. Smith, I should tell the other kids at the Academy what's going on," said David.

"Honey, why does this boy keep calling you Mr. Smith?" asked Cindy's mother.

"Because that's what I told him my name is," said apparently-not-Mr.-Smith.

Marylou looked at him with one raised eyebrow.

"I panicked," he said. Then to me, he said, "You can call me Patrick."

An hour later, a pick-up truck pulled up and three men got out and walked into the house. They each kissed Marylou on the cheek and she greeted them by name: James, Hugh and John. They joined Cindy's family and David at the kitchen table, staring at the soup pot on the stove.

"Would you boys like some soup?" asked Marylou with a wry smile.

"Pat, we need a better code than a card game. I just thought you meant a card game," said James.

"How about quilting?" asked Marylou.

"No. Someone might hear."

"So who's the boy, Pat?" asked John.

"This is David. He's a stray Cindy brought home. He's from the Academy up in Ireland."

The men froze. David swallowed a mouthful of soup loudly.

"He's emitting," said Hugh.

"It's true then," said James.

David placed down his spoon. "I thought you already knew we were really faders. Cindy said..."

"Cindy overheard us talking about a rumor. To tell the truth, I didn't think it was true," said Patrick.

"So, what are we going to do with him?" asked John.

"We're feeding him," said Marylou. "Then I think we should help him get as far away from here as possible."

"I'm going back," said David.

The men stared at him.

"The others need to know the truth."

"Now David, if you attempt to go back to that place, they'll kill you."

"They won't kill all of us, not if we all know the truth."

Patrick looked at David with pity in his eyes.

"Don't be hasty. What if they did all find out the truth?" asked Hugh.

"This could be the chance we've been hoping for," said James.

DAVID SLEPT ON THE COUCH, but in the morning, he was still resolved to return to the Academy.

Sitting at the table, eating breakfast, David could hear Cindy crying upstairs.

"She won't come down. She thinks something bad is going to happen to you and she feels responsible," said Marylou.

Patrick dropped David at the bus stop near the Academy

and had one last try to talk him round. David was adamant that his friends needed to hear the truth.

"I hope to see you alive again, boy," said Patrick, before driving away.

David blinked in for the twentieth time that morning. He wasn't emitting. Had he glanced around, he would have seen the fader trail leading to the woods from where the trunk of Patrick's car had been.

David walked up to the security post.

"Where have you been? Most of the Agents and trackers are out looking for you."

"Sorry, Bernard. It got late, so I stayed at my girlfriend's place," said David. He would have told Bernard the truth, but an armed Agent was standing next to him.

"I wouldn't look forward to going home. You and your pals will be cleaning the bathrooms with your toothbrushes for the next month. You know we're hosting a conference over the weekend, don't you? The place is in chaos. The last thing they needed was a missing student when they're expecting visitors. Report straight to the administration office."

David had forgotten about the conference, and that his friends had gone to a concert. Part of him wished his life had been simpler over the past weeks.

As he walked into the Academy grounds, he considered his parents, both trackers. Both had caught faders. Now he would have to tell them the truth of what they were, what they'd done, and what the Agency had done to them.

The first building he reached was the science block. Most of the kids had already left for the holidays, but he knew his friends would be around somewhere, and there were still quite a few who could carry the message back to their families.

He walked through the block, hearing laughter coming from a classroom. Walking in, he found a group of kids playing with a Bunsen burner, lighting up powders which burned different colors. They jumped up, but relaxed when they saw it was him.

"David, the whole place is going crazy looking for you," said one boy.

"I've got something to tell you. I need to tell everyone..."

He told them everything, and the microphone in the corner of the room picked it all up.

The others were horrified. They blinked in.

"You're not emitting; you're a liar," said one boy.

"It's stopped for now. It finally happened yesterday because I stopped taking the red pills a few weeks ago."

One girl dropped a glass jar, smashing it and scattering powder around the room. She ran away crying.

"I'm getting my little sister and getting the hell out of this place," said a boy, heading for the junior block where the younger kids were practicing for a concert to entertain the conference visitors.

"What's going on?" said another boy.

David shared the news with groups of kids as he saw them and watched them run off in different directions to spread the news.

"David, David," called a voice from outside.

David looked out of the window to see his friend Melissa running across the grounds from the convention center. A boy opened the fire exit for her from the inside, then ran off into the hallway.

"There's a fader here. We've got to get out of here," said Melissa.

"Lissa, I've got to tell you something," and then he told her.

A naked Cindy appeared at his side.

"David, they know. They're mobilizing armed units and shutting down the exits. They plan to kill everyone here and blame the faders."

"What? I don't know what to do," said David.

"I'm going to warn the others," said Melissa. She turned and burst back out of the fire exit. David's eyes followed her as she ran to the other building. He saw Kim open the fire exit for her.

He heard the crack of gunfire and, even from where he was, he saw the spray of blood and gore and watched her drop, lifeless, to the ground.

"What have I done?" he said.

Then the mayhem really began.

The few Agents who weren't out searching for David were systematically moving through the buildings, murdering kids and teachers. Through the windows, David saw them bring up their guns and shoot.

Without Cindy, David would have been shot several times. This naked girl he barely knew would fade, check out the path, return and tell him which way to go. He managed to get to the tree line and circle the buildings.

David sat down against a tree, looking out into the woods. He was blinking and shaking his head, unable to comprehend what was happening, and jumping at the staccato sound of gunfire.

"David, we need to get out of here." Cindy was shaking him.

They looked from their hiding place in the tree line through the large windows into the kitchen. He could see his friends, Chris, Kim and Alice. They were with an adult he didn't know. He couldn't see Mark.

He was too far to throw something at the window, and

was in the act of standing to wave to them when he saw the door open. Craig entered the room; he seemed agitated, but didn't shoot them. Craig was a good guy. He was friendly. Perhaps he was as confused by all this as David's friends must be.

David watched as Chris left the kitchen with Craig. He crept along the tree line, keeping low to the ground as Craig and Chris exited the conference suite and ran over to the armory. Craig took out a set of keys and began sorting through them. Chris turned to keep watch. David had no idea if they knew the truth.

If ever there was a time to make himself known, it was now. David stood up at the same time that Craig lifted his rifle and shot Chris in the back. Chris spun around, and his eyes met David's. He looked surprised. Craig began to turn, but Chris stabbed something into his shoulder. Craig cried out and shot Chris again, in the face.

David went to cry out, but Cindy appeared with her hand around his mouth and dragged him behind the large tree. She then faded and looked out. Craig was pulling something metal from his shoulder. He looked up into the woods, his eyes searching. He glanced at the metal object in his hand and pocketed it, heading back to the conference building.

Cindy was shaking David again. It was all too horrific. He couldn't understand it. He couldn't get the sound of the Agents murdering those young children out of his head. It was all his fault.

When Cindy was finally able to move David again, they returned to the kitchen and saw Craig at the window.

"Did he see you?" asked Cindy.

"I don't know—I don't think so," said David.

He was relieved that Craig had left the rest of his friends

alive.

"I think we should move further back into the trees. Just in case that guy saw you." Cindy was pulling him back, and he allowed himself to be led.

Moments later, Craig appeared outside. He crept along to where David and Cindy had just been standing. He raised his rifle to his shoulder and shot through the glass. Someone in the room returned fire, but Craig was well hidden behind the tree. David and Cindy were too far back to see, but Craig returned a volley of shots, and it was all over.

Craig stood and made his way back around the side of the building.

"Wait. What are you doing?" asked Cindy.

"I have to see." David had stood and was running down the hill. Craig wasn't even out of sight yet. David reached what was left of the window and climbed through.

Alice was dead. He now saw Mark's body too. The man who had thrown himself over Kim was dead, his body riddled with bullets. David felt Kim's pulse. She was still alive.

He rolled the dead stranger off Kim and lifted her over to the window, laid her on the countertop and climbed back out. Once again picking up Kim's unconscious body, he made his way back up into the trees where Cindy was scouting a safe route ahead.

Kim awoke briefly. "David?" she whispered.

"It's okay, Kim. I've got you. You got grazed by a bullet, but you're alright."

She seemed unable to focus on him.

"I'm sorry, Kim. It's all my fault. I shouldn't have come back. Now everyone's dead."

She was dazed, but apart from the graze on her head

and a bandaged hand, she seemed okay.

Cindy kept out of sight not wanting to distress Kim when she awoke. She walked mostly faded to avoid hurting her feet on the undergrowth.

Cindy would scout ahead and return to guide them. David carried Kim as far as he could, but when she regained consciousness, she walked, leaning against him.

THEY STOPPED to rest when they felt they were a safe enough distance from the Academy.

Kim shared what had happened to them. She told David about the man, Tom Harvey, who'd sacrificed himself to save her. She proudly said that Craig had told them how Chris had died protecting him.

David didn't correct her. He just stopped speaking, overwhelmed by grief and guilt.

They started to walk again, Cindy once more going ahead. It was just the two of them. David's eyes were wet and sore from crying. He fell to the ground, and Kim went with him. A wind came out of nowhere. David stood and tried to get his bearings, but he fell again.

When Cindy found him, he was alone. She back-tracked to try to see Kim, but there was no sign of her.

"I can hear my dad's car," said Cindy. She got to her feet, wearing David's coat, and stepped out of the woods. Then she went back to get David and helped him down to the car.

She bundled David into the back and climbed in with him.

Patrick, who had looked like he was going to shout at her, took one look at both of them and just drove.

"They're gone. All of them. Even the little ones. All the red, all the red."

17

I stepped out of the ribbon to find myself in a large convention venue. A sparkling chandelier hung from the top level, down through several floors in the middle of two sweeping, curved escalators. A man stepped out with a tray, offering glasses of champagne, and I took one.

I was directed to the third floor where Dad was waiting with a glass of wine in his hand, looking in his element. He walked towards me with a smile on his face and deftly swept the glass from my hand and placed it onto a passing waiter's tray.

"Dad, I'm nearly eighteen," I said.

"Unfortunately, sweetheart, the drinking age is twenty-one here."

Connor followed along behind Dad and snagged an orange juice for me. A group of men and women were huddled a few feet away, watching us. Some were taking notes.

"Thank God you're here," said Connor.

"What's wrong?" I asked.

"Your dad has been talking to these people for the last hour. The plan was to sneak in early with him and hang around quietly waiting for you, but the Mayor turned up and introduced him to these academics. When they discovered he's from our Earth and that he's a scientist, they went crazy over him. It's boring."

"I can help you with that. David's ready, and he's waiting for you. He's nervous."

"He's always nervous. I'll go get him."

Connor made to walk past me down to the ribbon, but stopped and turned back.

"You look beautiful." He stepped close and kissed me before fading and stepping into the ribbon. A few minutes later, he was back with David. Finally, Heidi, Zoe and Hannah stepped out of the ribbon.

"Well, that's just not fair," I muttered to Dad as Zoe and Hannah both took a glass of champagne. As I waited for them to make their way up to the third floor, I gazed around the room and noticed for the first time that the artefacts weren't just kept in museums. I saw a woman in a Madonna t-shirt and a Ramones baseball cap.

I dipped my hand into my bag for my lipstick and realized the glowing cube was still wrapped up in the socks. I wondered if I could ditch it somewhere. I walked to a shiny metal-lidded trashcan along the balcony and dropped the bundle into it, glad to be rid of it.

Wandering around the room, I looked at the art on the walls. A large, older man held out his hand to me, and I shook it. He was sweating profusely and his thin hair was dyed impossibly black.

"How are you finding these pieces?" he asked, sweeping his hand in the direction of the paintings.

"Nice," I said and tried to continue past him.

His eyes narrowed and he looked slightly offended. I guessed he was the artist.

"I especially like this one. The red and golden tones bring a realistic warmth to the..." I looked at it properly "...fires of hell burning people," I finished.

"It's called *The Incompletes Meet Their Maker*," he said.

"Well, it's smashing," I said, moving away.

He reached out to shake hands again, and when I complied, he gripped my hand tightly, stroking the top of it with his other hand and licking his lips.

"I'd like to paint you. You will come to dinner at my home and tell me everything there is to know about you."

"Well, there isn't much to know, really," I said, starting to feel like a deer in the headlights.

Just as I decided it might be best to blast him, Hannah appeared.

"There is something you should know, she's allergic to Rohypnol," she said, taking my arm and leading me away, depositing me in front of Connor.

"There you are! Where have you been?" he said.

"I was just chatting with the artist."

"He was going to paint her like one of his French girls." Hannah laughed and walked away.

"Would you like a drink?" Connor asked.

"If Dad's not looking, see if you can snag me a glass of champagne. I'm determined to try it."

While Conner was chasing down a waiter, a few people spoke to me, asking me predictable questions like 'Is it different on your earth?' and strange ones like 'Do you really eat lobsters on sticks?' Connor was returning with one champagne and one orange juice. I looked at Dad to see him watching. Sighing, I took the juice.

My eyebrows raised in surprise.

"This is nice," I said.

"Shh! It's got champagne in it."

"Where is everyone?"

"Heidi took Zoe down a level to see more exhibits. Hannah's talking to Callan, and I saw David down at the ribbon about half an hour ago." He looked around the room. "I haven't seen him since."

"Maybe he's looking at the exhibits too. Let's go see them."

Going down a level to find Zoe looking at some beautiful paintings.

"Jenna, come here," said Zoe, grabbing my hand and dragging me over to the wall.

I looked at the painting. It was lovely. It depicted the ribbon winding around a beautiful woman and following her arm up to the sky.

"This was painted by a brightling. All of the paintings in this section were. Isn't it wonderful. He just got on with his passion while he was the brightling. And look, this one shows a brightling and a red-mister. Where's David, he has to see this,"

"I don't know, he wasn't upstairs. Are you sure he's not on this level?" I asked.

We began searching for David.

"What's wrong?" asked Heidi.

"Have you seen David?" I asked.

"I saw him going down to the lower floor about ten minutes ago. He seemed fine."

We headed down together and finally found him on the main floor, standing between the ribbon and the wall which was a couple of feet behind it. David's eyes had glazed over, and when I blinked in, I could see a red mist around him.

"David?" I said, too scared to get close in case we ended up somewhere unexpected.

"Something's wrong. I was speaking to Vanessa again, and we were... well, cut off, I guess you could say. It's like something was jamming the signal at her end. I can still hear others over there. Jason's been in Calgary all day and says he saw a convoy of black cars going through the town a few hours ago. He called Vanessa and told her, but he couldn't know for sure it was the Agency."

"Let's get the others," I said.

Once we were on the escalator Heidi turned to David.

"It's you, isn't it? The mind-talker. You sent the message before. The one about the trackers."

"Yes," said David.

"I knew you were hiding something."

"I know."

"Why did you lie?"

"People are uncomfortable around me when they know. It's like you not telling people about your ability; sometimes it's just easier."

I wondered what Heidi's ability was, but didn't like to ask. Instead, I went and found Dad and Connor standing with Zoe and Hannah.

"There a man wandering around asking everyone if they know what Rohypnol is. How strange," said Dad.

"Weird," I said.

We returned to the top floor and told the others what was happening. As we had already been at the party for a couple of hours and James had shown off Zoe to everyone, we decided it would probably be okay to get back to the house.

Dad, Connor and David wandered down to the ribbon and walked around to the other side, out of sight. Connor flashed his tag, faded David and Dad, and they went straight back to the house.

The rest of us made our excuses to James and headed back down to the ribbon. Zoe stood behind me on the escalator. I turned around to speak to her. As I glanced up to the level we'd started on, I saw one of the waiters. He was wearing white gloves so I couldn't check out his tag, but I was sure he'd been one of the men at the museum. I blinked in to see several faded security people around us. I considered asking if it might not be better if they were solid.

The man had moved to the end of a wall, next to the shiny metal trash can I'd thrown the cube into, its light still hidden inside many pairs of socks.

"Heidi..." I began, but she was already turning to look up.

I had barely said one word when he stepped back around the wall while pulling out a gun and leveling it at Zoe.

Instinctively, I threw out my arm and ball of energy flew from it and hit the wall. As the gun came up again, I threw my mind at the cube in the trash can and told it to burst, hoping it would distract him long enough for the security agents to take him down. The container tore apart in a huge explosion and engulfed one of the artist's gruesome pictures —no loss there. The man leapt out from behind the wall. He was on fire and screaming.

Heidi was looking at me.

"Let's get Zoe back to the house," I said, avoiding her stare.

The officers were all now solid and surrounding us, telling us to fade. We did, then went straight through the ribbon to the house.

"Can you get us back now?" Dad was asking David.

"Yes. We'll have a long way to go to reach the others, though," said David.

"Are you all okay?" asked Callan, walking out of the ribbon into the garden, sweeping the area. "He must have had a bomb..."

He halted, looking at my dad. "How are you here?" he asked.

"Who had a bomb?" asked Dad at the same time.

The ribbon sprang to life, and James came through.

"Are you all okay?" he asked, clasping Dad's shoulder. "Anyone hurt?"

"We're fine," said Dad. "What's this about a bomb?"

"How are you here?" James asked.

It was time for the truth.

"I blow things up sometimes. I mean, not always, but on this occasion, it was me. Sorry. He was aiming at Zoe; I panicked."

Connor waved a hand. "I can fade other people, like him." He pointed at my dad.

David added, "I read thoughts."

"We have a situation at home, we're leaving," I told Callan and James.

"I thought you were staying," said James to Zoe.

Zoe turned to me.

"He's right. I gave my word. And as I said before, if I go with you, I'm putting you all in danger. Hannah and I are staying."

"Do you still want us to go with them?" Callan asked James.

"Yes. Go. I'll stay with the ladies and increase security around here." James reached for my dad's hand. "Stay safe, Neil."

"Where are your friends on the other side? Are they close?" asked Heidi.

"They're in Canada," said David.

"Then we should go there first and cross over from there," said Callan. "I don't want to have to travel for days in a land as dangerous as yours."

"Are you sure you want to do this?" asked Zoe.

"We told you we weren't going to stop you from returning to your world if that's what you wanted to do," said Heidi. "We meant it. But we're going to do everything we can to keep your friends safe."

"Do you need to change before you leave?" asked Hannah.

"Some flat shoes would be great," I said, looking down at my spiky heels.

"Where in Canada do you need to go?" asked Callan.

"I know the GPS grid reference," said David. Callan stared at him. "But you have no idea what I'm talking about, do you?"

"Not a clue."

"It's less than a hundred miles east of Calgary. I have the latitude and longitude."

"Now you're talking a language I understand. We can get you where you need to be."

We were back in traveling clothes, but they could have been warmer for where we were going. I hugged Zoe and Hannah, promising to be back as soon as possible.

"Calgary, Canada," said Callan, waving his hand tag across the panel on the gate.

Connor took hold of Dad and David, then faded.

"He just faded an inc," said Callan, shaking his head.

"I know, right?" said Heidi.

Callan looked at her strangely.

"Sorry, Hannah keeps saying that. It rubs off."

We faded and entered the ribbon. A few minutes later, we were standing on another platform.

"I thought it might be cold," I said.

"The temperature inside the domes is pleasant all over the world," said Heidi.

"That's a point. It might be cold when we get to the other side," said Dad.

We walked to a store and bought coats, gloves and hats, along with more sensible clothes.

"I'm glad the residence tag still works," said Heidi. "I wouldn't have been able to afford these clothes on my salary."

"We can ribbon to a small dome to the east. It will get us to within fifty miles of our destination," said Callan.

"Is it a new town?" David asked.

"I don't know how long it has been there. Is that important?"

"It could be a problem if it's wilderness in our world. We'd be stranded. I think staying in Calgary is our best bet. I'm familiar with our Calgary, I helped to set up the ranch we're going to, but I don't recognize anything around me here. We also need to meet up with Jason."

"Where can we get tourist information for Calgary?" asked Dad.

Ten minutes later, we were poring over the history of Calgary on a pad.

"We're looking for old buildings or sites. Ancient ones," said David.

"But what if they don't exist on our side?"

"I'm hoping something will look familiar."

David browsed through digital page after page.

"This. I've heard of this place. They renovated it a few years ago," he said.

"Hunt House?" said Callan. "It says here that it's one of the oldest buildings in Calgary, but it's falling apart now."

"Let's go visit," said Dad.

"Just a moment," said David. He walked back to the ribbon and stood before it. I blinked in to see the red mist moving out to the ribbon. "Jason, we'll meet you at the last gas station on the way out of Calgary in about an hour... I'll tell you when I see you."

We walked to the house, which was about twenty minutes from where we were. When we found it, it was indeed a mess. It had a sign saying "Hunt House circa 1890, Preserved". A small dome protected it.

"Can we fade in?" I asked.

"No. There will be protection on it. Do we need to get inside, David?"

"I don't think so. I'm pretty sure it's clear around the building on our side. We're not going to end up underground or underwater or fifty feet in the air. That's the important thing."

We stood on the grass outside the little building. David spent a few moments breathing with his eyes closed, then looked at us all. Knowing we were ready, he nodded at Connor, who faded himself and Dad. We all moved in a little, standing close, afraid to be left behind.

David faded, the red mist surrounded us, and we lurched to the ground.

It wasn't the soft grass I had been expecting. We were sitting in a car park. It was late. It was cold. We were home.

David was lying on the ground with his arms covering his head.

"There's too much noise. Shouting and crying," he moaned.

"We're here to stop that. Let's see what we can do," said Callan.

David opened his eyes, sat up, looked at Callan, then closed his eyes again. He breathed in and out for a full minute before opening his eyes once more. Callan reached out his hand, and David took it.

"Think twice about fading. Your clothes will probably end up on your Earth," I said.

"Oh. I'd forgotten about that. I'm sure my nanites will keep them with me." Heidi sighed, unsure.

"Where's Connor?" asked Dad.

I looked about us and blinked in. Connor was gone.

"Did he come over? Did we leave him?" I was panicking.

A few seconds later, one of the cars on the car park revved up. The lights came on, and an SUV pulled out of a parking space. It drew up beside us. Of course, Connor was behind the wheel.

"Darling, I fear your boyfriend has sticky fingers," said Dad.

"I wouldn't have him any other way." I smiled.

We piled into the car and headed off, meeting up as arranged with Jason. He left his car and jumped in with us, his face full of concern.

"I'm so relieved to see you all okay. David, everyone was trying to contact you. Vanessa says you were out of range."

"Yes, you could say that. I picked up a couple of friends who might be able to help us," said David, introducing Jason to Heidi and Callan.

"I hope you've got an army hidden in your pockets because I think that's what we're going to need," said Jason.

We set off, and about twenty miles from the ranch, I said,

"Can you pull over? We don't know what we're heading into here. Connor, have you ever faded a car?"

"Nope. And if it goes wrong, we've got twenty miles to walk," he said.

"No, you can't, or no, you've never tried?" I asked.

"I've never tried a car. I've faded a motorbike, though. What are you thinking?"

"What's the point of that?" asked Jason.

"You'll see. Maybe," I said.

We drove until we were within five miles of the ranch and couldn't risk getting any closer, then pulled up at the side of the road. Getting out of the car, we stood beside Connor as he psyched himself up. He tried to fade Dad and the car. He couldn't do it.

"Try fading just the car and going over with David. Then come back for us," said Callan.

"Over where?" asked Jason, beginning to sound annoyed that something was going on and he wasn't in on it. At that moment, we heard noises in the distance.

"That can't be shots, can it?" I asked.

"No, we're five miles away," said Dad.

"That's by road," said Jason. "It's probably two and a half miles across country from here."

Connor redoubled his effort. He hugged the car and they both faded. David faded, and they all disappeared.

"Wow!" said Dad. "I did not think that would work."

"What the hell was all that red mist? I've never seen anything like it." Jason was transfixed.

David and Connor reappeared. David drew in a sharp breath. I realized he was still hearing the voices.

"Where's the car?" asked Jason.

"Jason, I'd love to give you a choice between the red pill

and the blue pill, but I'm afraid it's the red pill all the way for you, soldier," said Dad.

We gathered ourselves together, faded and arrived back in the Full Earth.

Jason was staggering around as though he'd just come off a fairground ride.

"Welcome to the Full Earth," said Heidi, holding onto Jason to steady him.

"We need to get to the others, now," said Jason as he jumped into the car.

"I feel like he should have been more impressed," I said.

"I know, right?" said Heidi.

We were no longer on the road; we were in a field, which worked out well for us. It was a bumpy ride, but David told us when we were almost on top of the farmhouse. We parked and then walked until David told us to stop. Heidi and Callan got their bags out of the car, and once more, we huddled in a circle.

"Right, the floor might be higher or lower, so don't reappear immediately," said Connor. "Prepare for a drop or allow the floor to push you up."

We stepped across to our home earth...

18

———

... To the shattering sound of gunfire.

We all dropped to the ground. Heidi dived on top of David, and both Dad and Connor tried to leap onto me.

"What the hell's going on?" shouted my dad.

"Holy feck! Where did you spring from?" asked Orla, pulling a shotgun back in from the window. "Hit the deck," she shouted.

Windows and walls were blasted from the outside.

"Those poles are too far away to hit. I hope you've got an escape route," said Orla. She crawled over to Jason and kissed him. "I'd have preferred it if you'd stayed where you were. And where have you been? Vanessa said she'd had a call from David, but she wouldn't say where you were."

"I'm so glad you asked where we've been," I said. "First of all, I'm happy to announce that I know where our bloody clothes go."

"Where's Zozo and Hannah?"

"They're still in Oz."

"Huh?"

"Good to see you, Jenna. Why is your dad emitting?" asked Anna as she crawled back towards another room.

I looked over to Dad and blinked in.

"Well that's a turn up for the books," I said.

Callan and Heidi just looked at each other.

"Yes," said David, obviously reading their thoughts. "I think it might."

"What?" asked Dad of all the people looking at him.

"Neil!" came a yell from a doorway. Sofia came crawling across the floor and took my father's face in her hands. He buried his face into her hair as she burst into tears. A lump formed in my throat and I had to look away.

"Neil, how are you emitting?" asked Callan.

Sofia pulled back and looked at Dad.

"Santa Maria," she said, crossing herself.

"Maybe I'm a late bloomer," said my dad.

"Where have you been? You were so far from a telephone you couldn't let me know you were alive?" asked Sofia, punching my dad's arm.

"I don't think you'd believe it," he said.

"What's this gold thing on your hand? Some kind of tattoo? You had time for tattoos, but not to call me?"

Once more, Sofia grabbed a hold of him and kissed him.

I looked at Dad's hand. Sure enough, the silver nanite pattern had turned to gold.

"I can explain everything. We all need to get together to fade out," said Dad.

"We can't fade out of here," said Sofia. "The Agency's set up a perimeter. We can't get past it."

"It's okay. David can get us out," said Dad.

"Jenna!" called a voice from the doorway.

"Ava, you're okay, thank God!" I said.

"Mom's here, thank you for finding her. But she got hurt, and so did Vanessa."

Ava pointed into the next room. I crouch walked over to find Jodi on the floor with blood all over her clothes. Her face was white.

"I got my girls back for a while," she said.

I looked at Anna who was holding her hand. Her face was tear-streaked and grave.

"Where's my grandmother?" I asked.

"I'm here," came a weak voice behind me.

I turned. I wanted to scream. Vanessa was covered in blood and looked very close to death. I went to her and held her hand.

"I'm so glad I got to know you, dear. I imagine my Theresa would have been strong and compassionate, just like you."

Vanessa coughed up blood. Dad and Sofia sat down on the floor next to her.

"Jenna's just like her," said Dad.

"I'm sorry we weren't here," I cried.

"I'm sorry I wasn't with you all those years. I should have come for you," Vanessa said, looking at me, but I knew she was seeing my mother.

"Heidi!" I called. She crouched her way into the room. "Have you got anything that can help them?"

I could hear my voice wobbling. I didn't want to lose my grandmother, and I couldn't bear for the girls to lose their mom again.

Heidi looked at my grandmother and back at me, her eyes full of the pain I was feeling. She shook her head and moved over to Jodi, swinging her bag off her shoulder and rummaging around. Pulling out the pen-like device she'd used to tag us when we'd first arrived on the Full Earth, she looked at a display on the side.

"I've got a few nanites. They might tide them over. It'll take a minute to set up. We should cross over first."

David and Connor huddled down with Jodi, Anna, Ava and Milly, then attempted to take them across.

"It's not working. Those poles out there are stopping the flow of energy from the ribbon," said David.

"But it worked before," I said.

"The ribbon was flowing through the ground we stood on."

"The what?" asked Orla, crouching in the doorway, reloading the gun.

"If those things work the same as our blocking fields, we're stuck," said Heidi.

"Could this help?" Callan pulled out two extendable posts from his backpack.

"You brought a travel-sized gate? That might help," David said.

"I don't have a clue what's going on around me," said Orla.

"Don't worry, love, it's stranger than you could possibly imagine," said Jason.

Callan pulled and twisted each post and stood them against an internal wall. He took out two power cubes that were dimly lit.

"I hope this will be enough," he said as he dropped a power cube into the top of each post and clicked them into place. The posts hummed for a moment before a hazy, barely visible ribbon of energy appeared in the space between them.

"What the hell is that thing?" asked Anna.

"Think of it as Uber for faders," I said.

"Heidi, have you got your posts and cubes?" asked Callan.

"I was going to use one of the cubes to charge the nano pen." Heidi held out her remaining two cubes, both as dim as Callan's. They stared at each other, then at the women on the floor.

"It's okay," said Jodi. "Get my girls out of here."

"I think we'll be okay," I said.

I snatched one of the cubes out of Heidi's hand and pressed the button. It flooded instantly with a bright, piercing white light. Heidi and Callan stared at it with their mouths hanging open.

"We really need to talk," said Heidi, not for the first time. She pushed the other cube into my hand before connecting the nano pen to the brightly illuminated cube and smiling at the display. Lifting Jodi's shirt, she pressed the pen against her side.

Callan took Heidi's bag and the two cubes, then nodded once before fading and walking into the ribbon.

"Where will he end up if we don't have gates here?" I asked.

"He'll be okay," said Heidi.

A voice came over the public address system.

"Okay, boys and girls, I'm tired of this. You have two minutes to come out, or I'm going to shell this whole place, and I know you have people in there who can't fade."

"Oh, Major Tom's here. Let's see if we can disappoint him again," I said to Jodi, and she smiled weakly.

"Wait," said my dad. "We can't risk the Major getting hold of these cubes."

"Orla, get my boys, will you?" said Vanessa.

Orla went to a metal box full of ammunition, pulled out two hand grenades and held them up. "Two of this season's most popular accessories. They are absolutely to die for."

Callan reappeared in less than a minute.

"We had a two-minute warning about a minute ago," said Heidi.

"I've set the gate up on the shore of a lake. Get moving."

Connor began fading everyone through. Felix, in the pet carrier in Ava's arms, seemed to know what was coming and meowed loudly. Anna walked hesitantly towards the ribbon, eyeing it suspiciously.

"It's this or them," I said, nodding towards the front of the house.

She allowed Connor to fade her and went through.

Connor returned and faded Orla and Jason who were carrying Jodi. Heidi, Vanessa and I were the only ones left.

"Can you help me lift Vanessa?" I asked Heidi.

"I'm beyond help, Jenna. But I have one last 'screw you' for the Major. Can those posts be moved closer together?"

Heidi nodded.

"Sit me up and move them. The width of a doorway should do it."

We sat her up, and she gripped onto the grenades.

"I don't want to lose you, Grandmother." I wondered why it had taken me so long to call her that.

"You'll do just fine, dear. Now I need to visit with my Theresa. I've waited long enough. And don't think I can't see you, Connor. I'm so proud of you, my son. Now get them out of here."

I blinked in to see Connor crouching down next to Vanessa. He leaned forward and kissed her head.

"Okay, you had your chance, time's up," called the Major.

There was so much more to say, but no time to say it.

"Screw you," shouted Vanessa as she pulled the pins on the grenades with her teeth and held them on the posts. Heidi and I faded, and the three of us stepped through.

WE APPEARED BY A LAKE. No one spoke. We'd left Vanessa to die alone.

Orla came over and hugged me. I looked around for Connor, blinked in and saw him faded, standing a little apart. Vanessa had been the only family he'd known for years. I knew exactly how he felt.

"Where are we?" I asked.

"Rocky Point, Montana? This can't be right," said Sofia, sounding shocked.

I turned to ask how she knew that, to find her staring at her cell phone.

"Oh good! We'll have you home in a few minutes," said Heidi.

"That was our home," said Jason.

"Who are your friends?" Orla asked me.

Callan offered his hand to Orla.

"We came to assess your situation to see if we could help."

"I think you've already achieved that," said Orla.

"Everyone, this is Heidi and Callan. They're from an alternate universe that you're about to visit," I said. Then I faded and walked over to stand with Connor.

I reached up to his face. Feeling the resistance of our faded bodies, I stroked his cheek. He lay his head against my shoulder, and I felt the pulsing magnetic push as his body racked with sobs.

"I'm sorry, we have to get across and get help for your

friend." Heidi set about disassembling the posts. Connor and I reappeared and looked down at Jodi, who had a little more color in her face.

"Okay, David?" I asked.

He nodded. It was time to go back. He and Connor took us over in two groups. When I arrived in the second group, I was standing on the busy platform of a town built by the lake.

We had come out of a public ribbon gate.

"Oh! I expected we'd still be in the middle of nowhere," I said as I turned to find half of our party on the ground. "Oh yes. Watch out for the first step; it's a biggie."

"Thanks for that timely warning," said Orla, looking up from the ground.

"We build our biggest communities around the strongest ribbon sites. Without another gate, the ribbon took Callan to the nearest natural energy point on your side that would correlate to a station on our side."

Callan, who had gone over in the first group, was talking to several officers who looked ready to shoot first and ask questions later.

Heidi got straight on to her communicator. "Hi, Yolanda, we're back. We've got a few more visitors. We're at Rocky Point station, and the local officers don't look too happy. Okay, will do."

Heidi walked to the officers and offered her tag. They scanned it and moved quickly out of the way.

"Why didn't I think of that?" said Callan.

"Because I'm the one with looks and brains," said Heidi.

Callan's communicator squawked. "Yes, sir, we've got one new party member who's injured. Okay, we'll take them all back to the residence then." He turned to us. "Medics are going to meet us there."

Heidi tagged the newest visitors to the Full Earth with her nanite pen. Milly held the pet carrier out to her, but Heidi laughed.

"I'm sorry, it doesn't work on pets. You're going to have to rely on Connor for that."

Minutes later, we were walking into the garden at the residence. It was a hive of activity. There were loads of officers with blankets, gurneys and medical paraphernalia. Anna freaked at the sight of them.

"They're faders, like us. They're here to help," said David.

"Zoe? Hannah?" I called.

Yolanda walked out of the house. "They're not here. They got itchy feet and went sightseeing."

"Sightseeing?" I asked. It had been a long, awful night and my nerves were in bits.

"They went to the Citadel with the Mayor. If they choose to stay here, that's where they'll live. They'll be back tomorrow."

I turned to see Jodi speaking to Heidi while stroking the arm of a handsome medic. "What did you give me? I'm having the most incredible hallucinations."

I woke up with no idea of the time. It was still dark outside. I was teetering on the edge of my bed with Ava and Milly spread across it, soundly asleep. I could hear talking in the house.

Rubbing my eyes, I got silently out of bed. Felix jumped up and curled up in the warm place I'd vacated.

"If they can help, it would be incredible, but I can't help

wondering if it might be better for us just to stay here," said Sofia to Dad.

"I'm not sure they'd like me to stay," said Dad.

"What time is it?" I asked by way of announcing my presence.

"It's just gone 4 a.m.," said Dad.

"Any news about Jodi?" I asked. When the medics had ascertained that she was capable of fading herself, they'd put her in a wheelchair and she'd gone through the ribbon to the hospital.

"Not yet. The medics didn't look concerned, though," said Dad.

"What do you mean, they don't want you to stay?" I asked.

"Heidi is very disturbed that I seem to have turned into a fader overnight."

"Dad, I think everyone's disturbed by that."

"We've concluded that it probably happened because Connor's faded him so many times, it's activated a dormant gene or something," said Sofia.

"That makes sense."

"Callan and Heidi are concerned that I'm going to upset the balance here and this whole society is going to fall apart. They think I might not be safe here."

"They said that?" I asked, horrified.

"No, David sneaked a peek," he said, tapping his head.

I wondered if bringing people to this world had been the right thing to do in the long run.

Later that morning we were visited by Heidi. She found me sitting in the garden with a cup of coffee, watching Ava and Milly as they played with Felix.

"Won't David mind that you're in his seat?" Heidi asked.

"We won't tell him. How could he possibly find out?"

"I know, right?"

I chuckled. She was starting to sound like a valley girl.

"I'm driving Callan crazy with that. I've also started calling everything 'awesome'. I think he's going to ask for a different partner."

I looked at my coffee.

"You want to ask what my ability is, don't you?"

"Is it so obvious, or are you a mind reader too?" I looked at her.

"Nothing so powerful. I read emotions and intentions. I know if someone's lying to me; if they feel guilty or ashamed; if they intend harm; if they have a strong sense of justice; and if they are in emotional pain, like you."

"Oh, that. Vanessa was my grandmother. I'd only just met her. It seems so unfair to lose her so quickly."

"You've been in emotional pain since I met you," she said.

"It's been a difficult couple of years."

"You all seemed so desperate when we found you. David is heartbroken, isn't he?"

"He's a good person."

"I know that. But he's full of almost crippling guilt. It was more than I could take. And someone there was deeply ashamed. I couldn't work out who that was."

I shrugged. I felt uncomfortable discussing my friends. Heidi, of course, was able to sense this and stopped talking.

"I wanted to talk to you about your father," she said.

"About him not being safe here?"

She sighed. "Doesn't David have an off-switch for that?"

"I don't think so."

"But yes, that's what I mean. I don't know enough to understand the ramifications of this." As Heidi spoke, she twirled the little nanite pen through her fingers.

"Would it be possible for me to get one of those? They seem quite useful."

"Sure, take this one. I refilled it last night. I've got another one at the station." She handed it to me, explaining how the pen worked and its various applications. My only real interest was in its medical use.

"Listen, I've got an apology to make to you," I said.

"The cube?"

"You knew? Of course, you knew. I was mortified—you must have picked up on that. I was stupidly curious about them. When I pressed it, a bright light was glaring out everywhere. I panicked and wrapped the cube inside a load of socks, and stuffed it in my bag. Last night, when I realized I still had it on me, I dumped it in the trash can."

"The trash can at the party venue? I see. You should be careful. They're not meant to hold so much energy."

"I never thought of that."

"You're lucky one hasn't blown up in your hand."

We sat in silence for a few minutes as I pondered that.

"About Dad. Have you considered that it might not be as straightforward as you think? It might be that not all incs have this dormant gene, if that's what it is."

"You could be right. I just saw an inc turn into a fader and wondered what that was going to mean here."

"I know. No one to make the tea."

"That reminds me, I brought muffins."

"Oh great! That's really... dope." I couldn't help myself.

"That's what?"

"Dope. It means excellent."

We walked into the house. I couldn't wait for Heidi to start trying that one out.

AT MIDDAY, Zoe and Hannah returned.

"Oh my God, Orla, you're here!" said Zoe, hugging Orla as though she hadn't seen her in years.

"Well, you finally found a planet where they worship you like the goddess you always knew you were," said Orla.

Zoe rolled her eyes. "It's a complete pain in the arse."

"I hear the Goddess of Foul Language has returned," said Dad, coming out of the house.

"Sorry Mr. B," said Zoe, laughing and hugging my dad. "You're like the one person we can rely on never to change."

Dad faded.

19

———

I stood in Zoe and Hannah's room while they turned their backpacks upside down on the bed. Zoe's was half full of energy cubes. Some were dark, and some had a yellow light inside.

"Can I borrow a couple of these?" I asked.

"Sure, I've got loads of them now," said Zoe.

"What is the Citadel like?"

"It's a city with a wall around it."

I raised an eyebrow. "Mate, that's, like, the definition of the word citadel."

"Then let me tell you something you don't know. It's only bloody Glastonbury."

"You're kidding me." I laughed as we walked into the hallway.

"It looks way different to ours. The Tor is at the center, and you can't go up there unless you're one of the weird monks. And the city built around it has mostly incs living there. That part's really like home. They live a normal life where they're all solid and they walk or drive or cycle every-where. The Tor is the most high energy place on the planet."

"But the Brothers there don't fade at all," said Hannah. "Even though they could if they wanted. It's some religious thing, and most faders aren't allowed in there."

"Hannah had to get checked out before they'd let her go there with me," said Zoe.

"Checked out how?"

"A Brother came to the house. He looked at us and sniffed the air around us," said Hannah.

"That's actually what they're called, Sniffers. I mean, I wouldn't call them that to their faces, but generally, that's what they're known as," said Heidi on her way out to speak with James and Callan.

I wondered if these Sniffers were there to sniff out faders with abilities.

"You're probably right," sent David.

"Are you always in my mind?"

"I like the way you put things together quickly. It's like having Google."

I shook my head. Did David just compliment me? I wondered. But, I wasn't sure.

David called a meeting in the now overfilled house. People began wandering in from various rooms and outside. Heidi and Callan entered the residence with James after delivering their report.

"So, is there anything else?" asked James.

"Nothing, sir, we told you everything," said Heidi.

"Nothing?" Heidi and Callan looked at each other, then back at James.

"Artefact," said David as he wandered past them to his bedroom.

"Oh! Erm..." said Callan.

"Of course they brought something back for you. Unfortunately, it's parked in the middle of a field west of Calgary," I said.

"Parked?" asked James.

"We brought a transportation unit back for you," said Callan, catching on.

"An SVU," said Heidi with a huge smile.

"An SUV," I said.

"Yes, that."

James stood there with his mouth hanging open. "I thought maybe a book," he said eventually.

I followed David down the hallway to his room and knocked on his open door. He was writing on a notepad. I had been going to ask him to try pressing the little cube. I wondered what would happen.

He looked up. "Sure, I'll give it a go for science."

"You could let me ask first," I said, passing the cube to him.

He pressed the little button, and the cube filled with an odd red light. He pushed the button again and threw it back to me.

"Let me know if you find any use for it."

"I'm sure you'll know," I said.

As David and I walked back through the hallway, he passed James a piece of paper with coordinates written on it. James pocketed the details and thanked us three times.

Once everyone had assembled, David began. "We need to figure out how to get your families out of the Half Earth. I think they might not be safe, now the Agents know they can't trap us. There's not much benefit to keeping them as bait."

"Have you had any thoughts about how we can achieve this?" asked James.

The word "we" wasn't lost on me, and I could see the others had noticed it.

"I think the same approach as the ranch. Using maps and latitude and longitude up to the fifth decimal should get us exactly where we need to be. I want to start today."

We set about planning and discussing what order we were going to do this in. Orla's parents were in Ireland and her brother, if he was still alive, was in New York. Zoe's parents were in East London, Hannah's in Arizona, and Jason's father lived in Manchester.

We decided that the first thing to do was to try to contact Orla's brother.

David called the ribbon and emitted the red mist. As the red cloud moved between himself and the ribbon, it started to spin in the middle. I stood to the side, blinking in, transfixed by the shifting shapes which seemed almost to coalesce into something recognizable. It seemed like every time he did this, they became more tangible.

David's face was a mask of concentration. He turned his head this way and that, as though trying to hear snatches of conversation on the wind.

"If he's there, I can't find him."

I knew what that probably meant. I looked at Orla, who was staring at David as though willing him to find her brother.

"Wait... he's unconscious. Someone's calling his name. It sounds like they're in trouble." David stood. "We need to go, now."

"Where are they?" asked Orla.

"Richmond, Virginia," said David. "What's the best way to get there on this side?"

"We can get you to Richmond in minutes, but you'll have to find your way to the exact place," said James.

David put his hands on his head. "They need help now."

As David concentrated harder on the voice of the woman calling to Sean, the mist shifted, and I was sure I could see the shape of her crouching over him. Was I sure enough to do what popped into my head? I felt there wasn't a moment to explain. I faded and leapt into the mist.

I landed heavily on a wooden floor.

A man lay on the floor near me, and a naked woman scuttled away at the sight of me.

"Ouch," was all I could manage. I was winded. Or I thought I was winded until Heidi landed on top of me, and Connor on top of her.

"What?" said the woman, clearly confused.

"We're friends of Sean's sister," I said.

A loud crack filled the air. The woman had piled furniture against the door, but it was starting to move.

"I'm Sam. You need to get out of here. I'm not leaving him," she said to us.

"Neither are we," said Connor. He leaned down and faded himself and Sean. The rest of us faded as the door finally burst inwards.

Two Agents stood in the doorway and looked around.

"Get the tracker," one Agent called back.

A third Agent appeared with a tracker on a leash. A metal collar hung about his neck, and he squealed as the Agent pressed a button on the handle. I was infuriated.

"Where are they?" the Agent asked.

The tracker paused, and the Agent delivered another charge to his neck.

"Stay faded, for now, let them get into the room," came David's voice.

The tracker pointed to a door at the other end of the room. "They went through there."

I wondered if he was receiving directions from David.

"*Yes,*" sent David.

"Move it." The Agent pushed the tracker along by the object around his neck. When they had moved halfway into the room, Connor reached out his other hand and faded the tracker.

The metal circle fell to the floor.

"It's up to you, Jenna. I can't let go of these two," said Connor.

I waited until the two Agents were looking towards the door, and then reappeared with two balls of energy in my hands. I threw my arms out toward the Agents and watched them slam against the wall. The third started to pull out his gun out, but never got close to firing it. Heidi appeared behind him with what looked like a cattle prod and shot him with a voltage I didn't even want to guess.

We reappeared. The tracker passed his coat to the fader girl while I took out the little nanite pen and gave it to Heidi, who used it on Sean.

David appeared in the room. "That was a stupid thing to do."

"I figured I'd end up here or in LA on the other side," I said.

"But crossing without me? We don't know what's in between. What if you got stuck there?"

I shuddered. The idea of something in between the worlds hadn't even occurred to me. He was right; I had been foolish and felt embarrassed.

"Well... Connor and Heidi did it too," was my pathetic response.

One of the Agents started groaning.

"Let's get out of here," said Connor.

We huddled up and crossed over. Heidi took out her

nanite pen, fiddled with the settings and tapped the tracker and the fader girl on the hand.

The tracker was sitting on the ground with his head in his hands. "I don't have much time. When they wake up, they only have to flick a switch and I'm dead. I want to thank you for getting me away from them. I'd rather be dead than working for them."

"The nanites I've given you will disable the device," said Heidi.

"They will? It's over?" He began to sob into his hands.

"Where are we?" asked the girl.

"In the same place we were," said David, "just in another universe."

The tracker lifted his head from his hands. His face was purple. He began making choking sounds and foaming at the mouth.

Seconds later, he was dead.

"I don't understand, he should have been alright," said Heidi, her face a mask of horror. She got on her communicator and shakily asked for transport. We waited for a hopper to take us to the nearest gate.

The girl was sitting on the ground with the tracker's coat wrapped around her, talking to Heidi. "So it's a different earth, but if it's a different earth, then it's a different moon, sun, stars? The whole thing?"

"That's right, the whole thing."

"What happened to Sean?" I asked.

"It was my fault. There was a red dot on him. I realized they were going to shoot him from outside. I reacted. I pushed him out of the way, but into a low roof beam. He went out like a light."

"I wondered why you'd assaulted me," said Sean.

"You're okay. Thank God. I thought I'd killed you," she said.

"Who are you?" asked Sean, looking at me.

"My name's Jenna…"

"Jenna Banks? Orla's friend?" Sean sat up, then lay immediately back down.

"Yes. We're on our way to see her," I said.

"Thank God she's alive. Mum and Dad were in a right state. Then I couldn't contact them either, so they must be climbing the walls by now. I don't think it's safe to contact them directly, but I might be able to message a friend. Has anyone got a phone I can borrow?"

"I don't think you'll get a good signal from here. Let's get you back to the house first," said David.

When the hopper arrived silently and we watched it land, Sean finally realized that something wasn't quite right. "Where are we?" He raised his voice and sounded agitated. "What's going on here?"

"It's okay. You hit your head quite hard," said Sam.

Heidi sat behind him with her nanite pen and dotted him on the back of the neck. Sean flopped back and started snoring.

"Sorry," Heidi said to Sean, tapping his cheek.

"I think it might have been for the best," Sam said.

The medics brought out a wheelchair for Sean and a gurney for the tracker. I told them what I thought had happened. They looked horrified. I felt terrible that we didn't even know his name.

The tracker's body went to a medical facility, and we went back to the residence.

When we appeared through the ribbon into the garden, Dad hugged me, and Orla ran to her brother.

"What's wrong with him?" she asked.

"He didn't take the multiple earth thing very well. So I sent him to sleep. I think it will calm him to see you when he wakes."

David said, "I'm exhausted. I'm going to sleep for an hour. Then we need to go again."

MR AND MRS DESCHENE returned from the grocery store. As usual, Mrs Deschene went in first, switched on the kitchen lights and began moving products around in the refrigerator to make space for the new groceries.

Mr Deschene walked into the kitchen with four shopping bags in his arms. The refrigerator door was open, but there was no sign of his wife. He returned to the front door to see if he had somehow passed her without realizing.

The door of the house opposite flew open and half a dozen Agents ran across the street. Mr Deschene knew something was wrong. Where was his wife?

He turned back into the house, took one step, but his foot didn't touch the floor. He found himself sitting on the ground with his shopping bags beside him. His head was spinning, but he could see his wife a few feet away, hunched over something.

"Eleanor, what's happening?" he asked.

Eleanor turned towards him, "Charles, look."

He saw that their daughter Hannah was in her arms. "Hannah. Hannah!" he cried.

She ran to him and hugged him. "I'm sorry, I couldn't contact you. Mom says they put something in you. It's not what you think it is. We need to get it out."

"Where are we?" he asked.

"Oh boy, there's so much to tell you."

MR AND MRS Deschene sat holding hands.

"All those poor children," said Eleanor, still in shock from the revelation about the Washington State Academy.

"Charles, were your tracker glands removed or disabled?" asked my dad.

"They'd stopped the full removal by the time we left the service," said Charles.

"Are you interested in being able to blink in again? And fade, if you like. But that's up to you."

"Blink in again," said Eleanor, laughing. "One misses it so much when it's gone."

"The feeling that some of the people at our bridge night might not be human never goes away. Although, that's not true, is it? They're just people. They're us."

"If Hannah's going to live in a city in your England where most people don't fade, I'd be happy with that," said Eleanor, looking at Heidi and patting Hannah's hand on the table.

"We can arrange to have the capsules removed, though," I said.

"I think that would be preferable, dear," said Eleanor.

"Imagine that, our daughter a fader. Of all the things," said Charles.

Hannah stood up. "Since we're sharing, I'm also gay. I'm just going out there to do a thing." She walked quickly out to the garden.

"How adorable, honey, she thinks we don't know," said Eleanor.

Hannah's parents finished their tea, shook Dad's hand, told him again how pleased they were that he wasn't dead anymore. Then they went to the garden and called to Hannah that it was time to go to the hospital.

Hannah and Zoe came in and hugged me.

"We'll let you know how it goes," said Zoe.

"Why did I tell them now, when I'm about to be stuck in a hopper with them for hours?" said Hannah. "This is going to be excruciating. Maybe we should meet them there."

"Come on, you coward, face the music," said Zoe, laughing.

As they walked out of the front door, Jodi came in through the ribbon in the garden. Ava and Milly ran to hug their mother.

The door chimed, and Dad went to open it. It was Yolanda. Her face was grave.

"We've heard back from the medics who examined the stranger's body. It would seem you were right about the cause of his death. The nanites disabled the shell of the capsule, but it was filled with poison.

Sean opened his eyes. He looked to his right. Seeing Sam, he smiled.

"Nice to see you've got some clothes on."

He looked around the unfamiliar room, and his eyes landed on his sister, Orla.

Everything came flooding back. "Where are we?"

"We're just outside Los Angeles," said Orla.

"Okay. Did I meet your friend Jenna?"

"She's lovely, isn't she?"

"There was a big flying thing, only it wasn't properly flying." He rubbed his face, trying to get his head around the fragments of memory.

"That was a hopper. It's a form of transport here."

"Here?"

Sam leaned forward. "You're gonna love this."

After about two hours of talking, Sean was ready to meet people. Orla walked him around the house.

"This is..."

"Mr. Banks. I thought you were... erm, dead," said Sean.

"Hello, Sean. Nope, very much alive. It must be four years since you left Hilltop," said Dad, holding up his coffee mug. "I'm actually about to leave so I'll catch up with you soon."

"Is that you off to the Archive again?" I asked.

"You guessed it," said Dad. He put his mug down and hugged me, picked up his bag and faded.

"Jesus Christ!" said Sean.

"Show off," I shouted to Dad's faded back as he headed into the garden to call the ribbon.

NEIL STEPPED out of the ribbon to find himself in an empty room rather than the archives he had been expecting.

"Oh, I didn't know you could take a wrong turning in this thing," he muttered to himself. He shook his hand as though it would fix the errant nanites and turned back to the ribbon to continue his journey.

"THIS IS DAVID; he sent the warning you heard," Orla continued.

Sean nodded, hesitantly.

"We can talk about that," said David.

In the garden, Jodi and Anna watched as the ribbon sprang to life. They blinked in, but no one entered or left.

"Ha! Wrong number," said Jodi.

"You met Heidi. She's from the Full Earth, and so is Callan," said Orla.

"Ah, aliens," said Sean.

"I think since you're the visitor, you're the alien," said Callan, shaking his hand.

"I didn't think that through, did I?"

Milly and Ava came running in, chasing the cat. Felix stopped suddenly and hissed up at Sean before running off again. Milly stopped and looked up too, with an unhappy expression on her face.

Sean looked around himself. "What did I do?"

"There are a few others you'll meet. We've been getting more beds in and rearranging the rooms. It's getting quite full here. Until we figure out what's going on in the long term, you'll be crashing in with Connor and David. There's a room for Mum and Dad. They're not safe where they are."

"You don't say. My friends were taken down within minutes of that warning," said Sean.

"We think they're probably being watched and left as bait," I said.

"We need to go and get them, Sean. Now," said Orla.

"It'll take days, so we'd best get started."

"Well now, that's the good news. We know a great short-cut."

Sean sat down heavily and turned pale.

"What's wrong?" asked Orla.

"I don't know. I'm still dizzy, I guess."

"Heidi, can we call a hopper? I think he should go to the medical center," I said.

"There should be one outside. I'll check," said Heidi,

moving to the front door. She came back seconds later. "Yes, it's there."

Heidi went to the garden and called to Callan "Have you got this mission? Sean is dizzy; I'm taking him to the medical center."

"I got it," said Callan.

Heidi and Sam led Sean out through the front door.

"Wait," said Sean, turning back. "It's Friday night; they'll be at bingo."

"With both of their kids missing?" I asked.

Orla thought for a beat. "They'll definitely be at bingo."

Sean, Heidi and Sam continued out the door.

"Where's Jodi?" I asked Sofia.

"She took Milly for a nap. I think they're all having a nap."

"That's cute," I said. "We need to get started on this mission."

"Good luck. Our mission is to have dinner ready for sixteen people in a couple of hours," said Anna.

I went into the garden to see that David was already seated before the gate. Connor, Callan and Jason were ready to go.

"How are we going to do this?" I asked David.

"I'll find them. You and Connor go through. Let me know the exact location. Callan can report it, so we don't waste time getting support on this side if it's needed. Then Callan and I will come through."

"How will you find them if their glands have been removed or deactivated?" I asked.

"With the ribbon, I can hear trackers too."

He sat there once again with his eyes closed, turning his head like he was tuning in.

"Ha-ha, this must be them," he said.

"How can you tell?" I asked.

"The tracker is listening to Agents complaining about having to go to bingo four times a week." Concentrating, David spoke to the tracker's mind.

"*Hi. Don't freak out. My name is David. Do you know the truth?*"

David waited a moment.

"*They've put an inhibitor in your head with either an explosive or poison in it. We're going to get that out of you, but you need to help us... That's right. You're watching the McGinnesses, right? Which ones are they? Can you picture them clearly in your head?*"

David reached out and grabbed my hand. A picture of Orla's parents appeared in my mind. I realized I'd been about to leap out before I had any clue which of the older couples in the room were the ones we wanted.

As David focused on Mr. McGuinness, I watched the mist, and the picture became clear.

"I see it this time," said Connor.

"Didn't you see it last time?" I asked.

"No."

"But you still jumped in," I said. He shrugged.

"Yes, after you," he said.

"What is it they say? If your friend jumps off a cliff, would you?" asked David.

"It's more like, if the woman you love jumps off a cliff, would you? And the answer is yes, every time," said Connor.

I looked over at him and gave him my most dazzling smile.

"Then here we go again."

We faded and jumped, staying faded in the bingo hall. We walked into the ladies' bathroom, and Connor read out the location to David. David repeated it to Callan, who communicated it to his team already in Ireland, making their way to the McGinnesses' small town in County Mayo.

Moments later, Callan and Jason appeared next to us. We waited for David.

"David? David?" I called out with my mind, but there was no reply.

20

"You can come out. I know you're there," David said.

Vince appeared a few feet away.

David was on him in a second with fists flying. He was a thin, wiry man who would normally shy away from physical violence, but he was enraged.

Sofia and Anna, cooking and listening to music, were oblivious to the fight.

After landing several punches, David became aware that Vince wasn't punching back. He stopped and stood still, breathing heavily.

"You must be losing your touch. The cat knew I was here a while ago," said Vince.

"Why are you here?" he asked.

"I have friends who are in need of help that only you can give them. They're desperate to get home, but they can't go anywhere. I told them you would help."

"I wouldn't help you if..." David stopped and stared in horror at Vince. "They took Neil?"

"They redirected your ribbon. I'm sorry. I didn't think there would be another way."

David continued to probe Vince's mind.

"You won't find it there. I told them to take Neil somewhere but not tell me where, so you couldn't pick it out of my mind."

It was clear that David wasn't coming. I wondered how the hell we were going to get back.

All I could think was that we needed to press on with the mission.

Callan cracked the door. "The second we take the tracker, Orla's parents will be a target. I don't think the tracker will fare much better if we take the parents first. We're going to need a distraction."

"David could have asked the tracker to get them to move closer," said Jason, "but I guess that's not an option. Even if he sees something unexpected, he's just going to keep his mouth shut."

I looked out. "The Agents are in the last row of seats near the exit. We need to get Mr. and Mrs. McGinness closer to the tracker. Are we ready to move?"

Everyone nodded.

"Whatever happens, you keep the three of them faded," I said to Connor.

I looked over to the bingo machine and suggested to it that it might like to catch on fire. It complied.

The man calling the numbers leapt away from the machine as it burst into flames. The fire alarm went off, and everyone started moving to the exit. The Agents stood by the door, keeping the tracker behind them. One of them swiveled his eyes around the room, and the other didn't take his eyes off Orla's parents.

When they were close enough to the exit, Connor faded the tracker behind the Agents and said, "Stay in contact with me, move with me. Your life depends on it."

"You can be sure I'll be doing that," said the tracker.

Connor walked ahead through the Agents and put his arms around Orla's parents. They faded, and the Agents went nuts. They turned around to see that the tracker had disappeared. They took out little remote devices and started pressing them.

Connor looked at the little devices. "If I had a free hand."

Orla's father reacted first. "What are you doing to me? Get off, you filthy monster."

I said the first thing that came into my head to calm him down. "We've got Orla and Sean."

They froze, allowing us to lead them to the back of the hall behind the stage. The sprinkler above the bingo machine had showered water onto the fire and it was now smoldering. The heavy stage curtains kept the smoke away from us.

"What the hell have you done with our children?" said Declan McGinness. "If this new stupid thing they put in our heads worked, we'd have seen you coming and you'd have had a fight on your hands."

"Mr. McGinness, is that you? You're just a big yellow blob. It's me, Aiden Connaughty," said the tracker.

"Oh, Aiden love, they've got you too," said Mary McGinness.

"It's not that, Mrs. McGinness. Everything's gone crazy. The Agents have put new capsules in us with explosives in them."

"That's nonsense. I've worked for the Agency since I was ten," said Declan.

"Mrs. McGinness, I'm Jenna Banks. I discovered the Agency had a terrible secret and we had to run for our lives. The Agents have been watching you since we escaped in the hope they'd catch Orla trying to contact you. She knew that if she did, you'd be in danger."

"That's nonsense. We're trained observers. We'd know if…"

The curtain pulled back and two Agents appeared, each with a gun in one hand and little remote device in the other.

"We're going to have to call this in," said one.

"Shit! I'll call it in. You keep pressing that thing. The second they unfade, they're gone, problem solved."

"And no more bingo."

They walked back through the curtain. Orla's parents looked shocked as the truth dawned on them.

"How are we getting out of here?" said Mary.

"You need to stay connected to me at all times. If you reappear, your capsule will trigger," said Connor.

"I've got an idea. I have no idea if it will work. Jason, keep a lookout, I need to do something."

Jason stuck his head through the curtain. "It's clear," he said.

I reappeared and went through my backpack, pulling out the nanite pen and the red cube.

"What are you doing?" asked Callan.

"I'm going to try to get us back. We need to hop over to the other side."

"The other side of what?" asked Mrs. McGinness.

I connected the pen to the cube and drew up a little of the red energy.

"I'm not sure you should…"

I tapped it on my skin. After a few seconds, I faded, but the mist was still yellow.

"Maybe we should just get out of here for now," said Callan. He walked over to talk to Jason. I blinked in to see that Connor was facing them.

I pressed the pen and cube together until all the red had disappeared from the cube, and then I scribbled the pen up and down the length of my arm until it was empty.

"What are you doing?" said Callan, running back to me.

"Whoa," I said. Callan caught me before I could fall.

"What were you thinking?" he said.

I was hot all over. It felt like when I awakened, the pulsing of energy trying to burst out of me. This time, I instinctively knew what to do with it.

I grew a ball of energy in my hands. It was red. I didn't know what went through David's mind when he connected with another world, so I just thought of him, hoping for inspiration.

I threw the energy ball at the wall. It flattened and grew against the wall, becoming a clear image of the garden at the residence on the Full Earth.

"Holy Mother of God," said Mary.

"Am I seeing things?" I asked.

"What the hell is Vince doing there?" said Jason. The shock had made him reappear.

David turned to the gate, his face bewildered.

"Is that someone coming? Who is it? Don't do anything stupid."

"Get through," I said.

Connor's passengers were, unsurprisingly, hesitant.

Jason faded and went through. I waited for him to appear in the garden. The seconds ticked by.

"If I've lost Orla's boyfriend, she'll kill me," I said.

"That's my Orla's boyfriend? He's a handsome lad," said Mrs. McGinness.

Finally, Jason appeared in the garden. Then Connor took the McGinnesses and Aiden through. Callan followed, but as I was about to step through, the two Agents burst through the curtains with their guns raised. In the second they saw the portal, both of them faltered, staring at it, not sure where to point their weapons.

In a panic, I turned and threw a ball of energy at them. When the red ball hit them, they fell back into nothing. A portal had opened around them, and they drifted off into blackness.

I screamed and was unable to look away from what I'd done.

The portal wobbled, waved and was gone. I turned back to the portal on the wall and could still see the garden, but it too was trembling. I faded and ran through.

"What happened? I heard you scream," said David.

The thought of what I'd seen passed through my mind, and David looked horrified.

Jason and Callan took Aiden and Orla's parents straight through the house and out front to a hopper.

"Come out, you worm," I called.

"He thinks you'll kill him," said David.

"He's damn right."

"You need to stay calm. Vince's new buddies have got your dad."

"What? Who?" I felt like the wind had been knocked out of me.

"This has gone badly," said Vince, appearing on the bench.

I marched towards him, but David stood between us.

"What did you think would happen?" asked David.

Vince started sobbing on the bench. I didn't want to thump him any less.

"Where's my dad?" I asked.

"I don't know. He's okay."

Callan came back into the garden.

"Where have you been?" said David. "Just tell us. I don't want to spend another second inside that cesspit mind of yours."

Vince gulped.

Vince looked about himself. They had all reappeared, but Vince instantly faded again. He watched as they found his clothes, his phone, and discovered how he had been communicating with the Agency. He felt sick with shame.

The others walked down the hill, and Vince quickly threw his clothes on. The strange white barrier began to hum ominously, so he faded. His clothes dropped immediately into a heap on the ground as three officers in an unfamiliar uniform appeared in front of the barrier and made their way down the hill. Vince followed and stood with the others. The group was split into two and Vince chose to go with Neil and Hannah, not wanting David to pick up on his presence.

After a while, a strange vehicle with Lincoln Produce written along the side glided to a stop and hissed to the ground. Vince followed Neil and Hannah inside. It was full of apples in crates. There were some pull-down seats around the edge which Neil, Hannah and the officers sat on. Vince sat on the floor and remained faded while he tried to make sense of the whole thing. David had posited the possibility of a multiverse, and on the evidence around him, it seemed the most likely scenario.

About twenty minutes into the journey, the vehicle,

which was apparently called a hopper, jolted several times. It was clear someone was shooting at it. The hopper made an emergency landing, the apples and the people going everywhere. Vince slid straight through the wall of the hopper, landing on the ground on the other side from the door. He saw a man gathering apples that had rolled down the hill. The officers were chasing the rest of the attackers in the opposite direction, but Vince decided to take off after the young man with the apples.

The man got halfway down the hill and slid to the ground behind a water butt. He stayed there, breathing heavily, keeping low to the ground for ten minutes, until the hopper lifted off and continued its journey.

At the bottom of the hill, the man sneaked into a barn, and Vince followed. The man ate two of the apples and saved the rest. He then closed his eyes and went to sleep.

Vince watched him for some time. He looked sick; he was thin, with sores on his hands and face. Vince appeared and took one of the apples. He made his way to the far corner of the barn and wriggled under a pile of hay to sleep.

He awoke to noises outside the barn. Glimpsing out, he saw the farmer moving his sheep towards the barn. He went to hide, then looked at the sleeping man. He was going to be caught.

Vince went over to him and put his hand over the man's mouth. The man awoke instantly with panic in his eyes at the sight of the naked man leaning over him.

"The farmer's coming. Hide in the hay in the corner, quickly," said Vince, before fading.

The man blinked in, but there was no yellow trail. At the sound of someone outside, he gathered his apples and dived into the hay. The farmer led in the sheep, closed the door and left. Vince returned to his corner.

After about ten minutes, the man got up and walked over to Vince's corner.

"Don't you have a nanite tag? I thought you all got them. We have to resort to stealing your nanite sticks" he said, raising his hand. It was quite dark and Vince couldn't see what he was showing him.

Vince sat up, keeping the hay strategically placed. "Is that the pen thing?" He'd watched the female officer dot it onto the others.

"That's it. It spreads nanites with your DNA markers to your belongings, so they don't fall off."

"I could probably do with one of those Why were you after my friends?" asked Vince, although he realized he had no right to call them friends any longer.

"We were after the food. If we'd known the hopper would be full of police officers, we'd have left well alone."

"I'm Vince, by the way. I try to make a habit of introducing myself to people who see me naked."

The man smiled. "I'm Eric."

"What's wrong with you? The sores. You look sick."

"I'm dying. We all are. We're from what you call the Broken Earth. It's sun-sickness."

"I've never heard of the Broken Earth or sun-sickness. I don't even know what this earth is called. We came here from somewhere else."

The door cracked, and both men froze. A figure crept in and collapsed in the middle of the floor. Eric got up and made his way over to the still figure.

"Jeff?" said Eric, tapping the man's face.

"Eric? Hey, you got away. I thought I was the only one."

"What happened to the others?"

"Everyone ran. I saw a few drop down. I don't know if

they were hit or trying to hide. I just ran. I couldn't believe my eyes when all those officers came running out."

"Do you have your nanite pen?"

"Yes, there's not much left in it. I used most of it on me. I got shot." Jeff laughed, then cried. "I don't think it worked."

"You'll be okay in no time. You need to rest. Then we'll head to the meeting place so we can get out of here."

"That won't happen. They got Sarah," said Jeff. "I didn't even get an apple."

Vince stood from his hiding place in the corner, picked up one of Eric's apples and took it over.

Jeff looked at the naked man. "I see why you wanted the pen."

Vince passed the apple to Eric, who put it in Jeff's hand.

"I'll just smell it." He put it to his nose, breathed in, and breathed out in a long gurgle. The apple rolled onto the floor.

"What kind of place is this? Who is killing you because you're hungry?" asked Vince.

Eric took the nanite pen from Jeff's pocket, twisted it and held it out. Vince held out his hand and Eric tapped it with the pen.

"There are some clothes if you want them," said Eric, looking at his dead friend.

He returned to the corner and Vince removed Jeff's trousers and t-shirt. The t-shirt was light blue with a blood stain low at the back. Vince crept up the field to the water butt and washed the t-shirt in it. He turned to go back to the barn, but Eric was making his way up the hill.

"We need to get away from here," said Eric. "If they did get Sarah, we're stuck on this earth with no way back. She was our red-mister."

Vince ears pricked up. "Red-mister?"

"Our bridge. You can't make the jump between earths without a red-mister."

"I might be able to help you out there," said Vince, thinking about the red mist surrounding him and the others when they faded in front of the Major.

They made their way back up to the top of the hill. There were still apples strewn about the road. Vince and Eric went about, picking them up.

By the time they reached the meeting place, a grain house, Eric was leaning on Vince, without the strength to walk by himself. Finally, Vince had to carry Eric. He kicked in the door and staggered inside.

"Is anyone here? He's hurt," said Vince.

A man appeared and took hold of Eric. "Who are you?" he asked.

"I'm Vince. I was hiding out in the hopper you shot down."

"That hopper was full of police, there's no way you were hiding out on that."

Vince faded. The man blinked in and looked around. Vince returned.

"Like I said, I was hiding out." Vince helped the man lay Eric down on some bags of grain.

"Will he be okay?" asked Vince.

"I don't know. Our friend has a pen, but he's missing."

"Was that Jeff?" Vince realized how he'd phrased it. It wasn't the best way to break the news. "Sorry," he added. "Eric has the pen now."

"I'm Kyle," said the man, looking at the pen and shaking it. "Barely anything."

Vince felt ashamed for having used some of it to keep his clothes on.

Kyle tapped the pen onto Eric's neck. His breathing became less labored almost instantly.

"Is there anything those little nanite buggers can't do?" Vince asked.

"Cure sun-sickness," said Kyle.

Eric opened his eyes. "Kyle, Vince here has a friend who's a red-mister."

"I wouldn't call him a friend as such. He probably hates my guts right now," said Vince.

"Well, it's more than we had five minutes ago."

Vince looked around the garden and over to the house. "I look at everything you've got here. Food, beds. These people have nothing. Their planet has virtually nothing left. They came for food and help, but they're shot down like animals and imprisoned."

"It's not like that. They just appear and raid people's homes and businesses. We tried to help them years ago..."

"By locking them into camps. Yes, I heard," said Vince, looking at Callan.

"It wasn't like that. They've got all kinds of diseases. We tried to keep them together until they could all be assessed and cured. They broke out and thousands died from diseases they weren't capable of fighting."

David was looking at Vince. He seemed shocked that Vince was capable of compassion for these people.

"I'll help," he said.

Vince looked up at him from the bench. He seemed to be searching David's face for some sign of subterfuge.

"Not without getting my dad back first," I said.

David looked at me.

I sent to him, "*I will blast the lot of them into the inbetween before I let him use my dad as a bargaining chip.*"

"I don't feel good about this, David," said Callan.

"You don't have to do anything. We won't involve Zoe. In fact, if we can get this done quickly enough, it will be finished before she gets back with her parents."

From the doorway, Sofia said, "I know what it's like to be a frightened, hungry immigrant. Jenna, please don't turn them away."

I turned and walked into the house. I went to my room, sat on the bed and tried to think things through. Whatever these people were, I mustn't lose sight of the person I was. Vanessa died to protect disenfranchised faders. How could I do any less?

I returned to the garden. "Sofia, we need to get as much food as we can take, warm clothes, blankets and medicine."

Sofia put her arms around me and whispered, "You are your father's daughter."

Within half an hour, Sofia was handing out bags to everyone. They were full of everything I'd asked for. She held both of my hands and looked into my face.

"Bring him back to me."

I nodded and took a bag. Connor, David, Vince and I stood at the ribbon.

Callan said, "Wait," and walked over to stand with us. "Zoe will kill me if I let you go off and get killed. So will Heidi."

"Where are we going?" I asked.

"To the place we've agreed to meet," said Vince.

We called the ribbon and Vince spoke in an address.

We arrived in a room, empty except for Dad and several sick looking people. They were playing cards.

"Hello, darling," said Dad.

"Hi, Dad," I said.

"I Thought you were going to move him somewhere else," said Vince, confused.

"This chap is Eric. He was supposed to knock me out, but he collapsed. He seems quite sick. I was looking after him until his friends arrived. One of them had one of those little nanite pens and he's looking much better now. But they brought a lady in who's looking equally poorly. This is Sarah. She was the red-mister for the group, but she got shot in the leg. She faded back to Broken Earth and returned soon after to help her comrades. She doesn't have the strength to get them all back."

"You know they're your kidnappers, don't you? And you're their kidnapee?" I was bewildered.

"Well, yes. But they're quite a decent bunch," said Dad.

"Honestly, I didn't know Stockholm syndrome worked this fast."

"What's in the bags?" asked one of the men.

"Provisions," said Callan. "Let's get you guys home."

Callan clearly wanted this over. He looked uncomfortable.

David called the ribbon and began to emit the red mist. We watched while the mist twisted and turned. He pulled away and broke the connection, hyperventilating.

"What happened? Can't he do it?" asked Eric.

David nodded. "I can do it. I wasn't prepared for the pain. They're all in so much pain."

He began again. The strain showed in his face as he tried to tune out thoughts of a world full of people in pain. Connor faded and created a link between David and Sarah.

"That's it, I see them," said Kyle, looking into the mist.

We gathered together, faded and stepped into the red mist.

A dozen sick-looking people with guns surrounded us. David collapsed onto the ground.

"It's okay, they're friends," said Eric.

Dad and Callan carried Sarah to a couch, and people crowded around her.

"David, are you okay?" said Vince.

"I can hear them. It's too much," said David.

A woman turned from Sarah and stared at David on the floor. She walked over to him and crouched down.

"Hello, David," she said.

David looked up confused as she held out her hand to him. It was disfigured and twisted with a lump in the middle. He looked at her for a long moment.

"Kim?"

I stared at the woman. This was David's friend from the Academy—the one he thought he'd left on the Full Earth. He must have come here, all those years ago. I was stunned.

David stood, staring at Kim. Tears flowed openly down his face. I realized he must have been taking in the sores on her face.

"I left you here? I'm so sorry," he whispered.

Kim moved forward and embraced David. "It's okay, David. I won't pretend it's been easy, but I've had love and moments of pure joy in my life."

"You're a grandmother," said David.

Kim took a step back and looked at him. "And you appear to be a red-mister *and* a telepath. And here I was, thinking you were just a book nerd."

They hugged again.

"And we're faders. I started emitting after a few weeks here. I couldn't believe my eyes. I didn't realize what was going on at first—I thought a fader was standing in place with me. I spent the best part of a day trying to run away from myself."

They laughed and hugged once more.

"Am I going to have to break this up?" asked Kyle, stepping forward.

"I see you've already met my husband," said Kim.

David nodded to Kyle, but took a respectful step back from Kim.

"Man, I'm kidding," said Kyle.

"The faders here are good, though," said Kim. "I don't know what went wrong with the faders on our world. I've often wondered if it might be possible to get a message back there."

I thought that was an ideal time for David to tell her, but he said nothing.

We handed out the bags of food, medicine and clothes. The people were in an awful state.

"What happened here?" I asked.

"We don't know," said Kyle. "It started about fifty years ago and never stopped. The storms and winds increased and people just got sick."

"That's what happened on our Earth," said Callan. "We built domes over the cities to protect them, but after a few years, the storms just went away. But we lost millions to the sun-sickness."

"We've lost billions," said Eric.

I could see just by looking at Callan's face that he was struggling with this. He had been brought up to believe the Broken were thieves and criminals, when all they were was Broken. He looked around.

"Could I just step outside for a minute?" he asked.

"We don't really do that here," said Kim.

"Not without ten layers and a face mask," said Eric.

"I'm sorry. I didn't think," said Callan. He pulled a few nanite pens from his pocket. The Broken looked at them with wide eyes. "Will these help?"

"Help? Some of us will live a few more months with these," said Kyle. He took Callan into a fierce hug.

I noticed Vince sitting alone in the corner of the room. I was still angry about what he had done to us, and then to my dad, but I could not deny that he seemed to have found some kind of redemption in helping these people.

I walked over to him. "You've done a good thing here. A lot of people are still going to be angry about what you did, but I'm going to try my best to forgive you."

"I'm going to talk to the Mayor," Callan was saying to Eric. "We should be able to do more."

I went to my Dad, who was talking to his new buddy, Kyle. "Dad, we need to get you back to Sofia. She doesn't know you're safe."

"I'll stay here," said Vince. "Dave and I have a strong connection. He'll be able to find us more easily if I'm here."

That wasn't the only reason Vince wasn't coming back, but that was okay.

I STOOD at the doors to the garden. From there, I could see Orla together with her parents, Sean, Sam and Aiden. They had been joined by two of Sean's friends, Chester and Leroy. Jason sat a little way from them, playing with a small white West Highland terrier. By the time we had reached Jason's family home in Manchester, it was clear there had been a struggle. There was no sign of his father, but his dog, Scruffy, had been locked away in the shed.

David stood with Kim, Kyle, Heidi, Callan and James in

deep discussions. Zoe and Hannah were in the living room with Hannah's parents, Anna, Jodi, Ava and Milly. Felix was on the back of Milly's chair, looking out suspiciously at his new nemesis, Scruffy. We had paid a visit to Zoe's grandmother in the nursing home, but she seemed fine, apart from advanced dementia. Moving her didn't seem the right thing to do, and it was unlikely that the Agency had any plans for her.

Dad was in the kitchen, trying to cook, and Sofia was stopping him from burning the house down.

Connor stood behind me and embraced me. He kissed the top of my head and spun me around to face him.

"You did okay, Beautiful," he said, looking at everyone and back to me.

"We have a long way to go. The Agency is still over on our earth, hunting down faders. People are dying on the Broken Earth."

"But, for now, you've done enough. Come on, this is a party. Zoe's moving back to England tomorrow. Let's go be with our friends."

Connor was right.

I made to move through the door, but he kept a hold of me.

"Well, in a minute."

Heidi walked past us.

"Aww! Look at you two. That's so dope."

EPILOGUE

Craig Tomowski sat at his desk in his office at the base, cleaning his sidearm. When the gun was clean and shiny, he would put it against his head and pull the trigger. His career was over, he knew that. There wasn't much left to stay around for. And if he didn't do it, someone else would.

A loud knock sounded at the door. He toyed with the idea of slamming the pistol together and doing it immediately, but the thought of killing himself with a dirty sidearm seemed vulgar. He put the weapon into the drawer.

"Come," he shouted.

An Agent entered with a small box the size of Craig's own pistol case. This was it, then. He liked the idea of the box. It seemed ceremonial.

"Sir, we found this at the ranch. No one knows what it is."

Craig sat forward. This was unexpected.

The Agent opened the box and a glow spread across Craig's face.

"I want a tracker in here, now," he said, almost too afraid to lift out the little cube.

A young man was pushed into the office. He had been severely beaten up, with cuts to his lip and above one eye, the other eye swollen shut. Craig surveyed the man's ruined face. Luckily, he only needed to be able to see out of one eye.

"Blink in. Tell me what you see," said Craig.

The tracker did has he was ordered. His expression was one of confusion.

"Yellow. The light in that thing is yellow."

Craig indicated that the young man was no longer needed and he was pulled out of the office. Craig lifted the phone and hit redial.

"Tomowski here. No, Mr. President, I haven't submitted my resignation and taken my worthless ass off base yet. I'm happy to report that the primary goal of Operation Changeling has been achieved. We have a power source."

He hung up the phone, snapped closed the box and headed out to the lab with it.

"Time for a little reverse engineering, I think."

Click here to grab *PORTAL*, book three of the Faders series.

mybook.to/thefaders3

Or turn the page to read chapter one now!

PORTAL - CHAPTER 1

I*f I'd known the consequences, would I have done anything differently?*

I WOKE with a start in my bedroom at the Brightling L.A., Residence on what the locals called Full-Earth.

"What?" I asked into the darkness.

Turning on the light, I sat up and looked around. The room appeared empty. I blinked in, sweeping the room with my Sight. There was no yellow mist indicating that a fader had walked through the room.

Was that you? I asked silently into my mind. There was no response from David.

I must have been dreaming, I thought.

My arm was itching again. I pulled up the sleeve of my pajama top. It had been a month since I'd used the red cube, and the itching in my arm was just getting worse. I'd already cut my nails short to limit the damage I could do. At this rate I'd be sleeping in mittens. I reached over to the jar of cream the doctor had given me and smoothed it over the skin. Lying back, I thought about what I'd done; taking the nanite pen and the cube filled with an eerie red light from David and dragging it up and down my arm until it the cube and pen were empty in the hope that I'd be able to create a portal. It had worked, we'd escaped, but shortly after that happened, I stopped being able to conjure energy balls or make the lights flicker. I couldn't make a portal. I couldn't even fade anymore.

I wondered, if I'd known the potential consequences, would I have thought twice about it? We were in a bad situation rescuing Orla's parents. Even if I'd known the risks, I'd have done it anyway. I couldn't let any harm come to Orla's family or her boyfriend, Jason. We might have been able to escape another way, but the agents had placed booby-trapped inhibitors into her parents, telling them it would reactivate their tracker glands. Believing the faders had taken their children, of course they were willing to have the procedure. The problem was, the agents had remotes that would activate the inhibitors and kill Orla's parents if they reappeared. Getting them off our earth was the only option for them. I stroked my itchy arm. It felt lumpy. Great, I thought. Now I'm allergic to the cream. Just what I need the night before the first day at my new job.

I flicked off the light and lay in the darkness listening to the quiet of the residence. It was nice to finally experience peace in the house. Zoe and Hannah had moved into the Citadel with Hannah's parents. I was sad to see them go but happy they were safe. They had visited a couple of times over the last month, and we were planning to visit them soon in their new place before the binding ceremony when Zoe would be forever connected to this earth and replenish its ribbon. I didn't really understand what that meant, but it hadn't done the previous Brightling any harm, and it meant that Zoe would be safe and treated well for the rest of her life. Orla and Jason were down the hall. Dad, Connor, David, and Sofia were all still here, and we had visitors every day. We'd rescued over forty trackers and faders from our earth. James, the Mayor of L.A., had worked wonders finding places for them to stay, setting them up with work and school. Jodi was living in an apartment in the city, and the girls had started attending a school nearby, but they visited almost daily as Sofia watched the girls after school until Jodi finished work. I closed my eyes and returned to sleep because I was about to start my own first day at work.

As I dressed, sounds of activity in the house filtered through to me. I opened my door and the smells of breakfast hit my nose and stomach immediately. I walked down the hallway just as the doorbell buzzed. The panel showed that James and Heidi were at the door. I waved my tag at the panel and said, "Open."

"Not recognized," said the panel.

I did it again.

"Not recognized. Initiating security protocols," said the panel.

"Wait, what security protocols?" I looked around.

"Anyone?" I called.

The door buzzed again and Sofia appeared beside me.

"There's something wrong with the panel. It won't open the door," I said.

"Open," Sofia said, waving her tag at the door. The door opened to reveal Heidi and James. Sofia shrugged and said, "Good morning, I'm making breakfast," and headed back to the kitchen.

"Hi, Jenna," Heidi said, hugging me.

"Good Morning," James said,

"What have you got there?" I asked, pointing at the bags they carried.

"Two hundred nanite pens and cubes, for our friends on BE. We're meeting Kim here to transport them before we go to work," James said.

"Can't we just get Kim and her friends off that planet?" I asked.

"Hopefully. I'm having meetings with anyone who will listen. But how about you? Are you looking forward to your first day at work?" James asked.

"Raring to go," I said

"Good to hear it," James said as he followed Sofia towards the kitchen.

Heidi's communicator beeped. "Oh. You have an intruder inside the front entrance," she said glancing around with her brows furrowed.

"It didn't recognize me. The house is initiating security protocols. Whatever that means," I said, shaking my head.

Heidi waved her hand at it. "Cancel security protocols."

"Why didn't you come through the ribbon in the garden?" I asked.

"The mayor insisted we come in that monstrous SVU," she said.

"SUV. He can drive it?" I asked, closing the door.

"Hell no," Sean said from the other side of the door I was closing in his face.

I jumped back and let him in.

"I'm the mayor's driver now. I'll have to get myself a hat," he said.

"You drove it back from Canada?" I asked.

"He had it brought back in a hopper. Then he had the audacity to take all the best parts out of it. It runs on those bloody cubes now. I just drove it from the outskirts of L.A.

Anyway, I'd love to chat but I smell bacon." He carried on in.

I closed the door. With Heidi there, I tried the panel again, and it still refused to recognize me. It threatened me with security protocols again.

"What are the security protocols? I'm half expecting little machine guns to pop up out of the floor."

"It alerts me. I would have sent the officers in," she said, scrolling through menus.

"What are you doing?" I asked from over her shoulder.

"I've never experienced this problem before. I'm just creating you a new profile and deleting your old one. You'll have to present your tag again, like the first time."

We went through the process again, and it recognized me.

"Thank the Gods!" I said and exhaled loudly.

"Strange. But it's okay now," Heidi said, taking her bags into the living room.

I stood, staring at the door, and muttered, "Technology!"

I heard a muttered comment and turned to see who had spoken.

"Hmm?" There was no one there. Perhaps I heard them speaking in the living room. I rubbed at my arm and walked through the house.

I had toast for breakfast and headed out with Sean, James, Heidi, and Orla.

"The roads are shocking here. Someone should complain to the mayor," Orla said.

"They don't get used very much, although that might change. I seem to have started a trend. The engineer who updated the power supply wants to build his own,"

"Don't the incs use them?" I asked.

"Incs tend to live closer to hopper routes for convenience. The roads get better in the towns because bicycles are popular, but they're not very wide"

"You'll be popular, hogging the road with this monster," Orla said.

"People don't mind. It's unusual, they wave," Sean said.

We were in the car for nearly two hours.

"Are we there yet?" Orla asked for the third time. Each time she sounded more and more like a petulant child.

Heidi was in fits of giggles.

"If you ask that again, Orla McGinness, you'll be walking," Sean said.

"Pah! You can't get the staff," Orla stuck her tongue out at Sean through the rearview mirror.

"Aren't you his staff, too?" Heidi grinned.

"Well, there's no need to be rude," Orla said with an exaggerated bristle.

"Isn't this taking a large slice out of your working day?" I asked James.

"Well, yes. It is a little indulgent. I think we'll need to revert to standard travel methods for the rest of the week," James said.

"But what about my job?" Sean asked.

"I've received a lot of requests to see the vehicle. Speak to Yolanda, she'll sort out a schedule of journeys for you," James said.

"Your man will have to bring you in tomorrow," Orla said, like I needed to be reminded that I couldn't fade.

Sean dropped us at a ribbon gate and hopper station. James entered the gate, and Orla, Heidi, and I took a hopper the rest of the way.

Twenty minutes later, we arrived at the office building. We entered through the lobby doors and followed a long hallway to the back of the building where a small area was filled with people waiting for an elevator. The elevator doors opened. It was tiny. Three people stepped in, and the doors closed.

"We'll be here forever," Orla said.

I counted the people ahead of me. It would have to make five more trips before I could go up. I wished I'd gone to the bathroom but I wasn't giving up my place in the queue now.

"This is ridiculous. Why don't they have more elevators? Or one that holds at least ten people," I said.

"It could be made of gold, too," said someone farther down in the line.

A few people chuckled. Orla laughed.

"Why are you waiting?" I asked Heidi.

"I have to get you safely to your office," she said.

"Well, I'm safely in the building. Won't that do?" I asked.

"Hell, to the no," Heidi said.

A few people in the queue glanced at her with quizzical expressions.

I raised my eyebrows at Orla, but she kept her face down.

"Could you not just flash your badge and say it's police business?" Orla whispered to Heidi.

"That would be a lie," Heidi said.

"Sure, only a bit of one," Orla said.

The young woman standing behind us in the line had tilted her head out slightly, to discreetly look at our tags. I held mine out for her to see. She blushed and averted her eyes.

"You can see if you like, I don't mind," I said.

"I'm sorry. I noticed your gold tag and wondered why you would choose to travel in this thing," said the young woman, indicating the elevator.

I looked at her. Her skirt suit didn't appear to be something worn by catering or cleaning staff, which was what most of the incs here were.

"Her fade is temporarily banjaxed," Orla said.

"Banjaxed?" the woman asked.

"Up the swanny, on the fritz, busted, broken," Orla clarified.

"I understand," said the young woman.

"I'm Orla, this is Jenna, and this is Heidi."

"Hello, I'm Maggie. I assume this is your first day," she said nervously to Heidi

"I'm just ensuring these two get to work safely. They get into a lot of trouble. I mean, a lot," Heidi said.

Orla guffawed, and Maggie smiled uncertainly.

"Look at that. You found your first work friend," Orla said.

I knew instantly what was coming.

"So, Jenna, sweetie. You know I love you to the moon and back," Orla said.

"You can go. It's fine." I sighed.

"I don't want to be a bad friend," Orla said.

"Just go. I get it." I rolled my eyes.

"I'll have a nice cup of coffee waiting for you on the top floor, but I just cannot do that tiny, squeaky death box," Orla said, heading back out of the door.

Heidi looked at me and watched Orla's retreat, indecision on her face.

"You can go, too, if you like," I said.

"No, I'll stay with you," Heidi said, glancing nervously at the elevator as we shuffled closer to it.

"She'll be flying out of the front door, shopping for shoes," I said.

"You think?" Heidi squeaked. She bolted.

"You really think your friend would go to shops instead of to work?" Maggie asked.

"No, not really, but Heidi looked like she was going to faint before getting into the elevator," I said.

"It's usually psychological," Maggie said.

"No, I think the elevator just looks woefully inadequate," I said.

"I mean the fading. Losing the ability to fade. It comes back. The trick is not to worry about it. Or so I hear. I'm sorry, you probably already know that," Maggie said.

"I didn't. Thanks. You're likely right," I said.

"Where are you going to be working?" Maggie asked.

"In the mayor's campaign office. Stuffing envelopes, I suppose. Where do you work?" I asked.

"I'm in the mayor's mailroom. I'll probably be mailing out your envelopes." Maggie laughed.

We chatted until we were at the front of the line. We stepped in. Maggie pressed the M button for me, the floor below it for herself, and floor seventeen for a man who got in with us and just went into a world of his own. The doors squealed so loudly as they closed, I winced. The elevator juddered and jerked its way slowly upward.

"You can actually hear the rust," I said.

The man flicked an annoyed look at me, then breathed in and appeared not to breathe out again.

"I try not to think about it," Maggie said.

The man stood there. He seemed to be focused on a single point while sweat patches appeared on his shirt at every shudder.

I took my cue from the man and held my breath pretty much all the way up. He got out on the seventeenth floor, and the elevator continued its erratic journey.

"It must be well-made. I mean, it's working, isn't it? They wouldn't use it if it were actually dangerous," I said

"One of these broke down in another building a few weeks ago. A lady had a heart attack in it. By the time they got to her it was too late,"

"That's shocking. Couldn't someone have just faded in through the wall with a nanite pen?"

"Emergency calls get diverted from incs all the time. It must be very different where you're from." Maggie shrugged.

"That's the truth. Where I'm from there are only a few faders. Most people are incs,"

"Did you live in the Citadel?" Maggie asked as the doors opened for her stop.

"No. I'm from what you call Half-Earth," I said as the doors closed on her slack-jawed face.

The doors opened on the mayor's floor, and I stepped out on shaky legs, glad to be alive. True to her word, Orla was standing there with a mug of coffee for me, and Heidi stood next to her with Yolanda, the mayor's assistant.

"I am never getting into that thing again," I said.

"Don't worry. It's not so bad going down. When the mayor's floor calls the lift, it comes straight here. You won't have to wait forever." Yolanda said.

"It turns out, the wait was the best part," I said.

We walked down the hallway to the main office and waved to Yolanda as she took a call at her desk. She smiled and waved back. Orla showed me to our desks. She'd already laid claim to the one by the window. I looked at the paraphernalia on the desks. Sure enough, we were stuffing envelopes.

"What are you going to do today?" I asked as Heidi took a seat in the corner.

"I've got a bunch of reports to do. Believe it or not, being your liaison comes with a lot of paperwork." She smiled.

We got started. Heidi didn't get much of her paperwork done as we chatted away. Before I knew it, lunchtime had come around.

"We're heading out to a cafe down the street," said Yolanda, appearing at the door to our office.

My first thought was that I was hungry. My second thought was of the elevator.

"You go ahead. I brought a book," I said.

"So did I. I'll stay here with you," Heidi said, pretending she wasn't staying because it was her job to keep an eye on me.

"Don't worry, I won't let her out of my sight," Yolanda said as she and Orla left.

"That means they'll both be shopping for shoes," I said.

"I'm not falling for that one again,"

I laughed.

"It's the elevator, isn't it," Heidi said.

"I've already called Connor. He's coming to pick me up after work," I said.

"Great," Heidi said, barely containing her relief at this news.

"There's food in the break room," Heidi said.

We went down the hall and entered the break room which had a couple of sofas and a few tables and chairs scattered about. One wall had a vertical conveyor about a foot wide, rising from the floor and disappearing into the ceiling. A couple of feet along the wall, it came out of the ceiling and slid downwards. Glimpses of bright ribbon light shone through the edges of the boxes as they moved along. A display showed different foods. Heidi selected a sandwich and a drink and flashed her tag. The boxes continued smoothly up until her sandwich appeared and was pushed to an open box at the side. Her drink followed.

My eyes widened at the sleek, modern contraption. I didn't feel like food anymore. I felt angry and could only think of one place to direct it.

"Are you okay?" Heidi said, clearly alarmed at the sudden shift in my emotions.

I pivoted, left the break room, and marched to James's office. He was at his door with his jacket and satchel.

"Are you heading out?" I asked. The sharpness in my own voice almost made me jump.

"Yes...er...I've got a meeting in San Francisco in a half hour. Can I help?" He sounded wary.

"You're on your way out? Perfect. Come with me," I said.

I led him to the door that was used only by the incs and held it open for him.

"Oh, I've never been through here before," he said.

We walked to the doors, and I called the elevator.

"Is there a problem?" James asked. He pulled at his collar.

Just as Orla had said, the elevator arrived quickly, with its doors squealing rustily open.

"You're heading downstairs. Let's go," I said.

James stepped in with me. He was a tall, broad-shouldered man, and the tiny space became instantly claustrophobic. I pressed the button for the ground floor, and the elevator squealed, juddered, and jerked its way, painfully slowly, to the ground floor. The doors opened, and several incs jumped back to see the mayor exiting their elevator covered in sweat.

"Well, that was an experience," James said.

"That's not the best part," I said.

We entered the hallway to the front of the building, but

partway down I opened the door to the ground floor break room.

"Do you see how smoothly this system runs through the whole building from top to bottom? It's carrying snacks. That thing at the back of the building is supposedly built to carry humans."

"Jenna, you make a compelling case. I can assure you, we are on the same page," James said, patting his forehead with his handkerchief.

Having made my point, I sighed loudly, the frustration leaving me. "I have to go back up in that bloody thing again. Have a good meeting, James." I smiled.

I made my way back to the elevator and waited. There were only three of us, so I was back in the break room in a few minutes.

"Better?" Heidi asked.

"Can I get a sandwich now?" I asked.

"You feel like you need one," she said.

I laughed.

I selected a sandwich and drink, then waved my tag.

"Not recognized." I slumped.

"I'll get it. It can take a while for the updated information to get around the whole system," Heidi said.

We ate and chatted. I wondered if James would be able to do anything about the elevator. There didn't seem to be enough space to fit a bigger elevator in the back of the building, but there were three vertical ribbons at the front which seemed excessive.

James returned from his meeting at four p.m. and glanced in at me as he hurried past our office. I managed an embarrassed smile before he disappeared into his office and closed the door. I wondered if this would be my last day of working here.

James announced at the end of that day that two vertical ribbons were enough and the third was going to be turned into an elevator, powered by ribbon energy, big enough to hold twelve people. Work would commence soon.

"He really is a good guy," Heidi said.

"I hope he'll still be my friend. I know this isn't my world and things work differently here, but sometimes, however I look at something, I can't help but see it as wrong," I said.

"Jenna, that elevator is definitely wrong. I think that's what James likes about you Half-Earthers. Seeing things through your eyes gives him a wider view," Heidi said.

"Are you causing trouble again?" Connor asked from the doorway.

"Do you even have to ask?" Orla asked.

He laughed.

"That's my girl. Are you ready to go?" he asked.

"I just want to say goodnight to a new friend."

We headed down one flight of stairs to the mayor's mailroom.

"Hi, how's your day been?" I Maggie asked.

"Very well, thank you," she replied.

She seemed a little cool. I wasn't sure what to make of it.

"Okay, have a nice evening."

We turned to leave.

"Erm...I heard what you did," she said. "And I heard the mayor looked like he was going to faint when he left the elevator."

"That's an exaggeration," I said. But not by much, I thought.

"Thank you anyway," she said.

Connor and I headed back up to the office to pick up my things.

"So, is she your friend or not? She seemed conflicted," Connor said.

"Hmm. I noticed that, too." I shrugged.

Connor faded me down to the ground floor and back to the residence. After that, he took me to work and picked me up every day.

Click here to grab PORTAL, book three of the Faders series. mybook.to/thefaders3

JOIN MY TRIBE

Join my VIP list for the latest news, release updates, and notifications of promo pricing from my publisher. https://dl.bookfunnel.com/olndiiuzje

Find me on Facebook at www.facebook.com/egbatemanwrites

ALSO BY THE AUTHOR